Gravenhead.

Richard Thorns

Gravenhead.

Deep asleep, deep asleep,
Deep asleep it lies,
The still lake of Semmerwater
Under the still skies.
And many a fathom, many a fathom,
Many a fathom below,
In a king's tower and a queen's bower
The fishes come and go.

"The Ballad of Semmerwater"
Sir William Watson (1858-1935)

(For Tony)

Richard Thorns

Gravenhead

Richard Thorns

Notes and acknowledgements

The keel for Gravenhead was first laid down as a hesitant first chapter of a 'Girl finds a lost village' concept, and the first draft of the novel was finished around eighteen months later. This was pretty quick work by my standards for a full-length novel, but in reality the future drafts, revisions and editing were to prove to be the real killers on this occasion; they outpaced the original draft by around 7:1, and I really would like to thank Leila Rashid at The Writers' Workshop who, using her unique editorial insight, refused to tell me what I desperately wanted to hear: namely, that the book could be called 'finished.'

That said, there were inevitably a few niggles that troubled me once the book was published and so, four years after being with one publisher and moving on to another house, this was a great opportunity to revisit the book and tidy up some areas that I felt let it down, and also insert some new concepts and ideas that, sometime after the novel had moved on to publication, had caused me to retrospectively go: 'Drat!'

Back to the acknowledgements, Leah Webb at EMI was incredibly helpful with her advice in the music licencing processes and the reproduction of the Genesis lyrics, taken from - appropriately enough as the book is set in a record-breaking summer - that wonderful summer of 1976! Leila, thank you!

Bill Reiss at J.l. Hawkins Inc, New York City also deserves a mention for his ongoing belief, patience and enthusiasm

Richard Thorns

for this concept: a complete novel written in the magic realism genre. Thank you, Bill

The cover of the book shows the spire of Derwent church peering starkly above the cold, murky waters of the Ladybower reservoir following the flooding of Derwent village. It is taken from the following booklet:

Silent Valley: A history of the Derbyshire villages of Ashopton and Derwent, now submerged beneath Ladybower Dam by V.J.Hallam. All rights are reserved.

Finally, the biggest debt of all! Gravenhead is set in the mid-noughties, at a time of economic and cultural ambiguity: the millennium had come and gone, yet the legacy of the collapse of the mining industry remained; technology was accelerating and making its mark on uncertain lives, but old formats like VHS still survived. One element, however, remained constant: Wales either sparkled in sunlight, or presented a brooding land of mist and quartz and it never failed to move me, not least the wonderful people in it! Thank you so much!

"SQUONK" WORDS AND MUSIC BY ANTHONY BANKS AND MICHAEL RUTHERFORD © 1976, REPRODUCED BY PERMISSION OF HIT & RUN MUSIC(PUBLISHING) LTD, LONDON W8 5SW.

Richard Thorns. 2015.

Gravenhead

By Morwen Lundy

and

Bethan Kennedy ☺

Richard Thorns

How we did this book!

Hi, my name is Bethan.

Morwen has asked me to write the ~~forward~~ foreword to this book. It covers two things: how Morwen was the very first person in over 500 years to rediscover the lost village of Gravenhead - way back in 2006, that strange, final summer of our troubled innocence (although she says she WASN'T the first, and that the credit should go to the man who died there, but I don't think that's fair), and secondly, why we wrote our book in this way (which was Morwen's idea).

But I wouldn't be writing this now, and the whole book wouldn't exist if I hadn't lent out Garreth (who was my boyfriend at the time) to Morwen on one summer Sunday, because it all started that way! Morwen came up to us both at school just as the summer term was ending, and she told us about some wonderful, fabulous discovery she'd made in the mountains, but she couldn't film it because she only had some crappy phone worth £9.99 that she'd got at Tesco's and Garreth had a Nokia 6280 (which was THE phone of its day!) You could film video on it and upload it onto YouTube, which was quite a big deal back then (this was 2006, remember). ☺

It was a really cool phone, but that was the only thing that WAS cool about that summer because it was the hottest one ever!! I can still remember the feeling I had in the playground in that scorching, endless heat: six weeks of summer and NO MORE YEAR ELEVEN!!

(Maybe when you look back to your last days of childhood, to when you were discovering the

Richard Thorns

New World (like Gravenhead was to us both), maybe your summer memories ALWAYS jump first to the front)??

  Anyway, Morwen found Gravenhead, and Gravenhead was the reason Morwen moved on with her life and didn't spend the rest of it screwed up for good. I hope you'll like Morwen; she's tall and skinny and she's got dry black hair she can't control and pale freckled skin like milk and nutmeg (she once said) and she was always really good at English, and she had a brilliant way of writing; really lyrical and gorgeous, which is why she's at the London School of Journalism now.

  Morwen wanted so badly to get out of Rosengrave and into university to somewhere really good, and now she is doing this book as her diss-whatever and I am sending her my contributions and the result is going to be that (when the book is all finished) you will probably see this bit first. Morwen always used to say I was a real summer child, all hip pacifism and summer cotton bracelets and she was always so prim and serious and brooding in those days, but then again she had a lot to be serious and brooding about. The truth is she should have hated me anyway, because appearances can be so deceptive behind all those summer cotton bracelets, and I owed her so much, back then. ☹

(I don't want to talk about that now I'll leave it until the book). ☺

~~Sometimes when you find~~

Morwen found a box in Gravenhead's church, and it was wax-coated so all these ancient papers in it were dry, and they pointed to a way of killing the thing still there in the village. Morwen packaged all the papers up and sent

Richard Thorns

them anonymously to the British Museum and there they are if you want to go and have a look at them. They were sort of like sermons and they used the Book of Acts in the Bible to kill the thing, so that's what we've done; written our story like a Sacred Book: the Book of Morwen and the Book of Bethan (me) and the Book of All.

You see, speaking of lost things, there are four other lost "Books" in this story, but we can't ask Morwen's gran to write the Book of Nora (because she's too old and doesn't want to) and we can't ask Garreth to write the Book of Garreth (because his new girlfriend might beat us up); we can't ask Professor Hartley to write his Book (because he's dead) and we can't ask *Wales Today*'s demon weathergirl Louisa Caybourne to write the Book of Louisa (because she was a bitch).

So we have gathered (a) what we know and (b) what we imagined it was like for these people and we have written the books ourselves.

Morwen feels she owes it to the dead man's family not to steal his glory! I think she's missing the point, and she'll hate me for saying this but in a way I sometimes think that Gravenhead WAS Morwen, because Morwen, like Gravenhead, was abandoned and lost and hidden under such deep water, and I think her past must have had terrible monsters in it. But at least we can remember it and when we do, we agree it was like our last childhood and summer always leaps to the front. ☺

I can't think of anything else I want to put here so here it is.

Richard Thorns

PART I

VAGABOND AND DELICIOUS

Hasn't a friend to play with the ugly duckling.
The pressure on, the bubble will burst before our eyes
And all the while, in perfect time
Tears are falling on the ground
But if you don't stand up you don't stand a chance.

Rutherford/Banks. 1976.

Richard Thorns

Chapter One

The first secret.

Late July, 2006. North Wales.
Somewhere between Rosengrave and Tryffynydd

The Book of Morwen

LEAVING THE cool shade of the railway station had been a *great* idea, I thought savagely to myself, as I pushed my bike up the hill towards the fast-receding figure near the summit.

'Hang on a mo, Garreth!' I called out. My voice seemed to leap away from me in the thin air.

Richard Thorns

It was so *hot* today, as hot as a pie factory! Hot hot hot!

Leaning my tall (and a bit slim - some would say skinny) frame over the bike, and panting, I looked down the hill, surprised at how far up we'd climbed: Treffynydd station lay baking in the Welsh foothills; the hot air misty and blue. Far below me, the diesel train gathered its skirts and took a run to get going, bellowing faintly in the valley.

Still resting on the bike, and almost in the sky itself, it seemed to me, I found my shadow very small against the dark spoke patterns on the road. I looked upward; yes, I was so high up the sun actually did look a little closer; even in mid-morning I could feel it digging warm hooks into my face.

A small memory suddenly popped into my head: in much earlier teasing, *milk-and-nutmeg* was the name my Da had given to my face; for its light dusting of freckles over stark paleness, made even more obvious against my black tumble of hair. My hair was really damp with sweat and I pushed it out of my eyes (eyes so dark my Mam always said I could only ever be Welsh). After today, I thought, not so much a milk-and-nutmeg face, but maybe a shiny red capsicum if we didn't get out of this heat soon! I gave the bike another push.

At the top of the hill, Garreth had put his bike down on the road and was sitting on the grass verge, looking at me. He looked... well, you know that skater look that some lads try and get: thick long hair and wisps of their first adventures with a razor? I think it's either pretty sad, or really lush and gorgeous if it's done right, and Garreth had it great. Up there at the top of the hill he looked like summer itself, very brown with thick, shoulder-length blond hair and a honey-coloured T-shirt covered in navy graffiti, grey long shorts and leather sandals (Garreth's girlfriend Bethan obviously thought I was a proper munting if she trusted him with me today!)

He grinned as I pushed up to him, puffing like a steam engine.

'Come on up, Morwen,' he said, 'I'm loaded down with fishing stuff and I managed to get up here pretty quick.'

'Yeah, well, don't forget I *am* only a girl!' I panted from behind the handlebars (which was pretty much all I could manage).

But then we were coasting quickly, the muscles of my legs filling up again with blood, and the warm wind flooding into my face. We went past Llothwell Farm and beyond to the Raven's Head pub (where Sunday roast smells nestled briefly in my hair). Then we left the pub a long way behind so the corners of the high-banked lanes wrapped themselves around us. Until we reached the old track, nearly extinct, that I knew of old.

Still further - up the track, the mudguards of the bikes scraping on stones; stray brambles scratched at my bare legs. I grinned a little in revenge, listening to Garreth's muffled curses as he followed me.

Richard Thorns

To the end of the track. And I gazed down through the trees into the basin. I parked my bike and climbed carefully down towards the glassy water.

I wasn't wrong in February, I thought triumphantly...

The lake sulked under the heat of the day, untroubled by ripples or winds. The trees were baked into silence. There were grey patches of bank beneath my feet, and opposite, drying in the sun.

A trickle of sweat ran down my face, and I smothered it with the sleeve of my T-shirt. I'd never known a summer like this; even the birds couldn't sing in it.

A crunch of sandals sounded behind me, treading down the acorn cases. Then came another sound, and another, as Garreth made his way down the bank. I could hear his nearly-slipped giggles, and I knew he was grabbing at roots. Then, with one of those *can't stop* runs - the only way to stay upright - he bolted down the last part of the bank, hoping to stop as he neared the edge of the water.

He did. Just. He clutched me in excitement.

'It's... like a sheet of glass,' I murmured.

The air hummed gently with unseen flies; the lake lay very still in the heat. I squinted in the bright sunshine, and looked over to the opposite bank. Yes, we had come to exactly the right spot.

In the middle of the lake squatted a black pyramid of around a metre-square. A twisted, weed-encrusted tangle of iron clung awkwardly to the crest.

'Well,' I said, turning around, 'There you go.'

'That's the *steeple?*' exclaimed Garreth. 'Wow!'

'Complete with weathercock,' I confirmed to him. 'Unseen for five hundred years and it's going to make us both stars!'

But Garreth had other things on his mind. He was a fishing nut, after all!

'How deep do you think it is, then, Morwen, about a hundred feet, maybe?'

'No!' I scoffed at him, 'nowhere near! Maybe forty or fifty at the most! That little church is definitely late fifteenth to early sixteenth century; do you see the shape of the gable, and that squat steeple?'

I stared at it over the flat surface of the lake. The church was far away but perhaps twenty feet below the level of my eyes, and those dark lines on the opposite side of the bank gave me some idea of how much water had evaporated in this blazingly hot summer - maybe thirty feet or so in total.

That, I thought, was a lot of water.

(too much water?)

I felt suddenly a little frightened in that hot, silent forest. I shook my head as if to chase away my uneasiness, and shrugged:

'Right! I'll just get the camcorder set up; *where* are my notes?' I tossed my shoulder bag onto the forest floor and began to rummage in it.

That school camcorder would have been *well* wicked an' happ'nin' and cuttin' edge - when Duran Duran were last in the charts, pop-pickers! The little Hi-8 tape Panasonic was a great demonstration of our school's crappy funding and priorities. It was hiding away in the corner of its bag as if ashamed of itself; it reminded me of a kitten in a sack that didn't want to be chucked in the lake.

'Come on there, sweetie; I'm not going to chuck you in the lake,' I murmured, my heart still full of pride at my discovery, and that delicious summer feeling you get when you feel that anything can happen, and everything's limitless in the world! I pulled its cover off.

I found the notes as well and straightened up. Garreth was standing over me, looking reproachfully at me.

'Bethan isn't going to be very pleased about you booking out that camcorder,' he pointed out, 'she's booked it. She's doing that project for Media Studies.'

'Yes, but she didn't book it out for *today!*' I pointed out, extending the legs of the tripod and clicking them into place, 'Don't worry, we'll get it back! She won't be at the school on a Sunday, and she's got a note saying she can have it during the break. She told me.'

'I don't know why you brought it along in the first place,' grumbled Garreth, 'I thought you wanted *me*… along with my videophone.'

'I do, I do,' I said, my Welsh accent coming out in the sun, 'but all it takes is a flat *bat*-tery or something and that's a long journey all for nothing.' I walked over to him and squeezed his hand. 'Look, I'm not nagging, or having a go at you,' I said to him, 'anyway, look at that lake, stupid! - it's a bit better than the *EastEnders* omnibus.'

That cheered Garreth up. Squinting, he looked out over the lake.

'You know what,' he said thoughtfully, 'I reckon there might be pike in there.'

His battered fishing rod and tackle box lay on the ground in the idyllic scene. *We're so lucky,* I thought, breathing in the light, green scent of summer leaves as I watched him opening everything. Optimistic summer thoughts flooded unchecked into my mind:

And I'm the luckiest, I thought, *to be getting out.* To start the long, two year haul through Years twelve and thirteen in September; the surely-magical years through which I could kick towards the bright surface and breathe. And *then,* at LAST, OUT from pokey Rosengrave High, with its stupefied, new-frontier dreams; off to London to study journalism; maybe even minor in literature or poetry if I wanted to. Mr Evans said I was good enough at English and if I applied my-

Garreth's voice cut into my thoughts:

'Okay Morwen, both the phone and the Panasonic Hi-8 are going; I'm getting a good level on the sound. Just back up towards the lake.'

'How about trying for a good close-up on the steeple?'

'Can't, if I zoom in on the steeple I zoom in on you - you'll fill the shot.'

I nodded, walked to the edge of the lake and turned around. 'Is this okay?'

Garreth nodded. 'That's fine. You'll be fine.'

I turned away from him to look at the lake. Where branches met above me the water was calm and olive-dull, but in gaps the lake shone a blue reflection of the sky. I decided I liked the gaps; it was as if I could stand in the sky. I could, however, see a couple of long pale legs in khaki shorts reflected among the clouds (I noticed that, despite all my prayers and wishes, the legs above knee height still remained obstinately the width of my calves).

I made my lips up and quickly did the rest of my face, murmuring my lines as I did so, until I heard Garreth give a grunt. He was pleased:

'Okay, ready to roll, then, Morwen. On the count of five.' Fixing his left hand very still on me, he then held up his right, his fingers extended.

'Hang-on hang-on hang-on!' I found I was suddenly breathing quickly. Nerves had got to me. Garreth waited patiently, and pointed reassuringly at the camcorder:

'Just go in your own time; we can edit all this out. Hey, Morwen! Don't forget; you've *just* been handed over from the studio; they might need it to look like that!'

I gave a quick nod in answer as my breathing returned to normal. I held out my hands in enthusiasm, and fixed a smile on my face.

'I'm ready now,' I said.

'Five - Four - Three -' *Pause - pause:*

'*Thank* you very *much!* Well, as you can see this heatwave tells us Britain has *never* known a summer quite like this one, and the predictions are that the long, hot spell will continue for quite a time yet. But here in this peaceful countryside, twenty miles from the town of Rosengrave, something very peculiar is happening:

'The lost village of Gravenhead, long thought to have vanished in the sixteenth century, is once again making an appearance. Daily as the lake level drops behind me in this incredible heat, you see more of the ancient village emerging from beneath the water. You can see, for example,' I went on, gesturing with an expansive arm over the lake, 'that the church steeple and its strange, encrusted weathercock is sticking up from the surface, and also the dry patches of the banks can show us that this lake is being sucked up into the sky at an alarming rate; the product of this strange, baking summer.'

I waited.

'Cut.'

'What did you think?' I asked him anxiously.

'I don't know whether you'd really say: "baking,"' Garreth offered doubtfully, 'it makes you sound a bit young and girly, but otherwise it was good, Morwen. You're a natural!'

'Thanks, I reckon it was a good job,' I said, a little flatly.

'Oh sugar, let's get all this switched off! Hang on a minute,' Garreth stopped the recording on his phone, and walked over to the Panasonic, looking out over the lake. He stopped for a moment.

'Don't you reckon?' I said.

Garreth wasn't listening. His eyes were screwed up in the sun as he looked past me across the lake.

'What is it?'

'Morwen, that weathercock just moved.'

I spun around. And Garreth was right; the weathercock *had* turned to face us. I found myself feeling uneasy; there was no wind, and the weathercock had to be full of five hundred year-old slime and gunge, yet it had spun easily on its spindle. It seemed to be scowling at us.

If this is a staring competition, I thought, *I've already lost.* I pulled my eyes gladly away. 'It's probably just a high breeze,' I said to Garreth, 'which wouldn't show up on the water?'

Garreth snorted. 'In this heat?'

'Well, whatever,' I snapped. 'Come on, let's get going - or are you going to set that thing up?'

'You *bet* I am,' Garreth bent down and started to pull the fishing rod out of the bag. 'Beautiful day, peace and quiet and a great couple of hours' fishing ahead!'

'Why don't you come down on Tuesday?' I said, 'after tomorrow you've got the whole summer,' but now I knew I *was* nagging, and wasting my breath.

'Well, I'll take the camcorder then,' I said finally.

Garreth was silent, looking at the camcorder on its tripod.

'*You* were the one who said to get it back for Bethan,' I pointed out.

'Yeah, but you know, if there *are* pike in here they're going to be big, I reckon. I might get lucky, and then I'll be kicking myself if I can't record it.'

'What about your phone?'

Garreth laughed at me, 'You've never hooked a carp or a pike, have you? You need both hands; it's not like putting on a lippy!'

Slightly offended, I shrugged, and left to pick my way up the bank. At the summit I paused, with my arm locked around a root as I looked down to say goodbye. Garreth was bent over the tackle box, and I could even see his finger caressing a compartment as he searched for the right stuff. I smiled to myself, and the smile froze on my lips:

Garreth wasn't aware... but the weathercock had begun to move again, as if it had seen all it wanted to see. I had a sudden cold thought in the heat: *It knows us,* I thought. Disdainfully, almost contemptuously, the weathercock turned away, against what wind there was, until it was back in its original position.

The Book of Bethan

I remember walking very hot and flustered down shady school corridors, frowning and dodging the cleaners with their enormous, sweeping floor polishers. Muttering: 'oh, get out of the way!' and thanking my stars that the school had opened on the weekend before the summer term ended! I skidded around the corner that led to the library, tugged the doors open and went in.

There were only a few volunteers working and they were staff - no year ten helpers today. In despair I looked to the Media desk, and with relief I saw Ravel (an ex-year thirteen student as from tomorrow, and leaving for uni in the autumn). He was zapping in a few books. He smiled up at me because I didn't check my walk even in the library (that old hag Mrs Jennall would've said something!). I walked up to the desk. And Ravel is actually fit (he's known as *Library Fine* behind his back; I don't know if he knows that), so I should admit I was reddening a little.

'Hey there, Bethan,' he said to me. 'Not getting Sunday lunch in today, I see.'

'Hi Ravel, 'I heard myself saying, trying to catch my breath, 'I booked the camcorder for tomorrow, but if I don't make it in… please can I have it today? I've got my note!'

Ravel took the note off me. 'Two weeks starting from tomorrow. Okay. And you're still alright; no-one's taken it. Well, they can't actually; it hasn't been brought back yet.'

I dropped my arms in dismay, 'You're *joking!* Who's got it?'

Ravel smiled at the state of me in that near-deserted school. I felt flustered, and not just because of the hot summer. I've been called pretty before and I do really hate it but, let's face it, sometimes a girl wants to look her best. I know I'm quite small, and I was in torn, painted jeans with my face all sun-squinting; my streaked blonde hair all over the place and matted, because I'd been walking fast in the heat. I wished I wasn't carrying my denim jacket that had been drawn on in lessons, and I *really* wished my T-shirt wasn't informing Ravel that IF YOU STOP STARING I'LL STOP SCREAMING! Still, what's a girl to do?

'Bethan, I really hate to do this to you,' Ravel was saying to me, 'but Emma was on the desk yesterday and Amanda Devlin....'

I closed my eyes; Amanda's Da had once taken his TV remote to a darts match. It obviously ran in the family; the lost property office was considering offering Amanda loyalty points.

'*Please* don't let it be Amanda Devlin!' I breathed.

'Hang on, hold on a moment,' Ravel ran an inky finger across the sheet. 'Okay, it was booked out for this Saturday. Mr Davis signed for it. There's no name on the booking form, just his signature, so...' He keyed in the barcode number of the camcorder off a separate sheet into the library's computer.

'Morwen Lundy!' he announced in triumph. He frowned, 'that's funny; she's one of the more reliable ones.' But I wasn't listening as I tugged my mobile out from my jeans.

'I'm going to *kill* her!'

'That's nothing to what you'll get if you use that in here, Sunday or no Sunday!'

Richard Thorns

Despite myself, I laughed, pushed my damp, streaked hair out of my eyes and walked out of the library into the sunny, deserted playground.

The Book of All

Plunk!

As Garreth spun the reel the float dipped under the water briefly, and then sat smartly upright. He drew in the slack and then placed the rod on its rest. Now that he had stopped moving he noticed the post-midday heat settling heavily on him; Morwen had been so right before she'd left him about forty minutes ago - it really was very hot! Turning off his mobile, Garreth lay back in the sun, enjoying all the sensations of isolation and exhaustion. Everything about the day was still and slow. Occasionally in the lake, circles lazily expanded, touched from below by the mouths of fish.

In the direction of Gravenhead's drowned steeple he had thrown some bread pieces into the water, and he noticed that the glassy surface had begun to flicker; a small school of little roach had found the bread and were trying to feed, pushing it around with their heads. Garreth smiled to himself and settled back, his head against his tackle box.

Caught in his doze, Garreth didn't see the float move once and then be tugged smartly under. It bobbed up again.

He didn't hear the low chuckle that seemed to blow across the lake, but much nearer the acorn cases snapped behind his ears. He turned lazily, thinking Morwen had come back. His eyes widened suddenly in disbelief.

An enormous, ragged-feathered crow was standing less than a metre away from his face, its head cocked slightly to one side, watching him intently with one yellow eye.

'Go on! Get out of it!' Garreth snapped, and threw a handful of leaf litter at the bird. With an indignant croak the crow flapped up into the trees.

Garreth smiled, realizing how spooked he'd been as he watched it fly. It must've been after the bait. Then his heart sank as he realized that the tree was *full of crows* - he could see the branches of the tree bending under their weight as they hopped from bough to bough like black lice. But Garreth knew that normally the din would have been appalling: these birds had been utterly silent, as if *they didn't want him to know they were there.*

Garreth got up slowly, fixing his eyes on them, and then, as they seemed to notice his movement something seemed to burst in him and he ran heavily through the woods. He had been right to do so; the black cloud flapped and swooped down and he heard the line fizz out. He turned briefly, and out of the corner of his eye he saw his rod jump and fall, its rest collapsing as a bird collided with it.

Light flashed in the trees as he ran. Garreth knew he was running open-ended and that he would stop only when he felt safe. Brambles tore at his legs and low branches threatened to batter him unconscious...

Richard Thorns

Only after a long minute of pure sprint did Garreth finally stop. He leaned against a tree. It would be alright now, he thought. He allowed himself a brief smile. The crows must have had young nearby. Scared by a flock of birds - the great director! He remembered an old rhyme about magpies: "one for sorrow, two for joy. Three for a girl and four for a boy." What would you get for a hundred? Then, with dread he heard a low snapping above his head, and in sudden fear he looked up at the trees.

Noiselessly, the birds had followed him. And this time Garreth knew that there could be no escape and that no amount of running would help him now. He turned away from the tree to run again, and there was suddenly no ground beneath his feet; he tumbled into a deathly-dark blackness like Alice down a rabbit hole.

The Book of Morwen

The ringing on my mobile seemed to come from a very long way away.

My head was skidding against the slippery window of the train as it swayed, growling, towards Rosengrave on its journey. I smiled in a half-dream at the sweetest, newest memory of my obsessive escapes out into the mountains: before the 13.30 train had lumbered into Treffynydd (where trains to Rosengrave on a Sunday were every 90 minutes) my feet had thundered woodenly through the dusty ticket office and then I had slumbered on the platform, staring at flowers and butterflies in the droning summer, listening to the birds.

'Hello?' I said.

'Morwen? It's Bethan.'

'Beth',' I said warmly, 'how's it going? How are things at your Aunt's place?'

'We didn't go! Mam got in so late last night, and she thought she might still be over the limit. Da's away going long-haul to San Fran' so I'm at the school. I've been trying to get the camcorder.'

I jumped; Bethan knew phrases that a chef with his hand caught in an oven door wouldn't be able to keep up with.

'Oh, right, Beth',' I said a little nervously, 'so do you need it back now? Today?'

'Well, are you coming in? Or you'd better be in tomorrow because I *do* need it. I booked it,' Bethan's announcement ended lamely in my ear as she tried to hide the frustration in her voice. She wasn't doing so well.

'Bethan,' I said to her, my heart thumping, 'I'd bring it in now for you if I could, but the camcorder's still with Garreth. We're at... well; anyway, he's got it.'

I heard a sigh down the phone as Bethan tried to justify a long walk to the school for nothing – and couldn't.

'Well, he's switched his phone off; he's *got* to bring that camcorder in tomorrow! I need it!'

I felt an old familiar rising of panic in me the moment anyone showed any kind of aggression to me. After Year nine and what happened to me, it throbbed away at me like old scar tissue.'

'Bethan *I'll* call him. I'm *sorry* I'll try to get-'

'No, Morwen. Look, don't worry about it, okay?' Bethan's voice snapped in my ear, as at a distance she finally gave in to her temper.

I stared reproachfully at my mobile as it hummed up at me. Switching it off, I put it down on the empty seat beside me. *A fight with Bethan is all I need,* I thought. On top of the scar tissue, something else stirred: it was guilt; Bethan and Garreth had been my lifeline after Year nine. Oh, sure, everyone had stopped all they did before, but nobody had ever came up to me and tried to make friends. *Make friends with a* squonk? *Are you* joking?

The train growled and swayed through the valleys on its way back to Rosengrave. Yes, before Bethan had called I had indeed dozed, and the low droning of the train and the rocking of the carriage had lulled me almost into a hot sleep. Now I was awake I wanted to tell Bethan - anyone - that I was finding it hard to get the ugly image of the turning weathercock out of my mind. And now my head weighed ten tons and I lulled again and the dreaming came again...

And in the dream I was swimming deep under the lake, and down the ancient main street of the town. The half-beamed houses reared mistily into view either side of me, like ghosts. Gravenhead church lay on the remains of the village green ahead of me, its long-vanished grass now waterweed.

The water was keeping me upright; I landed lightly in the weed, feeling as if I had just flown there, and I gently pushed at the church door. It opened easily. I swam down the centre aisle, making a few fish dart suddenly through the water, heading for the gloomy safety of alcoves. Instead, I kept swimming the aisle, towards the barrier...

And then I turned to face the ancient remains of the Gravenhead congregation, silent and awful and grinning at me from the long-past; the current from my swim was still making them bob gently in the pews. One of the skeletons had its head slumped onto its chest, as if whatever sermon it was listening to had sent it to sleep, and I noticed with distaste that a small fish was swimming - in a tiny cage - within the skeleton's ancient ribs, as if trying to take the place of its heart.

Richard Thorns

Chapter Two

The birth of the squonk

The Book of Bethan

MORWEN HAD ARRIVED IN our class at the start of Year nine at the beginning of the autumn term. Right from the word go I knew she was going to get it, the moment she walked into my English class one dark and dreary morning. It was raining hard and the whole classroom smelled sour, with smells of wet hair and clothes; the lights were on in the morning and there were puddles on the floor from our bags. I'm not sure if this means anything, but it's a snapshot of that moment when Morwen walked into our classroom like a pale ghost.

You know when there's somebody at school who's going to get it; they're either fat, or ginger, or they've got braces or glasses, or whatever. Or maybe it's just because of where they come from, or the way they look; maybe because of something really dumb they're into that no-one else gives a toss about. Morwen didn't hold back there; she ticked all three of the last boxes.

As far as *because of where they come from*, for kick-off, Morwen came from the Longmeadow bit of Rosengrave, and Longmeadow has the kind of houses that make you feel you should wipe your feet on the way out. It was the bit of town that suffered the most from the pit closures in the eighties because all it really was, was just a little cluster of houses occupying the ridge that led up to the mine and the coalface. It was near the mine for a reason; close enough for the poorest of the face workers who had no transport, and rented from the National Coal Board. As a result, it was always the worst area; always grimy from the coal-dust that blew off the slag heaps so nobody's washing was ever clean. It also had the worst view in the world. And that's saying something for Rosengrave!

So it was bad enough even when Rosengrave was doing okay. But when the pit closures happened it *really* went down the toilet. The miners didn't know what to do anymore except get pissed all the time, and that led to boredom plus a lack of inhibition, both of which I think make babies. So then a whole new generation of kids gradually came along who never knew anything different; no sense of doing anything for its own worth; all people knew was what to depend on and where to get it from, whether benefits or drugs in some cases. If this is a bit depressing I'm sorry, but I think it's important to explain what Morwen had going against her, right from the off.

Because of the way they look. So, there was this kind of inherited tiredness and scruffiness about Longmeadow and the people in it, and this was a scruffiness reinforced by Morwen and the clothes she wore on that first day. Our uniform included what *should* have been a bottle-green sweater; Morwen's was lime-green; she was kitted out in designer gear alright, and it all looked genuine Sue Ryder. Nobody really said anything about this from the start; the school wasn't *that* bad. Gradually, though, a kind of victim mentality warily reared its head with Morwen, and that was what happened after about ten minutes, when Mr Evans asked us about a drama that was on the TV, which was an adaptation of some God-awful book by Hardy.

Because of what they're into that no-one gives a toss about. He'd asked us all to watch it if we could, because it might teach us deep down how books can be adapted into films (or something). Nobody had watched it; we all told Mr

Evans what we'd got up to at the weekend and *why* we hadn't watched it, though, and there was a lot of intellectual input like:

'Has it got any tits in it, sir?'
'If the characters are anything like you, Daryn, yes!'

So everyone had a bit of laugh. That was until he asked Morwen (who, you'll remember, had only just arrived, and so couldn't have been asked to watch it). She *had* though… *and* she'd read the book, and it's about a squillion pages long according to Mr Evans. So that went down really well; that was how Morwen earned her spurs on that first day.

Morwen was quiet and brooding, and she had this sort of… *desperation* about her that seemed to seep into everything; you couldn't imagine her ever collapsing into giggles at anything; which made that target on her back just that little bit bigger. I found out later that Morwen and her Mam had moved into Longmeadow (another black mark, and not on the washing this time; nobody ever moved *into* Longmeadow) because her Da had walked out on them both, and that was why she was like she was. I felt bad when I heard that. Not bad enough to stick up for her, though (I was hooked up with Garreth by then, and doing my own thing).

That was how the threads of Morwen's dysfunctional life kept coming; If Morwen was the trunk of her own tragic tree, then the branch from it was the story of her Da walking out on her and her Mam when she was only fourteen, and the sub-branch was that all she did at the weekends was go off into the mountains and be on her own, brooding about that break-up. And the twig from that sub-branch, and the bitter berries you might find on it was, at that time... who knew?

Looking back on it now, I'd say she was traumatised about her Da just upping off like that, and maybe more people should have considered maybe she was depressed and those isolated walks in the mountains weren't doing her any favours (telling people about them certainly didn't).

So by the end of the year we had, in the Red Corner: Katie Pressman, Georgie Taylor and Jestine Middle; a gang of three girls at the top of the food chain, or inner circle (or whatever you want to call it). In that hazy, vague aura that those girls had around them, swam the likes of Cara Leighton, Alison Dowding and Cathy Searle (who I went to primary school with). And to the nether regions of *them* (like the bits on sheep's wool at the back, I suppose), clung all those other hangers-on just waiting to move up the line. That was pretty much everyone taken care of...

And... laydeeez an' gen'lemen... in the black-and-blue corner... there was Morwen.

It really was that simple. That was how it all started; the persecution that I can write about now (just). I'll never forget one English lesson because just the memory of it makes a lump form in my throat.

It was still Year nine and we had all got back after our Christmas break to find the school experimenting with 'modules'; an idea to work into our lessons a few 'building-blocks of World Awareness,' ethical and cultural roles and all that bollocks. And so, for creative writing, everyone had to think of a mythical creature and tell the rest of the class about it. So, after the Loch Ness monster and Bigfoot had sputtered out like a wet firework, Morwen had put up her hand and told Mr Evans that she knew about a squonk (trust *her*... she was like a lamb to slaughter).

After the gales of laughter had subsided, Mr Evans cleared his throat and called for silence.

'So - for the benefit of the class, would you like to tell us what a squonk is, Morwen?' he'd asked her with the beady look of an all-knowing, co-conspiratorial sage (and probably thinking: 'what the blankety-blank's a bleedin' squonk, then?')

Morwen had gone red: 'A squonk is a creature in North American legend', she explained nervously. 'It's obsessed with its own ugliness, because it really does look hideous; it's probably the ugliest creature in the world. It wanders alone in the forests and the mountains all by itself

(Oh, Morwen, I thought a little sadly, *you're like a chicken stretching its neck out on its way to market)*

and all it does is weep loudly at its appearance and it avoids all contact with hunters, but because it's so rare all those hunters just want to chase after it and kill it. You can find a squonk only by following the trail of its tears by the light of a full moon, but if you catch it and keep it in a bag it will dissolve into a bag of tears. Or if you corner it and it knows you mean it harm it will collapse into a pool of tears. This will happen anyway eventually, but it comes on earlier if you-'

That was as far as Morwen got, because the whole class erupted. 'SHUT UP!' yelled Mr Evans as Morwen had shrunk into her seat.

And of course that was where Morwen got her new nickname from. 'Alright, Squonk?' she was always asked (not that anyone ever seemed interested in her welfare). Morwen never said anything at this; she always shrank into some quiet mass. And it would have stayed that way if a few girls decided she couldn't be all *that* bad, and if they hadn't invited her along to a pear orchard one evening to do some scrumping.

And something bad happened in that pear orchard that night.

Yes, it was something pretty bad, and I know what it was but it was so bad I don't know if it's my place to tell. I guess Morwen will, if she wants. But it was bad, because the nickname changed after that from squonk to something far bitterer, something so much more horrible, but little residues of the squonk nickname still remained; it then became interesting to know if squonks really *do* go to pieces in a pool of tears, when they're cornered.

And then it got *really* nasty.

It *must* have been nasty, because Morwen ended up in hospital and Katie, Georgie and Jestine all got suspensions, even though some got away with it. And we all had to attend a SPECIAL ASSEMBLY in which it was explained to us what CRIMINAL ASSAULT meant, and that was when everyone (*especially* Katie, Georgie and Jestine) decided that maybe it wasn't a bad idea to lay off Morwen (well, it was partly that, and partly because somebody else had arrived at the school with red hair).

Like I said, kids can be fat, ginger, spotty, you name it. If you have a face like a Domino's house special then you get called Pizza face or the Clearasil Kid and then it's up to you to deal with it. Anyone can be victims, though - given a twist of fate - and I guess that's where the scary bit comes in because I suppose it could have been me. I know I'm not munting or chopped liver to look at, and a few lads would always come up to me with messages about who liked me. So I guess I was always alright, but as far as victims go I've never met anyone like Morwen; it was the way *she* dealt with it.

You know, those girls might have picked on her and nearly killed her, but they never won. They never, ever won. They never saw the tears of the squonk, not ever. Instead all they ever got was that quiet shrinking and withdrawing; that silent, morose implosion of thinking and thought.

That was when I decided I liked Morwen.

Chapter Three

The legend of Gravenhead.

The Book of Morwen

THE SKELETONS IN THE DROWNED church disappeared into bubbles as the train bumped over points. I sat up, warm in the carriage with a metallic taste of sleep in my mouth, and hoping Bethan would still be alright with me. I think I would have given *anything* at that moment to dunk my head into a deep, ice-cold bucket of water to chase out the stuffiness in my head and the slight shakiness of shock I felt after that dream. Instead, I looked out of the window as the train slowed right down.

Rosengrave's great mining lift dominated the surrounding skyline as the train bumped and shrieked - it did from any angle. First begun at the close of the nineteenth century during the National coal boom, it now looked exactly what it was, I thought sourly to myself - a skeleton presiding over a picked-over town.

When the miners gave up their fight to keep the pit open and the town collapsed, Mam once told me you could almost hear the shops discussing it amongst themselves; Waitrose and Debenhams fled for the hills, settling instead over at Llancellwyn (Rosengrave's nearest big industrial town); Poundland and Primark turned up instead, hoping to grab the last of the local shop trade (and lots of my Mam's shop-owner friends went to the wall in solidarity with the miners). The bleak, economic winds that blew around our strange ghost town still blew, and every time I looked at this grim view as I came back from the mountains it fired at me every time and kicked me to do my best - my very, very best - to Get! *Out!*

I closed my eyes, deciding to doze in the carriage until the slamming of the train doors would properly wake me up. No panic there - it was the end of the line anyway. After five minutes, I found myself clawing at the carriage door. I went out of Rosengrave station, walked to the end of the street to the Place of the Dead and sat on the steps of the second memorial. I pulled open a bag of crisps.

The Place of the Dead was the name that me (and the few friends I had had in those days) had given to the area overlooking the shopping centre, way back in Year six. We liked the sound of it because in the winter (when it was getting dark on our way home from school) the mere mention of the name was enough to give us a thrill of terror when we knew we must walk past it. The name had stuck - unlike my friends from Year six.

Rosengrave's got two memorials, like a lot of mining communities. There's a war memorial, of course, paying homage to the dead of the two world wars, but a second one commemorates the dead of the two great mining disasters of the last century - the Fairfield pit collapse of 1903 and the Llancellwyn fire of 1938 (the cause of which had never really been established). A bronze miner, a child in each arm, stares out over the shopping centre and the KFC.

I finished my bag of crisps and got up, checking my watch. It said 15.04 and a few tired shoppers were still mooching around the Arndale on this hottest of summer Sundays, mostly looking as if they were having a rotten time. *I should ring Garreth,* I thought. I punched his number into my mobile:

Ring-ring - Ring-ring - Ring-ring - *"The person you are dialling is not able to take your call at the moment. Please leave a message after the tone..."*

I waited patiently for the beep.

'Garreth, I know you're there,' I said, 'listen! We have to get the camcorder back to the school because Bethan is there and she's really pissed off with us! Okay, 'bye.'

I ended the call, frowning as a thought came to me: *I thought Bethan said his phone was switched off?* It was just like Garreth to ignore it, anyway, *or* fall asleep in the sun, I reasoned. He'd be the most studenty-student in Wales when he finally escaped this dump of a place! I decided to call another number, and was slightly relieved when it also went to voicemail:

'Hi, this is Bethan. If you're fit, leave your name and number and I'll call you! Otherwise leave a message.'

I grinned and spoke into the mobile, hoping that Bethan's voice wouldn't suddenly break into the message I was leaving:

'Beth', it's Morwen. Look, I'm *sorry* about the camcorder; I didn't know you'd try to pick it up a day early! But I don't think today is going to be the day for you, I left the camcorder with Garreth and I guess he's asleep, I think. Anyway, he's not answering his phone. You can try me later if you like, but otherwise I'll see you at school tomorrow. Bye.'

Richard Thorns

I'd rushed the last bit, I thought, but what the hell. I left the Place of the Dead, and decided to get the bus home.

The Book of All

In the time it had taken Morwen to get home on the train and make her calls, things had changed slightly at the lake. Where once there had been a squat, ugly pyramid of black poking up through the surface of the water, the steeple now looked meagrely taller, as if it had grown up a little.

On the eastern side of the lake a fishing rod lay flat on the bank, its line leading into the water. And every now and then it shivered on the ground as the line tightened.

Nothing else had changed - the bank was empty. A collection of sandwiches, as scattered and stranded as the weed left behind on Gravenhead's steeple, dried slowly in the sun.

The Book of All (cont'd)

Garreth lay on his side, very still in the hollow; partly through fear, and partly because his breath had been knocked out of him. He craned his neck as he stared upward; the sunlight was so strong it was piercing even the tufts of grass and bracken that had hidden the hole from him. In his semi-darkness, parts of the earthen walls seemed to glitter and shine. Garreth's fingers crept around his prison: digging deep into the soft walls and they came back filthy, the nails blackened. Garreth looked at them.

'That's *coal!*' he murmured, '*this* near the surface?'

He was lying in a fissure around five metres wide and two metres deep. He had been lucky; he had fallen onto a little shelf, beyond which the hollow plunged a further three metres. Garreth looked from the depths back up to the surface: he could see shady black shapes, flitting and hopping. The birds were determined to find him somehow. They seemed to be interested in something. Garreth craned his neck towards the surface.

He could see a bright orange shape in the bracken, and he knew with a thrill of hope it was his mobile! He looked around the fissure and his eyes alighted on a long stick. An idea came to him. Carefully, quietly, he dragged the stick towards him, unlocking his fishing knife as he did so. Holding the stick carefully, he began shaping one end into a point.

The Book of Bethan

Our long, white-gravelled drive dug through my ballet pumps and into my aching feet. I sauntered up the drive towards the house, so tired I wandered from side to side in the hot sun. Eventually I found myself letting myself in through the front door; the shade of our big house settled on me like a cool glove.

Richard Thorns

The sun streamed in at the back of the house, and I could see my Mam asleep in a garden chair underneath the shade of a tree. I was going to announce my arrival, but then I saw a near-empty bottle and what was left of a lemon, shrivelled up in the sun and I saw there was no point; Mam would be out there until the creeping chill of dusk settled on her, and then she'd ease herself out of the chair, and totter towards the house in just the sort of sideways way I'd done earlier.

The fridge door was slightly open and I closed it with a sigh, now knowing I could have gone out with Morwen and Garreth all along. Dad would be in the sky by now, taking an Airbus or a triple-seven over to San Francisco on the red-eye; Mam couldn't even make it over to Auntie Helen's place in the car.

The Book of All

Garreth jumped out of his skin as his mobile suddenly activated. He had been poking around with the stick for a long time; of course it was bent and insisted in going the other way to where he wanted. The heat, the frustration and the fearful sight of the crows hopping around above his prison made the sweat seep out of him, and to his horror he felt suddenly tearful. But then the stick had a sudden hit and the mobile flashed into life.

It was on loudspeaker, and the welcome tone sounded loudly in the forest. Garreth sank back, exhausted and nursing his aching arm. Suddenly a shrill ringing stabbed the quiet air. Startled, the crows flapped noisily up into the trees. After three rings there followed a mumbling, manufactured voice.

And then, from deep within the bracken, there came a sound:

'Garreth, I know you're there. Listen! We have to get the camcorder back to the school because Bethan is there and she's really pissed off with us! Okay, 'bye.'

The Book of Morwen

The late-afternoon was cooling the air. It was around 17.40 in our tiny back garden. I felt myself relaxing after my long day, thinking about the end of term. The barbecue from next door was making me feel hungry, billowing smoke as it was over our fence (but unlike that fiery barbecue I was enjoying yet another yummy bit of salad, plus a few sausages from Spar's basics). *The mosquitoes are tucking in, too,* I thought sourly, twisting my nails into a white lump on my arm. I glanced quickly at the kitchen door; my Mam was inside washing up our soup bowls. I sipped quickly at my lemonade: there would never be a better time than this:

'Gran?'

My old gran, visiting us as she often did, was sitting opposite me at a table in our garden, and if she was feeling the heat in this sweltering summer she never let it show, what with the cotton trousers she was wearing, and her long-sleeved shirt. Maybe, I thought to myself a little sadly; maybe you just felt the cold a little bit more, once you got older.

I drew a deep breath.

'Gran, do you know anything about Gravenhead?'

She looked surprised, 'The lost village, you mean, dear? I'm surprised you've even heard about it. Why the sudden interest?'

I thought for a moment. *What to leave out?*

'Well... there's this thing some kids are doing at our school. Well, it's more of a taster, really, so they can get to know how to use the media stuff before our projects start properly in the sixth form. Most of us are taking it pretty seriously, though. The thing is... I wondered whether maybe I should do something on Gravenhead.'

My gran frowned a little.

'Well, it's more of a local legend than anything else, Morwen; there isn't a lot of fact there. I *do* know it was supposed to have disappeared in the sixteenth century - something to do with Henry VIII's troops on their way from Cardiff to Chester I think. You do *know* about the Dissolution of the Monasteries?'

With an eye on our kitchen door, I listened to gran's tales of Henry's vendetta against Rome at not being allowed to dump his wife and marry again; he'd obviously taken it badly, burning monasteries to the ground to get at the valuable lead in their roofs, confiscating treasures and seizing all the land; trumped-up charges for the abbots, and death - the agonizing end of being hanged, cut down and butchered.

I imagined Beth' writing about it: *"Henry VIII ruled from 1509 until his death in 1547 and he was a complete asshole!"*

'Well, anyway,' I heard my gran saying, '*anything* was fair game for soldiers and mercenaries in those days, so if Gravenhead ever existed in the first place it would be long-gone by now, I think. I shouldn't've thought that old story would interest you, Morwen. What about that pop group you saw last weekend at the Playhouse?'

'*No*, Gran, I want to do something *really* interesting,' I felt slightly desperate, my eye on the back door (I could see a shape moving about behind the glass with a bowl of trifle). 'I don't want to do it on some *group-*'

I suddenly jumped as a ringtone cut through the warm air. I glanced at the number displayed on my mobile. Garreth! About time! I grinned and held the mobile to my ear:

'Hiya! Catch anything?'

There was no reply for a full few seconds. And then...

A faint sound, stretching across the still-warm garden and through the mobile into my ear. A grey *sound! Unlike any I'd known before, drained of tone and colour. Like two sheets of rusting corrugated iron, banging lazily in the wind...*

But... old!

I caught my breath.

Richard Thorns

'Garreth? I whispered, 'there's something wrong with your mobile. Answer me, or try again!'

I snapped off my mobile and the screen winked and shut off. Then I reactivated it and called the number I had in my head:

A flat, smooth tone sang in my ear.

'Right, who's for trifle? All alright, Morwen?'

I looked at my Mam. 'I think so,' I said. 'That was Garreth. The signal on his phone sounded *well* scrambled! And now he's switched it off! All in a couple of seconds!'

My Mam shrugged at me as if to say: *what do I know?*

'Oh, spoons,' she said,

She disappeared back into the kitchen. I frowned; I was almost out of time now.

'Sorry, Gran, what were we talking about?' I said.

'You won't be doing your project on some pop group,' answered my gran with a wry smile, 'and so instead you want to do something on Gravenhead! You'll get me into trouble with your Mam.'

I frowned a little. '*Why?*'

I felt a sudden sting on my arm. Wincing, I slapped at it with my hand. A mosquito fell off, found-out and broken, leaving a big smear of blood on my arm. The blood was exaggerated - too big for the mosquito. Not *its* blood, I thought faintly. *My* blood! I looked up at my gran. She was sitting in her chair waiting for a spoon, and waving a hand now and again, as smoke from next door's barbecue drifted over the fence into the garden…

I felt a little shudder run through me; the thought was paradoxically almost a memory of the future, it seemed:

Blood and fire, and billows of smoke! I sensed innocence, then, and sunlight, but also an ancient evolution to be respected and somehow feared. Like a child on a sunny porch, playing with a spider.

Shaking my head a little, I said softly: '*Why* would you be in trouble, Gran?'

If there was anything other than surprise on my gran's face, she hid it beneath the soft folds of her skin.

She looked at me… almost reproachfully…

'For scaring you, dear.'

Chapter Four

At Treffynydd station

The Book of Bethan

THERE'S SOMETHING *going on.*

I could *feel* it somehow. Not that I was worried about anything going on between Morwen and my boyfriend. Not being horrible, I thought, but let's face it; we're talking Morwen Lundy. No, it was more that call to Garreth's mobile I'd made around five pm; I'd felt surprised (and annoyed) that once he'd turned it on again, he'd left it on voicemail. Maybe I shouldn't have left such a rude message, but it was just that I was thinking about my wasted journey to the school and my aching feet. Where *was* he? Morwen had called me and left a message while I was in the bog ages ago, and she'd said Garreth was asleep in the sun. Fair enough, but he couldn't *still* be out there! I frowned to myself. I looked at my watch; it was ten to seven. That was when the thought began to change in that cool, dusky big house of mine. It changed from: there's something going on.

There's something wrong.

I knew it; I *knew* from the way Morwen had seemed to change when she'd scampered up to us! During that last week of term we'd all marched towards 3.30pm, Friday afternoon! The teachers were trying to hide how they were *really* feeling, the rest of us were celebrating and *all* of us were thinking: *It's a wrap until September!*

But being so openly happy about something like the end of term; that wasn't Morwen's style, I'd thought. And I'd been right.

On Wednesday, Morwen had come bounding up to us both at school in the lunch hour, beaming all over her face. 'I've got something to ask you both,' she'd said, 'and in return, I'll have something to *show* you both as well!'

'What is it?' I'd asked, not really interested. Ah, but that was when that pale face of Morwen's became a bit cagey. She'd stuck out her bottom lip and refused to tell us, but then she'd asked if she could borrow a mobile that took film footage.

'What is it?' I asked again, and this time I *was* interested, Morwen had this look on her face. It was the first oasis of calm I thought I'd ever seen on it.

'No, I'm not telling you; I'm really not going to,' she'd said, 'but I promise you it's something amazing, and my phone is just - well, I got it at Tesco and it's no good for anything like that. I know you want the camcorder, Bethan; I know you've booked it, and anyway I shouldn't have to work with stuff like *that*... especially for *this!*'

I'd looked at Garreth: *he* was looking interested as well. I'm not being funny, but usually if somebody at Rosengrave High comes out with something like that you'd tell them to piss off, but Morwen, *she* was a serious one alright; when she said something you knew she meant it, and believed in it with all her heart.

'Is it something to do with that media study, then?' I'd asked her.

Morwen had gone red. 'Well, yes, in a way,' she'd replied evasively, 'if I decide to include it in that. But it's more than that. It's more important than that, I mean. And also...' her voice had trailed away in embarrassment.

'What?' Garreth had said.

'Well,' Morwen had stammered, 'you've both been the only ones who showed any faith in me or wanted to know me, and I'm not into big speeches but this is going to change things; *nothing* in Rosengrave is *ever* going to be the same again! And I want to share it with you.'

I looked at Garreth. I think he was thinking the same as me. Morwen was virtually hopping with excitement. She seemed so…, oh, I don't know, *free!* I suppose. Like she was at primary school on her first day and found out she was the most popular girl in the school. I remembered what had happened before, seeing her face after the attack; that bloodied face and those grazes…

'What are you doing this weekend, Garreth?' I asked him.

'Sunday's the only day I've got and you know that. I can't do Saturday; we're playing Gresford Harriers, and *you* said you'd watch.'

'I know, but I can't do Sunday either, though. I'm visiting Auntie Helen with Mam.'

(Morwen really *was* hopping now).

'Can I borrow your mobile then, Garreth?' she said. 'Please!'

Garreth sighed and looked at the floor. I remembered those grazes again as I looked at Morwen's face.

'Can she?' I asked him.

Garreth sighed again. 'Bethan, you know how much it cost, I'll be old enough to drive by the time it's paid for-'

'Come out with me, then,' blurted out Morwen suddenly

'What?'

Richard Thorns

'If you don't want to be separated from your phone, come out with me on Sunday. Out into the mountains where I found it.'

Garreth opened his mouth to tell her no, but then two things happened to make him change his mind: the first was that Morwen told him there was a lake there, un-fished, as far as she knew, and *that* made him prick up his ears alright! And the second thing was that I'd just taken a big grab at the small of his back with my sharp fingernails, because I'd never seen Morwen like this and she was owed a break. And then, funnily enough, Garreth had said 'yes'.

Saturday night. 'But if anything happens in those woods with Morwen tomorrow, Garreth, you'll wish your Da had never met your Mam,' I'd said.

The Book of Morwen

My arm itched from where the mosquito had bitten me. My mobile rang and I looked at the screen, frowning; it was a number I didn't recognise, a land line.

'Hello?' I said cautiously.

I don't know, but I think I instantly knew it was Garreth's Mam; there was a level tone to the voice, but at the outer edge of the voice there lurked a high, almost imperceptible edge to it; a shrillness, maybe of held-in panic.

'Hello, there, is that Morwen Lundy speaking?'

'Yes?' I answered, nervous now.

'Morwen, it's Mrs Rowe here, Garreth's mother. The thing is; we're wondering about... Garreth hasn't come home yet from a day out and I think he was out with you today, wasn't he (the voice dared me to say it wasn't so; if I had, I think that shrill veneer of panic would have cracked like toffee-apple).

'Yes,' I said carefully, feeling her panic beginning to be shared with me and not wanting it, 'Yes, he was; we went... on a picnic together, and Bethan was going to come as well, but she didn't. But Mrs Rowe, I can't tell you what happened to Garreth after that because we didn't... I came home by myself.'

'By *yourself*? Why?'

'Well,' I began, struggling for an answer. 'I had to get back and-'

'That was all you did, then Morwen? You just went on a picnic?'

'Yes,' I said, trembling.

'But what about that filming you did, then? Garreth said you wanted to film something you'd found in the mountains.'

I jumped. 'Oh... *that!* No, I just wanted to film some... I just wanted to film some birds, because there's a film studies module and I thought-'

'But he's not back yet, Morwen, and it's nearly eight-o-clock and he would have called us. I think there must be something wrong with his phone. Has he called *you?*'

Richard Thorns

I thought back to the earlier call on my phone. That dull clanging sound, that… *old* sound through my mobile that had seemed to scare the very teeth out of my head.

'He *did* call me,' I said to her, and I heard (or felt I heard) an exhale of relief down the phone into my ear, 'and there *was* something wrong with his phone, but you see that wouldn't be unusual, Mrs Rowe; sometimes when you're in the mountains the reception isn't too great! But all afternoon we were at Treffynydd station, or we were near it anyway. He's probably missed the train back.'

'Oh,' the brittleness of the voice seemed to be checked; the voice seemed warmer, somehow running smoother, 'yes, I suppose that would be it. But on a Sunday I can't think the trains would run much, Morwen. If he's missed the last one then maybe his dad should drive out there. Perhaps even the police; it's very isolated.'

'You know,' I said coaxingly, desperately wishing I could end the call, 'I'm really absolutely certain there's nothing wrong to speak of; Treffynydd's not the back end of the world and he's got his bike! I'm sure Garreth can look after himself and there's Bethan to think of as well; *she* wouldn't let anything happen to him.'

And, thank goodness, against all the odds there was a hint of humour from Mrs Rowe. She said something like: *'That's true enough,'* and then she ended the call and I took a deep, deep breath. I felt my heart hammering against my ribcage and I took a long gulp of squash.

'Is that a problem you've got there, Morwen?'

For the second time, I jumped; Gran was eyeing me beadily.

I shook my head quickly. 'No, nothing's wrong,' I said quickly, and fled inside to the bathroom.

I was frightened as I ran across the darkening grass of the back garden; where *was* Garreth? I remembered the scowling, fierce beak of the rusted weathercock. *What had I done?* Garreth was a friend; he'd tried to help me.

And he's fit, as well, a mocking feeling told me, as it floated after me like a joke Scooby-Doo ghost, *anything else about Bethan's boyfriend you'd like to mention?* But I soon outran *that* as I tugged open the back door (Mam saw me heading for the bathroom and I could imagine her mentally blaming the sausages).

I stood there in the locked bathroom, a wet flannel around my head to cool it, forcing myself to calm down. *What's wrong with me?* I thought. But I knew what was wrong. My own nature, which I had always thought of as rather sweet; that was the thing that was buckled and wrong; whatever had happened to Garreth, I knew it didn't matter as much as… well, it was very important to steer the course of the conversation away from the real reason, the real *place* we went out to today. I had to steer the conversation towards the station at Treffynydd because… because…

Because the station was a long way away from the lake.

Richard Thorns

Yes, that was it. Gravenhead's promises opened up before me like a summer flower, a sweet gift of fortune. I would film it and be the first to claim it. Then would come my name, presented to the London School of Journalism; the Natural History museum or something, and impossible to erase from that foundation-stone of record!

And then the end of another stone-block to my dreams of escape: the cold, unromantic stink of cash, and it would come winging in from all my interviews and newspaper features, and I'd wait for that magic moment of enrolment, of leaving my school for the very last time.

And then...

The Other Thing.

Yes, I knew it: I *knew* there was another reason for my determination to claim Gravenhead all for myself. But it hovered in my memory like a sweet thing, like a small burning candle in the corner of a dark room, or a call in a snowy wood; blanketed but clear at the same time. And I wouldn't let it in properly because it was there in that part of my brain that dealt with happiness and had once known happiness, and if that part of my brain was dead, then so too was that part of my happiness; my ambition. It said simply: *stay away*.

But I would deal with it, the Other Thing.

It was waiting.

The Book of All

Garreth's bicycle sounded like a sack of old bones thrown down a well as he hared along the rutted track. As the track met the smooth, asphalted road he gave a small sob of relief; in the darkness his parched, clattering track had looked nothing like the one that they had come along during the day, and with the terror of final reason Garreth had realised it had not been! He had cycled along a tiny thread of earth in the heavy dusk, hoping… hoping… before finally turning around and going back, dreadful thoughts turning towards the Sunday timetable and the last train!

But now his original track *had* hit the cool, grey road, and his descent was fast; a mixture of evening scents and temperatures. Firstly he felt the thin air of the mountain's height; air that smelled of dusty slate, quartz and other rock; stray gorse and thin trees. The sun, a great red-orange orb, had descended behind the furthest peaks, leaving behind a great panorama of sky: slate-blue and rose, and then the lane fell deeply into a pungent canopy of green scents; flowering bracken and air so warm after the mountain air it felt like the tropics, before levelling out to a gradual downward sweep of grassy fields and sheep. Here the mist had already gathered in the fields. The air was damp and chilled to summer perfection.

Now Garreth had it, he shivered in it. He cycled slowly along the lane. The fields were very black and in the

moonlight the sheep appeared to gleam in them.
Carnivorous crows and shining sheep; a scene between thriller and super nature, something collected from the deep past, and viewed like an old wartime silver-screen flick. Didn't it feel like that?

No.

It felt older.

Ahead of him gleamed the faint spot of a luminous eye, and he knew it was the lamp of Treffynydd station. Caught between that yellow, grounded eye and the full moon, white and glaring in the heavens, Garreth felt as if the giant sky was squinting interestedly at him. In the great space and silence the yellow light became closer as he cycled and, as he did so he heard the distant rumble of a train. He quickly checked his watch and a thrill of horror ran through him; *the 9.00 pm last train!* A grumbling lifeline between Pizza Hut and the Arndale Centre in Rosengrave, and abandonment here in this terrible place, with its misty silence...

Ignoring the muscles in his legs as they protested their innocence, Garreth put on a spurt.

The Book of All (cont'd)

The cool air had turned to swathes of mist now; visible and not hinted at. At Treffynydd's railway station the last train of the evening hung patiently at the platform, waiting for its timetable to catch up.

The train's hypnotic purr rose and fell: diesel-breathing that felt comforting to Daffyd as he walked the amber length of the twin coaches. Inside, there was just a single occupant, a young lad with a bike. *This service will be pulled soon,* thought Daffyd, *can't run a railway like this.* He checked his watch.

Satisfied, he blew on his whistle, sharp in the night.

The two-tone blast of the train's reply made him jump out of his skin. His mouth set in a hard line: he wished Ted wouldn't do that. One of these days, his (Daffyd's) heart of sixty summers would pack up at that sound and it would be Ted's fault! He stuck up his arm, thumb aloft.

'See you tomorrow, Ted!'

The train's purr became a steady roar, as the heavy engine began to rev. From deep inside the carriage, the sound to Daffyd seemed a low growl from a maw. The carriages moved slightly.

As the train began to move, that young lad in the carriage was staring at him, pointing over the fields to the lane. Daffyd's old eyes stared back at him. Well, his mate would have to cycle back to Rosengrave. Or walk. Bloody kids!

The noise died, and then rose again as Ted had another go. The carriages moved smoothly down the platform to where it sloped down to oil drums and dirty grass, and then the train was away down the line. Daffyd watched the red lights hang in the air until, with a faint blast of triumph, the train disappeared around the corner.

Silence descended on the station, broken only by the scraping croak of a pheasant.

Daffyd buttoned his jacket and went inside the station. Just a few bits of litter lying on the floor. Daffyd looked at the broom and then thought better of it; his thoughts turning instead to a pint at the Raven's Head. He unlocked the ticket office door and pulled down the blind.

Shaking his coat on its hook, he checked for the jangle of his moped keys. He opened the till and began to take out the day's takings, and it was then that he heard the sound of the station door opening. He tutted as he thought of that lad. He should've locked the door before he'd begun to close up. Now there'd be a scene while he explained he couldn't call the train back.

'You're too late, mate. Last train's gone.' he called out.

There was no reply, but Daffyd heard the door close. A dragging sound was coming from the ticket hall floor. So it's an old guy after all, thought Daffyd. Deaf, as well.

'LAST TRAIN TO ROSENGRAVE'S JUST GONE, MATE! THE TAXI NUMBER'S ON THE WALL!' he bellowed. Daffyd turned off the kettle at the wall but he *knew* the chap was at the counter. He really fancied that pint now. His mouth set in a firm line.

'*Look,* I *told* you we're...' he began, as he tugged at the cord of the blind...

The blind sprang *up,* and Daffyd's old heart suddenly roared in his ears as he stared at what was in the ticket hall. There was a pain at the back of his head, and he knew he had somehow struck the floor, yet the pain couldn't match that terrible tightening in his chest. His last memory was that... even on a Sunday, he hadn't had time to make the sign of the cross.

Outside, the clock CLACK-CLACKED patiently and the pheasant croaked mournfully into the mist. It was just after nine.

The Book of Morwen

I was awakened at 22.30 by the ringtone from my mobile.
'Garreth's home,' said Bethan
Relief flooded over me, 'Thank goodness!' I said to her, 'well, all's well that-'
'And his Mam says he's lost his phone and he's shaking like a leaf,' Bethan continued, and I could feel the sharpness in her voice, 'so it wasn't exactly the best weekend ever, Morwen.'
'No,' I said from my bed, grinning all over my face, 'I'm sorry, Bethan.'
'I think Garreth's maybe the one you should say sorry to,' Bethan said. 'His Mam says he won't be in school tomorrow and I don't think she's very pleased with *you!* It might not

be too good an idea to go round there, not unless you want to be fed into the microwave!'

She rang off, and I snuggled down into the duvet before realising how hot it was. I threw it off instantly and lay there in the darkness.

So Garreth had lost his phone. Well, that was shame; it would've been nice to have additionally had my footage on it. But then again, Garreth might also have tried to put my precious Gravenhead on YouTube, that discreditable land of geeks and hoaxes that had only been going a year; nothing would come of *that!* I pushed the image and possibility firmly from my mind: Garreth had lost his phone, but it didn't matter because for backup *I had brought along the Panasonic camcorder!*

So Garreth was safe, the footage was safe and my fabulous secret was also safe. I lay in bed and the veils of sleep began to drift and charm me in the hot room. It was summer and everything was alright, and I need never go back to the lake and see the ugly turning weathercock ever again. It was over.

Chapter Five

The typewriter fly

The Book of Morwen (cont'd)

I OPENED MY EYES SLOWLY, drowsily. I heard a blackbird singing in our back garden and the morning greeted me very gently. There was a low, buzzing sound at the sunny window, and I heard tiny taps; a fly was trying to get out. It reminded me of a typewriter fly: tap-tap… tap-tap… tap-tap… 'ping!' would go its desperate heart, and it would fall to the windowsill like a black, still typewriter word, perhaps to lie there until spring.

Richard Thorns

The typewriter fly and the singing blackbird meant that in the hazy air I forgot that our back garden had a punctured plastic football in the stinging nettles; kids from next-door who stood on their climbing frame and peered into our business. For a moment some sly, romantic little faerie seemed determined to place me instead in a lazy princess's summer-bed, with droning, soporific air with dust motes dancing in it, hazy petals on my pillow.

That blackbird was singing its little heart out.

Yes, sunlight was flooding into my room, a room that suddenly seemed full of CD's that Bethan had lent to me, and my clothes littering the floor; a wardrobe door lay open and an old glass of squash stood on a chest of drawers, with a sheet of paper on top to keep it clean. I sighed a little to myself but not in a bad way; this little princess better bag herself a prince who was into Lily Allen, I thought, and maybe a bit of Kate Moss as well; someone who wasn't too picky and didn't mind a bit of rough living.

My eyes settled on a newspaper lying on the floor, a copy of the *News of the World* from yesterday. The paper was open and there was a figure in one of those hard-done-by poses, sitting on a step, face-on-fist; elbow-on-knee. God, that bloke looked miserable!

"Now an alcoholic and living alone, Walter Emerson says he would give anything to see his daughter again after so many years."

'I know she's now a star, but I'm not after her money. I just want her to be Daddy's little girl again.'

I smiled. I knew exactly why I'd kept it now; I liked reading about that sort of thing. The Other Thing that had hurried away from me yesterday evening in my bathroom, warning me to *stay away;* my eyes flitted instinctively to the picture of my Da on my bedside cabinet. In the picture he was holding me up as he passed me over a gate to my Mam on the other side. I think I must have been, oh, maybe seven or eight? And this time as I stared at the picture the Other Thing really *was* like a lost call in the forest, thin and clear, but unlike before it seemed… *louder.*

'I do miss you so much, Da,' I whispered to the photograph.

But then Mam yelled upstairs that I was going to be LATE FOR SCHOOL! And this broke that mischievous little faerie's spell, and I got up and went into the bathroom.

The Book of Morwen (cont'd)

Downstairs, I froze with a spoonful of cornflakes halfway to my mouth, staring at the TV screen:

"Police investigating a death at a remote railway station say they have not yet ruled out foul play. The body of a sixty year-old stationmaster at Treffynydd, was discovered in the early hours of the morning. Police say a head wound, and the discovery of an open till, means they cannot discount robbery as the motive for the death."

Richard Thorns

Treffynydd railway station lay sunning itself in the bright morning, the idyllic picture fouled and spoiled by the "POLICE CORDON - DO NOT CROSS" tape (I noticed faintly that it was upside-down) stretching around the scene. I felt myself going pale; so unfamiliar to everyone - so familiar to me! I felt myself recognising... *everything!*

That was the dusty place we'd echoed through yesterday; that little station office. I saw the poster warning against travelling without a ticket; that stretch of road behind the station that led up to Fawkes's Hill; the place I'd guided Garreth's Mam to yesterday thinking it wouldn't matter, when she was talking about ringing the police...

So did *she ring the police?*

'We were at Treffynydd station, or we were near it anyway. He's probably missed the train back.' I looked at my cornflakes and the thought of another spoonful made me want to throw up.

'And now, with what promises to be another *scorching* day ahead for us - Louisa Caybourne's got the weather.'

'Thank you very much. Now you make sure you pack your sunscreen because it's going to be-'

I bit my lip and whispered...

'Oh, no.'

The Book of Morwen (cont'd)

I just about made it to school and kept quiet during tutor group, but that was normal for me so nobody said anything. This really *was* the final day, loose ends to tie up; careers advice in the holidays for Year 13, workshops for Year 11. There was some sort of amorphous good mood sweeping the place, because everybody knew the rules had been relaxed.

The first fire alarm went off at ten as I was walking to the library. Ricky Arren ran away from the smashed box on the wall, stuck a finger up at me and launched himself, backside first, onto the three-step vinyl-coated bannister. Whooping, he set off down the corridor, followed by his mates.

There was movement ahead of me: Mr Hughes and Mme Percelle came around the corner ahead of me and then hesitated, torn between justice and the school's Health and Safety policy. Mr Hughes looked straight at me, his face grim. Clutching their registers they walked into the playground, shaking their heads. I followed them, as distant classrooms rumbled with chairs being scraped back and doors opening.

Squinting in the bright sunshine, I touched my face tenderly. It was a hard, hot mask; I had burnt badly at the lake. I found my tutor group and joined the line, looking around me. Girls in ripped tights, pigtails and pencilled freckles were dotted around the playground. Some capered and strutted about excitedly, looking forward to the long summer. Friends on the other side of the fences waited for them for probably the last time; some appeared nervous and deep in thought (takeaway-careers beckoning), as if wondering: *What have we done!*

'SOME OF YOU OBVIOUSLY THINK A FIRE AT A SCHOOL IS A LAUGHING MATTER!' bellowed Mr Baynes through a megaphone, making a ripple of laughter skitter across the playground. Tutors looked around the playground suspiciously.

I felt a little better. *Oh, come on,* my mind had started to say to me, *we were just there - what did we have to do with anything; why would it be a problem?*

Because, a little sneaky voice inside me peeked at me, *you can't hide behind that little station-story of yours any longer! You'll have to tell the police where you really were. And when you do...*

Bethan sidled up to me. 'I bet it was Ricky Arren,' she said.

You think your secret's safe? It isn't safe yet!

I dragged my brooding thoughts gladly back from the forest. 'It *was* him,' I said to her, 'I saw him do it right in front of me! Good riddance to bad rubbish after today; he won't be allowed near the sixth form.'

There was an awkward silence.

I began: 'Look, Beth' - '

'Oh, forget it,' Bethan said, but she still looked a bit waspish, 'it was a bad time all round. I was worried for Garreth, and I didn't need a walk in the heat like that!'

'You've caught the sun,' I remarked.

'Not as much as *you*, Morwen! That's really gross!'

I grinned at her.

'Thanks!' I said.

'So what's this discovery of yours all about, then?'

I started, 'Hasn't Garreth told you,' I asked.

'No, no! I don't think he's even here! I called this morning and he was still in bed at gone eight.'

I nodded.

Anyway,' Bethan went on happily, 'all I need to do is tell the library Garreth's got the camcorder, and I can transfer it over and that's that! I'll just get it off him!'

Bethan looked as if she hoped I'd ask her about her project, and when I didn't, she went on breathlessly: 'I'm filming the inside of the Playhouse? You know we have to include at least one interview: I've got the drummer from *Forbidden Janet* because Kelly Winter's brother knows him. I'm doing my project on their gig we saw last weekend.'

I smiled again, 'Maybe you should talk to my gran,' I said.

What?

'Nothing. It was a joke. Look, why don't we just get into the library after this and sort out this transfer? I can come with you.'

'Okay,' agreed Bethan as the fire alarm suddenly cut into silence. We began to walk across the playground, but then my tutor tapped me on the arm. Placing a tick on the register, he said: 'Morwen, Mr Hughes and Mme Percelle want to see you in the House Office - right away!'

My heart sank. 'He doesn't surely think that was *me?*' I almost screamed. But all I got was a: "couldn't-tell-you" look and he continued ticking off names, moving off down the line.

Bethan was humming a little snatch of *Smells like Teen Spirit*, trying to raise a laugh, but I wasn't in the mood for humour. We walked quickly to the House Office, and I knocked nervously on the door.

'*See you out here,*' I mouthed to Bethan.

'Come in,' said the voice from inside the House Office. It was Mr Hughes's voice.

The Book of Morwen (cont'd)

My heart sank as I walked in because the police were waiting for me, just as I knew deep inside they would be. There were two of them; they both seemed such giant figures to little me, with their uniforms and their Hi-Viz. Mr Hughes and Mme Percelle were both there, as well, each holding a mug of tea.

'It wasn't *me* who set off the fire alarm, Mr Hughes,' I blurted out.

'No, funnily enough, Morwen, I didn't think it was you,' answered the tutor with a smile. And in a flash I saw how stupid I'd been.

There was a silence.

'How's the media project going, Morwen?' Mr Hughes said.

I jumped. 'Well, I don't know that you'd really call it a *project,*' I said, stammering slightly as I stared at the police. 'It's only optional, so I'm not even sure I'm going to do something? I mean, what I'd *like* to do is something to support my journalism but you can't really

(slow down; you're babbling)

I took a deep breath. 'So I thought... maybe I could film...' I remembered just in time what I'd said to Garreth's Mam, 'some... wild birds. Maybe do something on rare summer birds?'

'We only need to ask you something, Morwen,' said Mme Percelle gently, holding up a hand as if to say: *enough already!* 'Morwen, you aren't in any trouble, but... did you watch the TV this morning, as you got ready for school?'

I found myself going red.

'Yes,' I said.

'Did you want to sit down?' one of the policemen said to me, with an air of someone not used to talking with kids (or with anyone else). 'Just wanted to ask you a few questions about an incident we're investigating that happened at Treffynydd last night.'

'I did watch the news, I told you,' I answered shakily.

'Treffynydd would appear to be quite an isolated location,' droned the policeman in a sort of report-speak that reminded me of a filing cabinet. 'Because it involves an incident at the station and because your friend's mother alerted us to the fact you were there yesterday, we'd like to ask if you saw anything suspicious, anyone hanging about near the station?'

Blankly, I shook my head.

'We didn't see anyone,' I said, 'I'd tell you if we did! But we didn't.'

The policeman nodded, 'Not at the station then? How about on the train itself?'

I shook my head again, 'There wasn't anybody else on the train and I'd like to help you,' I said honestly, 'really I would! I'm sorry about that man! But we didn't see anything. I promise!'

The policeman laughed. 'It's okay, Morwen,' he said, 'you are allowed to use public transport you know! And incidentally, don't worry; incidents like this are very rare, especially out in the sticks at a place like Treffynydd! But maybe don't go out there again in the short term?'

'I'm not planning that,' I said truthfully (and a little too heartfelt for my liking).

The two policemen thanked me and began to say their goodbyes. The second one hadn't spoken at all and I wished he had. He seemed nice, with an open, round face that was a little too red from the sun. He smiled at me as they began to leave, after shaking hands.

'Oh, excuse me?' I said suddenly. They turned around to face me.

That lad I went out to Treffynydd with,' I said, 'his name was Garreth. Have you managed to speak to him?'

'We will do that,' the filing cabinet said. 'To be honest, we were hoping to do that this morning with you, but he isn't here, I gather?'

'No, he isn't,' said Mr Hughes.

'And that's a pity,' said the policeman with that irritating way of speaking as if other people hadn't opened their mouths, 'because he could be useful to us given that he got the last train. You should bear in mind that you two are just the ones we know about, thanks to your friend's Mam. There are probably lots of people who got different trains.'

'But are you planning to speak to him?'

'We'll speak to him.'

'Why are you so concerned, Morwen?' Mme Percelle asked me, frowning slightly.

Because Gravenhead's not safe yet! I've checked nothing on the camcorder! And Garreth's phone is lost.

I smiled back at her, 'I just wanted to know whether he'd be able to help the police, Mme Percelle,' I said to her. 'I just wanted to help; that's all I meant.'

The Book of All

Two hours later, a bumblebee hummed lazily across the police station's rear walled back garden. It poked itself into flowers, and then buzzed weightily past P.C. Arnold's nose...

Richard Thorns

Well, this is a bit better than being stuck at the desk, or tramping around schools!

Arnold sat back in his garden chair and took a sip of tea, enjoying the warm morning on his red, round face. He was confident that the sign he'd left at the desk, telling anyone to ring the bell would do the trick. Who'd nick from a nick, anyway?

Arnold relaxed in the chair, closing his eyes as the sun shone down. He'd better watch it, he thought; this sun was going to warm his brains like ice cream.

It was a beautiful summer morning.

Almost.

Arnold just about managed a frown. What on earth had made that dead old man at Treffynydd *look* like that? Arnold had heard about burglars who could literally frighten the elderly to death, but he'd never seen it at first hand. Poor bugger! Years in the police force made Arnold instinctively wrestle with feral, untamed thoughts that included *oh, pack it in!*

And that lad - Garreth, was it? Even though the lad was a Rosengrave lad, and Treffynydd out in the sticks. And when the judge rang the doorbell because he'd got the ice cream the verdict would be-

Hang on: that last bit wasn't a thought... it was a dream.

The telephone was ringing.

Shaking a cloud of hot dizziness away, Arnold scurried inside. He sat down in the shade, listening to Crooks, who had driven back to Treffynydd:

'It *wasn't* a robbery,' Crooks said down the line, 'the station till balanced. You'll be glad to know it wasn't murder either; there'll be a different slant to the story on the evening news now, that's for sure! Bloody hysteria!'

'What makes you sure?' asked Arnold. 'They said the old fella had a head injury; they wouldn't be wrong about that.'

'No, they weren't wrong,' said Crooks (trying, Arnold noticed, to keep the smugness out of his voice) 'but the door to the office was locked on *his* side. He probably slipped - after all, there was loads of water slopped about on the floor in the ticket hall.'

Relief flooded over Arnold. Suddenly the day seemed bright again.

The Book of Morwen

'How can you drink tea in this weather?' Bethan said to me.

We were sitting in Rosengrave's local *Pile-Upz:* a horrible place of hot griddles and cooking smells. The door was open as it was so hot, but there were still veils of blue smoke drifting near the ceiling, and the place stank of cigarettes. I traced a laminated menu with the edge of a foil ashtray, staring at whatever it was I'd ordered. I knew I couldn't eat it.

'Okay, so you went on a picnic together,' coaxed Bethan, a little more gently. 'You should say something if you saw him last; the police might be able to help.'

'We *said* we were going on a picnic,' I corrected. 'What I wanted to share with you? It was supposed to be a secret; it's pretty incredible, Bethan.'

I paused:

'It's just that... we were so near where that guy was found. We actually got off at that station yesterday.'

Bethan looked quizzically at me: 'Yeah, what *were* you both doing all the way out there?'

I instinctively felt protective and uncomfortable at the same time; past and present all became jumbled in my head: 'Well, like I say, it was pretty amazing what I'd found, Beth'. But I left Garreth there and now that poor man's dead and everything seems to be falling apart!'

And in that hot little cafe on Rosengrave High Street, I knew I had fear in my heart. Because in the bright day, when the temperature's 32° in the shade, and nightmares become daft as they flee away, it wasn't working. My mouth turned down, and I suddenly knew that for once I was near to tears.

I knew there was nothing daft about Gravenhead - I knew I was wise to be afraid.

Bethan thought for a moment. She reached into her bag and took out her mobile. She pressed a few buttons and then placed the phone on the table. I heard my own voice floating across the table. My voice was a day old, and stale, I thought:

'... I left the camera with Garreth and I guess he's asleep, I think. Anyway, he's not answering his phone. You can...'

I listened through to the end of the message. I felt, in that hot little cafe, suddenly, oddly, at peace: Bethan was there and the phone message seemed to connect everything - it was only a day old - when things were so easy and safe, from a time before the image now in my mind's eye: the weathercock, turning balefully to fix on me with its rusted, dead eyes.

Before I'd visited and filmed Gravenhead, showing it off like a performing bear. Prodding at it, using a fishing rod as a stick!

'Why *did* you leave Garreth behind, anyway, Morwen?' cut in Bethan's voice, 'did he *want* to be left?'

I nodded. 'He wanted to fish,' I said, and it occurred to me that Bethan was fishing herself; she wanted to know exactly what it was that had sent us both on a train, all the way out to Treffynydd.

'We were at a lake that's north of Treffynydd station,' I said. 'You know how I like walking and bird watching and being outdoors and all that stuff?' Bethan nodded.

'Well, in mid-February I was up that way all by myself; it was on a Sunday. You remember when the spring arrived in

February, surprising everyone?' Bethan nodded again, helping herself to one of my chips.

'It wasn't a freak warm snap,' I said, 'it *was* spring; it stayed with us, do you remember? And then April blazed away at us? Well, it was in April I went back there because I'd seen something really weird in the lake, a couple of months or so before.'

'What did you see, Morwen?' asked Bethan.

I hesitated.

'It was the head of a bird. It was the iron head of an iron bird. I went away and I thought: *I went bird watching and the only bird I saw that day wasn't real!* And it was so funny I kind of forgot about it. But then at Easter I was walking past Rosengrave church with my Mam and she mentioned the blue sky. I glanced up and there was a flash of gold. What I saw made me realize... it hit me like a punch in the head...

'Morwen... this is the most amazing-'

'I'd seen a weathercock,' I went on remorselessly, 'and I knew then that I'd found a village. Ah, but which one? But a book in the library said there *was* only one and it was Gravenhead, lost in the sixteenth century.'

I leaned forward in my chair.

'Don't you *see*, Beth'; when we were filming, the water was *already* a quarter way down the steeple and it's hotter now than it's ever been. We said yesterday that in a few days' time the village might even be sitting there in a dried up lake bed, right in front of us! We'd be the first visitors to the town in over five hundred years!'

I stopped, feeling slightly breathless, and I stared across at Bethan who was sitting opposite, looking as if she'd been shot.

'Morwen,' she said eventually, 'you might even get an 'A*' for that!'

I smiled for the first time in ages, it seemed.

'Thanks for the support, Bethan!' I said with feeling.

'Oh, that's okay,' answered Bethan, adding pointedly: 'And I'll tell you something else it *well* beats filming the inside of the Rosengrave Playhouse!"

Chapter Six

The dream.

The Book of Bethan

IN ROSENGRAVE, ESTATE AGENTS SEEM as rare as Ferrari dealerships, because I suppose there's no point in having a shop if you can't sell anything. That's why Nettos and charity shops are doing okay here, I guess, and if you want a kebab here in Rosengrave you'd probably be alright (if you want a kebab and a punch-up on a Friday night you'd *definitely* be alright).

Anyway, if a miracle happened and you wanted to move to Rosengrave and buy a place here, then you'd probably fall somewhere between Morwen's place in Letsbe Avenue and my own dear mummy and daddy's pad up here in the Fairwater hills. The Meads is where you'd probably end up, a big estate with mainly bungalows, where the cars are different to Morwen's neighbours' ones (they still have wheels on), and where neat front lawns jostle for space with garden pots and stuff. The Meads was where Garreth lived, and it was The Meads where I found myself around seven pm, around five hours after Morwen had shared her incredible secret with me. To be truthful I'd thought about nothing else:

I'll say one thing for her, I thought as I rang the bell, *she knows how to celebrate the end of term all right!* The summer air that evening had a pearly quality about it: it felt like silk on my skin. In the warmth of the evening, windows were open and thin net sheers hung lifeless and the sky was beautiful; a soft, fondant blue. Faint scarlet lines from planes scratched the sky here and there, and it seemed so peaceful on that Meads estate. The summer stretched out in front of me after our last day. All that remained of school was my summer project lurking in the wings.

And there was something else.

There was Morwen.

Richard Thorns

Something about Morwen was beginning to trouble me. I knew I was a little island in her world, because I at least talked to her and I was interested in her, and I'd sure helped her out by renting Garreth out to her. And that was all okay; I wanted my help to be good enough to make up for what she'd suffered from Katie and all those girls who'd put her in hospital. But I also knew that once I felt I'd done enough - when I was ready, I mean - on that unspoken Morwen-ometer of mine, I'd get the hell away from her and her paleness and her secret.

Because she'd told me her secret. And I knew that sooner or later, once I'd exhausted all my help and favours then maybe there'd be nothing left to give anymore and then maybe I'd share my secrets, too. Maybe I wasn't as great as Morwen thought I was. Maybe -

'Screw it,' I said to myself as Garreth opened the door, I could smell beer on his breath and my first thought was one of mild, amused irritation that he'd started without me. But then I saw a faint line of colour flush in his cheeks and he began to stammer about having a visitor as he ushered me down the hallway to the front room. I went into the room, and the look on my face must have been obvious:

Morwen was sitting primly on the sofa, a glass of squash in front of her on the glass table (I *knew* she'd refuse a beer!) and she had the grace to look embarrassed at my face as I came into the room.

'I'll get you a beer, Bethan,' said Garreth gratefully, and fled into the kitchen.

Morwen's cheeks were flushing and fast joining her sunburnt nose and forehead.

'What's up?' I said, and although we always meant it as: *how are you?* This time I meant it for what it was.

'I'm fine,' said Morwen, deliberately misunderstanding. She looked at me anxiously. 'I hope you don't mind, Bethan. I just had to see Garreth quickly. I'll go.'

I pulled a face.

'Don't mind me,' I said.

'No, I really do want to go,' Morwen said quickly, 'Your Mam will be home soon, Garreth and I don't think she likes me very much after yesterday. Anyway, you had plans and I know you want to look forward to no more school this summer. Garreth's been really looking forward to you coming round as well, Beth',' she said to me hopefully (and a little too pointedly for my taste). Garreth came in with a can of beer and handed it to me.

'Garreth's got something to tell you,' Morwen said.

I stared at him and, I don't know, what did I expect him to say? That he was dumping me for this tall, pale ghost sat on his sofa in front of us? I don't know. Maybe. Morwen's voice was pragmatic and fact-laden. I got a feeling this would be the same flat voice she'd equally use if she announced she'd won the lottery, or told me her Mam had just died.

Or told me she was taking my boyfriend...

'The media stuff's still at the lake,' Garreth said.

I swallowed,

'Is that it,' I said without thinking.

Garreth stared. 'I thought you'd go off the scale after yesterday.'

I smiled (I felt slightly teary with relief and I didn't know why).

'I wasn't in any hurry to stick around and look for it or pack it up,' Garreth said, 'so it's all still there.'

'Well, off you go then,' I joked (Morwen smiled a little at this). Garreth didn't laugh. I looked at his face.

'I didn't mean *now,*' I said.

Garreth shook his head. 'I'm not going back there,' he said to me flatly, 'so now you know what Morwen's found out there in the mountains. But I'm telling you what I told *her;* I'm not going back there. There's something about that lost village that's bad! You know I'm getting a visit from the police, don't you - I'm surprised it's taken them this long to find me.'

I looked out of the window, feeling surprised, too; they'd chased up Morwen quickly enough at school today.

'It's dusk, Morwen,' I said. 'You'd best not walk home tonight, especially as school's out today; there'll be kids all pissed up. I'll call you a taxi.'

'But that wasn't what I came around to see you about!' Morwen suddenly blurted out. 'There's something I need to ask you, Garreth, what with the police looking to interview you about that man.'

'Tell me in the hall, Morwen; Bethan is on the phone,' Garreth said as I held my mobile up to my ear.

I got through, just as I heard Morwen saying desperately, faintly in the hallway, *'Gravenhead...'*

'Please can you hold on a second?' I said down the phone. I crossed over to the doorway.

'Garreth,' Morwen was saying, 'please will you do one last thing for me? You can leave the project. I'll understand. I'll even collect the media stuff for you. I'll go... soon, I promise! But please, when the police call for you... don't say anything about the village. Please!'

I took in Garreth's outraged silence.

'Why *not?*' he almost shouted.

'Just don't. Please don't! About where it is or anything. They wouldn't understand.'

Then Garreth was going off on one about his lost phone, and I thought I heard the word: *'selfish!'* and his voice rose again and unable to stop myself I burst through into the hallway.

'LEAVE HER ALONE!' I screamed at the top of my voice.

I saw Garreth spin around to look at me.

'Bethan,' he stammered.

Stunned, and a little shocked at myself I said to him again: 'leave her alone,' and I actually felt my voice softer. 'Garreth, come in here with me! Yes, I'd like a taxi, please. From 41, the Meads to Longmeadow.'

But I guess that was one fare the taxi company felt they didn't need because they'd hung up on me. So I had to find another one and book it to come and take Morwen away (that sounds great doesn't it - like she was a lunatic or something). And that was our end of term, standing in Garreth's house in an uncomfortable silence for ten minutes before it arrived and Morwen got in. She still looked dismayed at being shouted at and essentially chucked out of Garreth's house; her earlier noises about wanting to leave long-forgotten. I took a long slug of beer and Garreth did the same as we smiled at each other to try and make up, and tried to drink Morwen and Gravenhead right out of our thoughts.

The Book of Morwen

The taxi swung out of the Meads and onto the road that led back into town. A quick scoot across the centre would take it through to the cinema and the Arndale Centre, and then it was just out to a B-road (hugging the base of the old coal heaps and slag piles from nearly thirty years ago) that would take the taxi into Longmeadow. I found myself thinking of the time I had squeezed Garreth's hand beside the lake. I frowned, remembering; he hadn't seemed so eager to pull away.

I sank back in the rear of the taxi. The driver had tried to talk to me earlier, maybe keen to get a bit of summer feeling from me after the last day of our term, but I hadn't responded and gradually he had given up: *The Meads; LongMeadow; Rosengrave; Gravenhead; the Raven's Head.* The words seemed to billow and mutter in my head, similar names trying to knit themselves together, like broken bones. Words jumbled as if to prepare the entrance to dreams. Instead, and in my waking state, the entrance to the Arndale Centre glided past the car.

The Book of Bethan

So we were going to drink Morwen and Gravenhead right out of our thoughts? Yeah, right! That was a laugh!

It was less than ten minutes after Morwen had left the house and now the light from Garreth's computer shone over our faces in his bedroom. The lights were off and there were dull thuds in the darkness as an action scene from the TV downstairs travelled up but I felt, in Garreth's bedroom high up, as if we were the only two people left in the world. The thuds were imprints on the air and on the atmosphere, like the definition of a phantom.

'Keep going, then? What do you reckon?' I asked Garreth.

The smell of beer hung in our faces. We were past page twenty of Googling Morwen's lost village of Gravenhead; our emotive LOST word was hitting up stuff by geeks about lost mines stuffed full of gold, shipwrecks and mystery animals, even on *pages from the UK*. So Garreth had gone into an advanced search and so far words had stared at us in blue with a pointing finger icon that seemed a bit rude, but appropriate given the circumstances; Google was for once being no help at all! A new page opened up:

I felt like crying:

"Rosen**grave** - a history of the town of Rosengrave, the mining pedigree and history of the Welsh mining community."

"**Grave**send - the official 2009 guide as published by the Kent Tourist Board. For a listing of hotels, attractions, and travel passes, please call..."

Garreth was staring at the screen beside me, probably wondering why he was feeling small stabbing pains in his arm, and suddenly, with a little trickle of fear in my throat I knew I was hurting him...

'*Look*, Garreth,' I breathed gently in his ear. Garreth turned around in the darkness to look at me and I smiled as I touched his can with mine.

"*The Comely Flood:* The **lost villages** of Middenwich, Cowminster and **Gravenhead.** 1979. Professor P.N. Clark Ph.D. *Out Of Print.*

'Cheers!' I said softly to him.

The Book of Morwen

'Of course!' I said softly to myself.

If there was a 'mead' in 'Longmeadow,' then a *mead* was an old name for a meadow, and I liked that; It reminded me of a poem by Keats I'd seen that I'd loved when I was a little girl. Somewhere in my room I had an exercise book with poems in, copied out with a child's pretence of originality. Something about: *meeting a maiden in the meads*. I made a mental note to find it. That was something else we had in common, on top of the fact that we'd both seen the lost village in the mountains and Bethan hadn't.

Startled, I jerked my head up. No! That wasn't *right;* how could *that* be right! Garreth had shouted and been horrible about his phone (which was understandable, but even so). And it was *Bethan* who'd tried to help me!

'Sorry, love, did you say something?' said the taxi driver.

Embarrassed, I shook my head. 'Can you turn left at that takeaway, please?' I said a little weakly, as the bright neon sign of an Indian with its ghastly outdated pun - *The Spice Grills* - floated into view. The driver spun the wheel quickly and warm air suddenly flushed into the taxi through the open windows.

'I've never known a summer like this one,' said the driver.

But she would *step in,* a sudden voice in my head gloated jealously, *because she wants Garreth all to herself. Isn't that right?*

(noleavemealone).

'In any case, she gave me ten pounds for the taxi,' I said aloud.

Richard Thorns

To get rid of you! She wanted you out of the house with no big scene!

It must be the weather, I thought. Through town, the smothering night heat wallowed in the doorways of gridded shops and in rubbish-strewn alleys. We chased the silent B-road along the side of the slag piles and the warm air also carried *scents:* sweet, green smells of nettles flowering in the heat fluttered in through the opened windows of the taxi… like a snake oil cure when the very air was running a fever. Bethan had helped me… hadn't she?

'What did you say?' I said.

'I was saying that's fine, love, a tenner'll be more than enough,' said the driver.

The Book of Bethan

'It's just that I want what's best for her,' I said softly to Garreth, 'I'm sorry I screamed at you like that, but after what she went through…'

I left the sentence unfinished.

'But you *have* to stop feeling responsible for her,' Garreth said to me, 'you weren't to blame; it was Katie and Georgie and Jestine, we know that; they admitted it, and all that's long gone! Morwen should stick up for herself.

And then there's you! I thought, with tears in my eyes. *You and Morwen on the sofa together! You can't see it but you looked so good together! I think deep down you know I don't even like watching you play football on Saturdays and you like poetry and stuff and I don't and she does!*

The Book of Morwen

'I've never known a summer like this one,' said the taxi driver again, as he poked at his meter, trying for the last time to make conversation.

I nodded, not answering. I paid the driver with the ten pounds that Bethan had pressed on me, suddenly glad to be home. The garden at the front of my Mam's house was tiny and silent, the streets deserted now.

I tiptoed up the pathway, feeling the shrubs for support. Then suddenly my foot gave way on something soft and there was a sharp, horrible screech. I lost my footing and fell heavily onto the path. My ankle felt as if it was on fire as I lay there, stunned. I moaned softly in pain, looking around me.

There were just shrubs, that sweet smell of stinging nettles flowering in the heat. And there was...

Morris, the Tregarthy's cat was staring at me, and the fur was up on its neck.

'Morris, you little idiot!' I said softly.

The cat parted its jaws and bared a tiny white fang (one had been lost in a car accident). It spat heavily at me.

'Morris!' I breathed weakly in dismay, trying to calm him.

Morris fled away from me, and squeezed under the gate. I heard him still spitting in the street as he ran.

I pulled myself painfully to my feet and limped into the house. My Mam was asleep and I felt glad my fall outside hadn't woken her! I tiptoed painfully towards my bedroom, trying to place the weight of my body on my left ankle.

My Mam's bedroom door opened and she stood on the landing in her nightie, squinting half in her sleep at me:

'Sweetheart, was that you? I can never sleep properly before I know you're safe. I heard the sound of someone falling outside; what's happened to you? Was it lads and lasses at you again?'

I shook my head as I tried to test standing on my right foot. It was a bad idea; I nearly passed out with pain.

'I fell over Morris,' I whispered almost tearfully.

'That cat! *Why* don't the Tregarthy's look after that beast properly? Away down the road with it and I'll not be sorry if it's gone!'

'It did go off, Mam!' I whimpered, 'and it treated me like a witch, or a ghost!'

'Never mind that cat! But it'll be cold water on that ankle for you,' said my Mam, and I let her show me that this was indeed for the best, and then Mam went back to bed and I fled (or rather hopped) into my room as soon as I could.

It was very hot in my bedroom, but it was going to get even hotter because I limped over to the windows and closed them very tightly. I got into bed and threw the duvet firmly away from me. There was a sick feeling in my ankle;

the pain was still warm in it like Tiger Balm. My feelings of anger and dismay were still there, also; every bit as shocking, but fainter this time. My head hit the pillow, and I waited…

I waited for my thoughts to become jumbled, as they had done for a moment in the taxi; for when my veils of sleep would drift and arrive like phantoms in the hot room. Little tricks I knew to jumble the thoughts up faster: maths equations and counting backwards. Old riddles made up all by myself, when younger… *What's wet but you can drink it when it's dry?* Wine! *What's gross to eat but sounds so sweet?* Sugar soap!

My mouth turned down slightly in the darkness…

What's lost and found?

What's a dead world still living?

I dreamed in the night. Almost straight away:

In my dream, a squonk moved slowly through the dense forest in the heat of the day, weeping at its own ugliness as it edged towards the lake that glittered in the distance. It was a very hot summer's day and the dappled light shone in the squonk's face, illuminating its tears. It was aware that the sound of its weeping would alert the hunters who shouted in the distance, one of whom the squonk knew (or thought it knew, or was told by one of its friends) possessed a great blunderbuss gun that could be fired at any moment. The squonk's ugly shoulders brushed against the trees; ripe pears swayed and shook in the sun.

Richard Thorns

Quietly, warily, the squonk approached the lake. The spire of the church wallowed invitingly in the depths; Gravenhead seemed up to its shoulders in the cool lake and was fresh and new, with no hint of decay. The lake was not a pool of tears, but fresh, cool water on this hottest of days.

The squonk slid carefully in, to hide its nakedness, swam out, and submerged, floating just beneath the surface…

And there I was, happy in brightness, face-down and observing, as the sunlight seared silver through the water. I made no attempt to descend this time - content to look far below. Morris spat at me and swam away as I stared down. Deep below I could make out a tiny, humanlike figure swimming steadily through one of the streets. Its head gleamed white. I wished it would look up so I could see its face.

I floated, high over my beautiful Gravenhead, with fish as birds. And this time...

And this time it felt so good.

Chapter Seven

Under the lake.

The Book of Morwen (cont'd)

My Mam was flicking through the morning post.

'This is for you,' she said, handing over a letter. I frowned as I took it. The envelope had: *"Rosengrave High - Build High For Excellence!"* stamped across it.

I opened the envelope. Well, there it was, bang on cue:

Richard Thorns

+ + + + + + Media Equipment 24 hr generated notice + + + + + +

"You are advised that the following item(s) are due for immediate return:"

Panasonic SV800 Digital Hi-8 Camcorder.
Tripod.
Hi-8 Digital C180 tape.
External Microphone.

Well, that was no surprise, I thought sourly. Garreth leaving it there, and that fragile state of nerves he possessed! He was like toffee-apple, just like his Mam!

'Come on, what's *that* all about?' asked Mam, handing over a mug of tea.

'It's nothing?' I muttered, folding the letter over, 'just a few things overdue from the library.'

My Mam tutted: 'You should've returned your books at the end of term before the summer break started,' she said, 'now think of all those fines waiting for you in September.'

'Yes, Mam.' My *don't hassle me* snap was stifled by sheer relief: Mam thought it was only books! She'd *freak* at the thought of all the media stuff abandoned in the woods - over twenty miles away!

Understandably, I thought, as I limped over to the window to open it. After all, nobody in *this* house could replace it! The sun was streaming in through the windows and dust motes danced in the air, exposing the worn edges of the

Gravenhead

furniture and the frayed curtains. The battered dresser that was holding the photographs of my Da, stuffed in there after he'd first walked out on us when I was thirteen years old. Since then, I found myself thinking, there'd been no new furniture; instead I'd watched helplessly as Mam had become steadily like the furnishings of our house: worn-edged and frayed.

'So,' said Mam, sipping at her tea, 'what are you doing today?'

I hesitated, 'I... might take things easy today,' I said. 'How about you, Mam?'

'Your gran's coming over at twelve and we're going to have lunch in the garden,' said Mam. 'You're sure you don't want to stick around, Morwen? She'd be so glad to see you.'

'I think I might be busy today,' I said, my eyes down.

The telephone rang. Mam went into the hallway and picked it up.

'It's Bethan for you!' she called, 'and don't stand on that foot!'

'Thanks, Mam,' I limped into the hallway and picked up the phone.

'Hi there, Bethan,' I said.

'Hi, Morwen. Look... um... I'm sorry about last night; I saw you were a bit annoyed. I wasn't... chucking you out or anything and don't worry about that stupid boyfriend of mine! It's just that he was in a bit of a state.'

(I noticed Bethan had subconsciously given me Garreth's status rather than his name).

'Forget it,' I said warmly. 'How is he?'

'Well, not all that good. He was going off on one about a flock of birds having him for lunch!'

I didn't laugh.

'Have the police been round to see him?' I asked her.

'Yeah, this morning, and you wait until you hear this. Only one policeman turned up; it was that one with the round face who was in Mr Hughes's office yesterday, the one you thought looked so nice!'

'So?' I said, frowning.

'Well,' Bethan said, 'he was talking about visiting our school yesterday, all the usual banter about breaking up for the summer, and about that man who died at the station? Garreth says you're in the clear; they said it was an accident and they're closing the case. It's a matter for the coroner now.'

'Good,' I said.

'But, get this: He asked Garreth all about why you were both out there at Treffynydd on a Sunday, and *then* he said there was nothing to worry about. Why would he have done that?'

I didn't answer.

'Anyway, it was a good job you left before his parents arrived home, Morwen; they were going bananas the other night!'

I felt myself prickling defensively:

'Well, I'm not his keeper! He should have looked after his phone then or called before he lost it; I *was* trying to find him from my back garden on Sunday night, you know I was, Bethan-'

'Morwen, he *couldn't* call! The phone was in the lake! He had time to punch your number in with a stick, before it fell down the bank. Morwen - did you get a call on Sunday night?

The prickling was still there, but in the hallway, I knew it was no longer defensive...

Sunday night! A mosquito, found-out and broken, leaving blood too big for its own body.

Blood and fire, and billows of smoke.

'Morwen, was there a banging sound of metal through your mobile? Really dull and... and *old?* Garreth was trying to reach you, Morwen; it was what scared the birds off.

The prickling was *fear...*

'Morwen, it was Gravenhead's church bell.'

The Book of All

But *that* part of the secret was safe for the moment, at least. Stranded in summer air above the glassy surface of the lake, there was nothing but silence from the belfry now. The silence settled on the hot forest and the cool lake, and on the man swimming in the lake (next to the church steeple and almost touching it), for there was an invader and breaker of secrets in the lake.

Silence, and *no view* to the right of the swimmer either; only an immediate, great grey wall. Gravenhead church's flagstones reared by his side, stretching up for a few metres until they gave way to the ancient, green slates of the steeple which itself stretched into the sky, crowned by a tiny, weed-encrusted tangle of iron.

Treading water, he buried his hands beneath the surface, picked up the breathing apparatus and sucked hard. Air flowed freely into his mouth. In the heat of the day there was no need for a wetsuit; the aqualung was tight against bare skin. He spat into the mask and rubbed saliva around the inside. Clamping the mask in place, he squinted in the bright sunshine and looked around. There was no-one about; the lake was completely deserted.

He touched a tiny point of stone poking up through the lake, against which the water lapped gently. It was the first beginnings of a window. Tiny pieces of coloured glass clung forlornly against the rusted iron webbing.

Turning turtle, the diver dived.

The warmth of the water began to cool. He sank and then kicked, descending deep against the church wall. Slowly, the ruin gave up its dimensions: first came the base of the window, then the long, low sculptured facings of stone guttering slowly peeped into view. There was a drop of around ten metres to the waving floor of the lake, and he could see the overhanging enclave of a yawning gap, which meant he was far over a door. In the gloom, something clung to the guttering above his shoulder, right on the corner. He exhaled a cloud of bubbles in excitement, feeling his way along.

A bundle of weed sat smartly upright, and the diver gently pulled away at the vegetation. It parted easily. The diver took his torch from his belt and switched it on…

Liberated from their darkness, in deep, green water, three ruined faces stared at him, nestling inside their stone cowls. With a thrill of imagination, the diver saw weed floating around the sightless eyes: the hair removing itself, it seemed.

He waved his hand harder and the water cleared. They were full stone figures, hunched over and carrying something on their backs. Perhaps it was a large sheaf of barley, or wheat? But somehow he knew he was hoping against hope: there was no place for the innocent joy of harvest in Gravenhead. In its deep water this place - he suddenly felt - was dreadful. And then he saw it was a rough, stone casket on their backs and, yes, there was something else: loops of carved rope hung between all three. He flapped at the water and holes appeared in the stonework. No, they were not loops of rope, the figures were chained together.

Shaken, the diver replaced the flashlight and sank backwards and downwards. He looked up: the crude faces were staring fixedly ahead as they slowly became obscured by the distance. So they were gargoyles, he thought. But he had seen gargoyles in Warsaw and Prague: *those* brutes seemed like Michelangelo's work, compared to the Gravenhead apparitions.

His bare feet sank into cool, tickling softness; the weed brushed his bare calves.

It was the floor of the lake; he was in front of a yawning black gap. Taking his flashlight out from his belt the diver shone it into the gloom. He could see the faint outline of sunken pews in the darkness.

But, somehow... he didn't want to go inside.

Kicking, he swam away from the church, powering swiftly along the floor of the lake. The waving weed was like a sunken meadow now, but beginning to arch gently downwards. He'd been watching the contours of the drowned village green for so long that he had not looked upward, and when he did he drew a deep breath of oxygen and nitrogen in delight...

The weed-waving street lay forlornly in front of him, and great shapes loomed either side: gloomy houses nestled eerily in the water, perch and roach darting in and out of his viewpoint. He shone the powerful flashlight about him. There were black gaps in the houses; it was as if the village was blind. Here and there he saw black hoops in the streets: perhaps they had once wrapped themselves around cartwheels.

As he swam over one of the rusted black hoops he felt a sudden sting on his wrist. He swallowed a little spurt of fear: it was as if the village, irritated at his intrusion, had bitten him. He turned instead to see his watch, the links snagged and broken, spiralling lazily towards the weed-waving street. It glittered in the water before being swallowed by the weed.

The diver instinctively kicked, but felt only relief. And he suddenly didn't want to put his hand into that sullen, waving weed. He powered towards one of the houses. A large one - maybe it had once been a manor house.

A drowned, unseeing window lay far to his right. Swimming fast, he then hovered in front of the manor house's grand, blank eye. He placed both hands on one side of the empty window frame, and swam inside...

The Book of Morwen

I collapsed against the wall of the hallway like a punctured balloon, all the fight going out of me. I thought of the turning weathercock again, and I was never gladder to know my history...

'The church bell was ringing by itself?' I whispered.

'Yeah, so now you know why he's not too keen on a return trip. Not to mention those crows or ravens, or whatever-'

'I'll call you back in a bit, Bethan,' I said, and hung up.

Bethan, in post-medieval times the church bell was rung for a reason.

I stood in the hallway, taking deep, whooping breaths. I knew it as clear as anything:

To warn evil to stay away. There's something still there!

Richard Thorns

'Is everything all right?' called out Mam from the living room, 'you're not standing on that ankle, I hope!'

'Everything's fine, Mam,' I called, my voice high. 'I'll be here for Gran!' I said on impulse. I looked at my hand; it was trembling hard. I knew I couldn't go to Gravenhead today.

I gulped down non-existent saliva and I picked up the phone again. I dialled a number and waited. I would be... *normal* I said fiercely to myself.

'Can I speak to Garreth please, Mrs Rowe,' I said brightly.

There was a pause. 'Oh, it's you, Morwen,' came the reply. 'Hold on a moment. I'll see if he's in.

I felt my heart sinking. The voice of Mrs Rowe was flat and cool. *Well,* I thought, *it's no more than I deserve.* The voice from the phone was muffled, but I could just make out the words: *'It's Morwen. Sounding a bit too pleased with herself if you ask me.'*

'Hi, Morwen,' said Garreth's voice.

'Garreth,' I said, feeling suddenly tearful. 'If you don't want to speak to me I'll understand. I just wanted to say how sorry I am. If I'd known you were trying to tell me where you were...'

I could hear Garreth's voice, away from the phone.

'Look, Mam, I'm trying to have a private call here!' There was a silence, some muffled words. Then: 'I don't care. I don't judge the people *you* work with!'

'Sorry about that,' said Garreth, 'the police left earlier; it was a good start to the summer break for Mam!'

'So that's all I am now, then,' I sniffed, 'just someone you work with, rather than a friend?'

I heard his voice soften. 'Look Morwen, I know this idea's fantastic. You'll go a long way with it. It'll get you into uni, in London or Oxford or whatever and I know how much you want to get away, but...' I could hear the deep breath being taken, 'the truth is, Morwen, I don't want anything more to do with it.'

'Garreth,' I said pleadingly, 'Alright, I suppose I'll admit it's all a bit creepy. On Sunday evening I spoke to my gran; I asked her about Gravenhead and I think it must be a real... what do they call it? Like an urban legend or something? Even gran said she didn't want to scare me. But look what we've found! You *can't* expect to just walk away from it!'

I swallowed hard.

I'd *have* to say I to him... it was now or never.

'Well, look, Morwen, if you really want to know what I think, I'd say you should listen to her. It's like I said to you yesterday, there's something about that village that's... *bad*. Maybe you should drop it. I really do think that.'

It was now or never!

'Garreth' I said, please can you just tell me one thing? I need to know if you did what I asked you yesterday. You didn't say anything about the village did you? Please tell me if you-'

Richard Thorns

There was a click as Garreth put the phone down on me.

The Book of All

Inside the house, he swam from the parlour along a gloomy corridor towards a door. The flashlight shone brightly, the beam sweeping the floor. The diver knew that in Tudor times the parlour had taken the place of the Great Hall living quarters; here, at least, this was true.

But the Hall itself - this vast room - would have been a *dark* place, he thought as he entered, for everywhere was great space and half-rotted oak: a ramp of oak reared in front of him, the remains of a great collapsed table. His hands gently rubbed at the weed, and the enormous wooden bulb of a Tudor table leg stared at him, its carving beautifully preserved beneath the slime. He swung the flashlight around; the beam picked out the cavernous black hole of a fireplace.

Oak. It was all oak. A chair lay on its side.

No, he suddenly realised, it was pandemonium; *all* the chairs were scattered around the room.

What the hell happened *here?*

A little feeling of fear washed gently over him. He no longer felt alone in the house. He realized he was breathing hard and he watched the nitrogen and oxygen bubble up towards the great, beamed ceiling.

The bubbles didn't stop at the ceiling.

There was a hole in the ceiling. Beyond was... blackness.

The diver swam upward and looked down. Yes, he could see the room better from up here. Tiny tendrils of what had once been a rich carpet bobbed and waved in the current, wafting around the wrecked room. Turning, the beam of the diver's flashlight entered the black hole in the ceiling.

It picked out a tiny flash of white.

And, against all his training - not the training of calculated diving techniques, but of older, more human training - on impulse, the diver swam up halfway through the hole and cast the bright beam around. He waited as the debris fell and the water cleared - his breakfast rose acidly in his throat:

A skull glared at him from the blackness of the room. It was so close its bared teeth and blank eye sockets filled his vision. He waved his torch. No, it was not just a skull: two sitting skeletons were bobbing gently in front of him, and behind them a third sat, slightly slumped forwards as if in interest, from inside a grand, rotted armchair. The ragged remains of their clothes waved gently in the water; they were awful in their near-nakedness, but the heads were... *dressed* in disintegrating cowls.

The forgotten people stared silently at him. The diver gradually made out a stone box, about the size of a tea-chest in their midst. It was thick-hewn, rough and ugly, and his mind flew back to the three gargoyles as they clung to the wall of the church, their carved hands clutching their crude possession. He gave a great start that nearly blew out his mouthpiece...

They're here! They're guarding it!

And he placed his hands on either side of the ceiling beneath his chest and tried to push himself out. He felt soft powder and he realised with dismay that his hands had gone through the wood and that the large stone box had moved. It almost seemed to *aim* for him, and it collided with him and the diver became aware he was plummeting through the hall. The lid of the box fell off above them both and the diver, in finality, thought he saw it turning and curiously petal-like, despite its weight. Then the diver landed on the floor and the weight of the stone box stuffed him bone-breakingly through. The lid landed with a crash onto the box, fell to one side, and lay still.

There was a chaos of debris and silt in the room. The stone box lay on the shattered floor, directly below the open timbers of the upper room; one corner and side sunk into the floor, the rest inanely half-out.

A tiny roach paused in the room, hovering and gazing at the great cloud of silt in the Great Hall. Perhaps it was food! It skittered about, gasping at the water. Then, giving up, it swam quickly away from the silt, over an abandoned pewter cup and on towards the safety of the shadows.

Chapter Eight

The Comely Flood.

The Book of Bethan

I PAUSED, GETTING MY breath back, at Morwen's front gate and looked at the Tregarthy's gatepost. A photograph of Morris stared out from the wood, fixedly drawing-pinned indicating that he was LOST. And because there was a REWARD, I looked instinctively up the street:

Richard Thorns

There was nothing except a few kids sitting on the kerb, digging sticks into the melting tar at the edge of the road. An ice cream van sounded in a distant street. I could see jealousy in the kids' faces. The bright, thin tune continued faintly. It didn't seem to be getting any nearer, or any further away.

Morwen's ankle had been a long time in healing. The bone had slightly chipped and the ligaments had been strained badly. She had come off better from the collision; of Morris there had been no sign, and Morwen told me that the continued tapping of fork-against-plate in the cool of the dusk, and the constant calling from next door had unnerved her.

'I keep seeing that tiny white fang and hearing that horrible screech in the night,' she had said to me, when I'd visited Morwen the day after we'd spoken on the phone. And I'd asked her to describe exactly what had *happened* in the night: I guess it was a clumsy attempt at remembered, childish mediation.

Morwen had shaken her head at me: 'No, I mean it's in the night when I *see* it,' she'd answered. And then she had said no more, preferring to lean back in the sunshine and relax.

Over those eight convalescent days Gravenhead, too, faded in the heat. Morwen and me lazed in her scrubby back garden, talked about normal things and watched repeats of the summer's best tennis at Wimbledon; gradually I wondered at what it was that had ever entered our dialogue:

how the words: 'lost villages' and 'drowned towns' had ever made their way into our conversation.

Which was why I'd run down the street to Morwen's gate, clutching a package in my hand. I'd walked past the photo of Morris, glanced up the street, noted the jealousy in the faces of the kids, walked swiftly up Morwen's front path and rang the doorbell. I'd waited patiently in the open doorway.

The kitchen door opened and Mrs Lundy came in; I guessed from the back garden. The shape advanced through the hall, and I noticed with guilt that it was pushing a slight smell of poor-ness about it that opened windows had not quite masked: an overall smell of poverty, of which faded sofa covers played only a part.

'Oh, hello, Bethan,' said Mrs Lundy. 'If you're looking for Morwen, you just missed her: she's gone jogging.' Seeing my astonished face, she smiled at me, shook her head and pointed at her ankle.

'*Insisted* on hobbling down to the shops for me,' she said. 'She'd had enough of lounging around and... well... you know Morwen.' I followed her through the kitchen and out into the back garden.

'How is she?' I asked as I accepted a cold drink.

'Oh, you know,' said Mrs Lundy, 'the ankle's fine - it's all the other stuff. Morwen's trouble is she never knows when to let go of something. She was the same when...' she hesitated

'Well, anyway,' she went on, 'the big thing right now is some school project of hers; she thinks she wants to do something now. Only she's terrified she won't think of something in time.'

I hesitated, feeling at my pocket.

'I thought maybe she had something in mind,' I said carefully.

Mrs Lundy looked surprised. 'Well, if she has, it's news to me,' she answered, with a peg in her mouth. 'I wish she would! There's a lot riding on this project, what with her desperation to get out of Rosengrave - not that I'd hold that against her.'

'Mrs Lundy,' I said, 'I've brought something round for her to have a look at. Well, it's for both of us, really. It might... help her a bit. Do you mind if I leave it for her?'

'Of course not, Bethan, but don't you want to stay? She said she wouldn't be long.'

'I... have to go,' I said, my voice tight.

'Well, you know where her bedroom is.'

I walked through the kitchen, and up the stairs. So, Morwen "hadn't found a project yet." If that was news to her Mam it was certainly news to me! There were only two possibilities, I thought, as I made my way past a pile of washing left on a dresser:

Morwen had decided to abandon her project; I wouldn't have blamed her for that. In a funny sort of way it seemed... *safer,* somehow.

But it would have surprised me.

Because I had the funny sort of feeling that the *real* reason Morwen's Mam didn't know anything about Gravenhead was because Morwen didn't want her to. But that was stupid. Why wouldn't she? But as I entered Morwen's bedroom I remembered Garreth's complaining voice, fresh and angry, back on the phone to me:

'All she cared about was keeping that village away from anyone.'

And that's the end of Morwen's friendship with Garreth, I thought. *Will it be the same for me, then?*

Morwen's room was like an oven. I opened a window. From outside, I could hear blackbirds singing in the heat, and the ice cream van sounded ever so slightly distant. *Will it be the same for me, then?* The sound of humming came from below, as Mrs Lundy pegged out the washing:

'She's terrified she won't think of something in time.'

I sat on the bed, and looked around the untidy bedroom; my attention was caught by a Sunday newspaper lying on the floor. There was a photograph of a drab, unshaven figure sitting glumly on a step. I picked up the newspaper, and looked at it:

"Now an alcoholic and living alone, Walter Emerson says he would give anything to see his daughter again after so many years."

'I know she's now a star, but I'm not after her money. I just want her to be Daddy's little girl again.'

Richard Thorns

I grimaced at the whine in the man's voice: it was like dirty sugar. I let the newspaper fall to the floor and picked up an exercise book lying there. It was dog-eared and had seen much better days. The book was open and recognised Morwen's writing, but only just: for some reason it looked slightly child-like:

A little verse stared up at me:

> *I met a lady in the meads*
> *Full beautiful, a faery's child*
> *Her hair was long, her foot was light*
> *And her eyes were wild.*

The words: "the meads" were underlined!

I felt fury rising in me. I threw the exercise book disrespectfully on the floor and took out my package - a brown paper bag - from my pocket. I carefully pulled a book up and out. I stared at the front cover:

THE COMELY FLOOD

The lost villages of Middenwich, Cowminster and Gravenhead

Professor P.N. Clark Ph.D.

I stared at the book, and then around the bedroom. Hang on a minute; those were *my* CDs lying in a heap on the floor. I felt something stirring, almost glittering in my stomach. Yes, that skeleton of a tune from the ice cream van was *definitely* much fainter now. Morwen's clothes lay in a heap. Would she ever pick them up? All the trouble I'd gone to: to run around for her and trail around that STUPID DREARY bookshop when I could've been outside and *all for someone who writes lovesick crappy poems for my-*

'What are you doing in my bedroom?'

I jumped out of my skin. Morwen was standing at the doorway of the room. Was her mouth set in a hard line? I didn't know.

'Morwen!' I stammered.

'So come on then,' Morwen said steadily, 'what have you noticed?'

I felt myself going scarlet, 'Morwen...' I began again.

Morwen rolled her eyes, '*Look* at me!' she said. She took a step backwards from me, and did a bit of a girly twirl.

'All the way to Somerfield and back again! Ta-Dahh!' she declared triumphantly. 'I reckon I'm on the mend!' She walked over to the bed and plonked herself down next to me and gave me a hug.

She handed over a magazine to me.

'Something to say: thanks for being my friend and looking after me, Bethan,' she explained, 'just so you know I appreciated it.'

As I looked at Morwen's smiling dark eyes in front of me, I realized with horror that my own were full of tears. I looked away.

'Bethan, are you okay?'

I drew a deep breath. I swallowed and looked around.

'Yeah, I'm fine thanks, you wally!' I managed, 'your sunburn's still no better; it *still* looks really gross!' The words were, by now, untrue and I flinched as I said them: when I'd used them in the playground, my motive had been to make up with Morwen. Was that why I'd used them now? Or were my words designed to wound, like she'd been wounded before by those girls? To take that long pale body of hers and-?

'You liar, I look great! I should be on Miami Beach with a cocktail instead of stuck in this dump, so come on,' Morwen affected an American accent in her good humour, 'did you go fix one yet?' Swept with the mood, I stuffed the package back into my pocket and followed Morwen downstairs.

As I did so, I realized that the tinkling of the ice cream van was the same volume it had always been.

The Book of Bethan (cont'd)

'I can't believe it!' Morwen said to me slowly as we sat in the sunny garden looking at the book. 'Where on earth did you get it?'

I sighed. 'Well, I kind of thought that... if this book really *was* doing the rounds in the late seventies, and as it concerns where we're supposed to be, then I thought maybe copies would be floating around locally,' I said. 'It was in the very first second-hand bookshop I went to.'

'Listen to this,' said Morwen, and she began reading aloud to me:

'"Although the exact site of Gravenhead is unknown (the last [unnamed for that region] parish records were recorded in 1489 - now in the British Museum), it seems likely that Gravenhead shared its trade locally with both Middenwich and Cowminster. These villages are also lost, but speculation remains that Gravenhead was once located in the region of the high hills that surround Treffynydd (perhaps due to the similarity of their names) and the industrial town of Llancellwyn".'

'That much we know,' said Morwen, grinning.

'"Indeed, excavations within the hilltops of Treffynydd in 1976 unearthed, at Fawkes's Hill, evidence of land disturbance that dated from the Tudor period, of around the earlier part of the sixteenth century".'

My heart seemed to skip a beat.

'They found it,' I breathed.

'No, hang on,' said Morwen in relief. 'Listen to this:'

'"However, the purpose of the Fawkes's Hill indentation remains a mystery, as apart from this ground disturbance there was nothing else to suggest there was any activity in the region in relation to the period, and indeed to Tudor life in general".'

'Goes on a bit, doesn't he.' I remarked.

Morwen scratched at her chin. 'So there was never anything to locate Gravenhead either with itself or with any of those other villages *except* for that building work they found in 1976,' she said. 'We need a map, Bethan. But why would they just... *dig?* Back in the sixteenth century, I mean? I don't understand.'

'You got me, but I'm glad they stopped,' I said, 'it means we're in the clear; you've still got your scoop, Morwen.'

'Yes,' said Morwen thoughtfully. 'I've still got my scoop.'

The Book of Morwen

I sat with Bethan in the shade of Rosengrave train station. The curved metal seat was painted red and holed to let out the rain. Rain, I thought; that was a laugh.

I stuffed the map we'd bought into my pocket, got up and walked to the edge of the platform. I had always loved coming here amid the bustle of people coming and going. I could get on the trains and take off for the silence of the mountains and the valleys where I could forget the flickering moments in my memories: *I'm coming home from school at thirteen, all smiles and clutching a drawing, to see my Mam smiling bravely back, saying: 'I've got something to tell you, Morwen. You've got to be very grown up.'*

I looked away down the line. Beyond the wet shimmer of heat coming off the rails the mountains reared blue in the distance, and much nearer a dirty old freight train clanked away to itself, its couplings kicking up a fuss. The air smelled of dust and oil and dirty cotton, the rails expanding lazily in the heat.

'Morwen!'

I jerked my head up, still half-dreaming. A train was crawling backwards towards us.

'Come on, Morwen, wake up - time to get going!'

But why would they just... dig? *Back in the sixteenth century, I mean? I don't understand.*

The Book of Bethan

'You don't understand,' Morwen said earnestly to me as the train rumbled through the valleys. 'You live in a great big house... I'm not having a go at you... but living in Longmeadow we really don't have anything very much anymore. Not since Da left us. And - well - being a news reporter means you've really got to have a nose for something really *special!* And I guess finding a village undisturbed for five hundred years is something pretty special!'

I tabbed a can of Sprite and took a swig. 'So *that's* why you're doing this, then. Sod our school project!'

She smiled a little at me, 'It's a bit wasted on a school project, don't you think?' she said.

'Maybe. It'll help you get out of this shithole, though.'

'Exactly! That's what I'm saying! I'll *use* it alright, Bethan, but my *main* thing is to send out copies to TV stations and universities. This is the idea: top marks from the school for the project, to help get me *into* uni; cash from the TV stations for my story to *pay* for uni; a bursary if the cash I get isn't enough...'

She talked on and on, and I stared at her, feeling slightly shaken. She'd certainly thought of everything! I realised how much I'd underestimated Morwen's hatred of Rosengrave; how desperate she was to get out! She was still speaking, her heart and voice singing with hope and reason: 'If I can get a part-time job, maybe I can even *save* the bursary; I don't want to graduate and then do a boomerang straight back to Rosengrave, find myself in *Chicken Kitchen* or selling shoes in *Meeks's.*'

I looked out of the window at sheep in the fields as they winked past.

'So, what's this village actually *like?*' I said after a while.

Morwen was silent for a moment.

'It's more what it's *going* to be,' she said to me a little quietly, 'I mean, I'm not an expert or anything, but I guess people would pay *millions* to have the water drained away so they could keep it as a museum, if the summer wasn't doing it already.

'And you know what, Bethan?' she continued, 'you know what? If the steeple is anything to go by, Gravenhead looks in perfect condition. Maybe there's not much oxygen in the water or whatever. But it looks in amazing shape to me.'

'The largest museum in Wales?' I offered.

'The *only* museum in Wales that's a complete Tudor village,' Morwen corrected, 'I was thinking, Bethan; old Tudor villages aren't *that* special; they're all around us. But they've all got telephone boxes and cars in them now, and the houses have all double glazing and stuff. This is the *only one* that hasn't; it's exactly as it was. That's some museum!'

I finished my can of Sprite and settled back in the seat as the train began to slow as it approached Treffynydd. 'Well, I know what *I'd* do, then,' I said to her.

'Go on, then,'

'Well, if that village *is* in perfect condition, the contents will be priceless. Kitchen things, farming stuff, you name it.' I held my empty can up to Morwen's eyes: 'you take something that's simple and everyday and you bury it for five hundred years and suddenly it's worth a fortune! You want to get out? *That's* your ticket out!'

She shot me a look of interest, 'I hadn't thought of that,' she said, 'but I was never able to hold my breath for very long underwater; somebody might get lucky, though.' She shrugged (not without regret at my unworkable idea). 'For us it's a case of getting the stuff and then making sure we go down in history as Gravenhead's rediscoverers! End of story!' She paused, considering, 'or *beginning* of story, depending on which way you look at it.'

'So get a boat and grab a gargoyle off the roof or something!' I said, 'anyway, don't look so doubtful; I'm not talking about *nicking* anything; finders keepers! At the very least, get a reward from the council in exchange for the location.'

'We'll see,' Morwen said absently.

The Book of Morwen

The journey on our bikes was every bit as hot as before, but Bethan didn't complain to me, as Garreth had. I found myself with plenty of time to think on the journey up the track; *is what we're doing actually* right? For the first time, I allowed myself to wonder: *maybe Gravenhead is better off left as it is.*

'Morwen!' Bethan's voice snapped me out of my thoughts.

'Nearly there,' I said. For some reason I didn't want to talk.

'It's not that, Morwen. Listen! Have you noticed how quiet everything is? What's happened to all the birds?'

I nodded, remembering my Keats poem, the one I had adored so much as a little girl:

The sedge is wither'd from the lake

And no birds sing.

I cast a wary glance into the trees, slightly ahead of me and to my right as I cycled. Through the branches, I could see the flicker of a distant tall spire. It was man-made.

I suddenly found myself with tickling butterflies in my stomach.

Deep down in my hidden heart, even though the pride in me had blustered at him, I knew that Garreth had been right; there was something bad about Gravenhead. I was safe in my house when he'd said it, and I hadn't listened; I'd ended any kind of relationship with him without any tender thought in my head. And now, as if to punish me, I was here. In the woods.

(Maybe you should drop it).

There was something bad about Gravenhead. I could *feel* it. I felt like a bug approaching an insect-eating plant, which uses its sickly, tempting gifts in order to...

I parted the leaves and the bracken fronds that hid the basin from the track, and frowned. I had not expected this; the air had *not* dropped a fraction of a degree, inviting a misty, sixth sense of water. Like Carter at Tutankhamun's tomb, seeing "wonderful things," I had never *dared* hope everything would be... like *this!*

There was a pushing of branches behind me. And I felt slightly jealous that Bethan was seeing it all for the very first time.

'Oh, *wow!*' said Bethan.

Chapter Nine

Around Gravenhead.

The Book of Morwen (cont'd)

THE LAKE WAS *gone!*
  As if in a trance, Bethan walked down the slope to the point where I had once been forced to stop, and she *continued* walking, for where there had once been the surface of the lake, flat and smooth like dull, olive glass, there was now a simple contrast between leaf litter and creamy, dry clay. Away from the shade of the trees, little eddies blew dust up into the warm air: I fleetingly sensed a dividing line, where the light of the known world ended.

Richard Thorns

Even viewing the drowned remains of the church from the lakeside, I had been so right about the earlier dimensions of my discovery, I thought (a small glow of satisfaction slapped the faces of my suspended tormentors); my basin was a cavernous bowl that looked very smooth and, surprisingly, the fifty feet or so drop to the floor looked very shallow. But in reality, I thought, this rim where I now stood would seem very high once we were down among the deserted houses; the church would tower over us, small as it seemed up here, with its short, added Tudor spire on squat medieval roots.

I shook my head. With Bethan gone, I searched around for the evidence of my last visit with Garreth, and presently I found a scrap of Clingfilm; the only part of Garreth's sandwiches, I thought with a slight stab, which the animals of the basin hadn't eaten. The ghost of our excitement seemed to hang in the air. It was here that I'd triumphantly breathed to Garreth: *'There you go,'* and now everything was changed and it was-

No - one thing at a time. The *camcorder!*

Casting my gaze around, I suddenly saw the Panasonic standing abandoned on its tripod and the camera bag stuffed nearby against a tree. I breathed a sigh of relief and ran over. I carried the camera and tripod, very top heavy, gently over to the bag.

'Hey Morwen! Come and look at this!'

I spun around. Bethan was beckoning to me in excitement. I hesitated, looking at the equipment. *Well,* I thought, *I've kept my promise for Garreth - and no fines to worry about for me; it's my time now!* I made a quick mental note of the location of the tree, and turned and ran towards Bethan.

Over the line that marked where the water had been, the slope was shallow, but then it took a sudden plunge. Seeing Bethan's slight frame disappearing over the edge, I followed quickly. I scrabbled down a slope of hard clay, grazing my hands behind me as I slid. I caught up to Bethan, bumping into her.

'*Careful!*' said Bethan. 'You nearly sent me flying! Look over there.'

She pointed silently at the furthest away house, which was also standing mute. The top of the house was smashed into pieces, so the elegant half-timber was jagged, stretching up alone into the blue sky. The timbers steamed gently in the sunshine. Looking at the ornate lower windows, I thought, it was as if the house had poked out its own eyes with the wood.

Bethan murmured: 'I've been waiting five hundred years for someone to come and fix my roof.'

But I was busy pulling the map from my jacket pocket. Shaking it open, I ran my finger over the paper.

'Past that house, Beth'. *Bethan!* Look! Straight past that wrecked house at the far end of the village... you see that high hill at the other side of the basin? That's Fawkes's Hill!'

'So what?' Bethan's eyes were still shining.

Richard Thorns

I gave up, smiling with joy. So - we had found it properly at last, and it was as beautiful as I had always known it would be. At the bottom of the basin, a low-lying mist curled gently around the houses as they lay clustered in the streets. It was as if Gravenhead was gasping in the heat like a fish out of water. And at the crest of the church, the weathercock seemed to stretch triumphantly at the sky.

I took a swig of water, poured some into my hand and rubbed the sweat from my forehead. I then handed the water bottle over to Bethan.

'Right,' I said, 'off we go then.'

The clay was full of rocks that could twist underfoot, and so neither of us spoke as we made our descent, each caught in our own thoughts. There was a brief moment when the slope levelled, and we ran giggling down in the sun, like children from a golden age to my lost town. But mostly we were quiet, and the silence of the forest and the forgotten village seemed to ache in my ears. Perhaps the reason for our silence, I thought, was the one I was feeling all by myself, until the ground became marshy in the shade of houses, and then Bethan suddenly said:

'Morwen?'

'Huh?'

'Do you get the feeling that... this isn't for our eyes?'

'What do you mean?'

'Well... it's been lost for so long and we're the only ones to see it and it's just - well, it's a bit scary here, that's all.'

Bethan's voice was small. I knew what she meant. Once, in my dark days in Year nine I had been talked into stealing pears from an orchard, where it was rumoured the farmer had a gun. Desperate to be accepted, I had watched my new friends darting around the trees, and I'd instead been frozen to the spot in pure terror, the nerves coming up through my skin - every second the one before the imagined roar of the gun. And *then...*

Uurgh! Look at Morwen! Run!

The memory flickered as I stood in Gravenhead's sunny, abandoned streets and plucked a twig from a hazel hedge; it formed the rim of a once-beautiful, grand garden. Beyond it were the remains of a great vegetable patch, leading around the side of a house. I could see the high rear wall at the back.

But it had been alright back then because when I'd arrived at my gran's with wet socks and legs and in tears my Da had been there and he'd said...

I snapped the hazel twig in two - the first act of destruction in Gravenhead for nearly five hundred years.

'I've come to say goodbye for a while, sweetness. This staying friends with your Mam; it isn't working out.'

(my two pieces of hazel-twig became four).

'No,' I said, 'you're alright, Bethan. It's just a village. I don't feel it at all.

Richard Thorns

The Book of All

In Morwen's back garden, her gran took a sip of tea and waited for the telephone call to end. She heard a faint 'Good-bye,' as the call was ended, and presently the garden door opened and Mrs Lundy walked out with a tin of biscuits, her face grim.

'That girl,' she said.

'What's she done now?'

'That was Rosengrave police station; a policeman wants to speak to Morwen.' Mrs Lundy poured herself a cup of tea from the pot. She waved a biscuit at her mother.

'All this time I've been trying to tell her to get off her backside and get something done in the summer holidays, and she's had that project up her sleeve all along!'

The old woman jerked her head up, startled. It was as if a little black cloud had rolled over the sun.

'You know the business of that dead body at the station? That policeman went round to see a friend of Morwen's the other day, and he's got told a yarn that Morwen's involved in right up to her ears!'

Morwen's grandmother carefully sipped at her tea, as her daughter continued, her Welsh accent singing in her indignation. 'He wants to ask Morwen about some lost *ci*-ty or something her friend claims she found under a lake. Well, I *said* to the police it must be some fantasy they've made up as kids do, and they should-'

Gravenhead

'But why did they want to speak to *Morwen?* Surely the police's job is to catch *criminals.*'

Mrs Lundy pursed her lips. 'That's what I'm cross about - they *are* interested. That case on the TV about the old man died at Treffynydd, Mam, now they say there's someone vanished; someone actually from Rosengrave this time.'

The old woman looked across the table at Mrs Lundy. She saw the anger in her daughter's eyes at the deceit. She saw something else. She looked around the peaceful back garden, sweltering in the midday sunshine. Everything seemed so normal. The climbing frame next door needed a coat of paint.

'You know, Mam,' said Mrs Lundy hesitantly, '*that's* what's daft: if Morwen... *had* found something like that she would tell us - wouldn't she?'

And rush home all excited screaming: 'Mam! Mam!' to explain everything. But she won't. She's a teenager; she'll never do that again.

But Morwen *had* tried to tell... her gran. She remembered Morwen's high little words:

'I wondered whether maybe I should do something on Gravenhead.'

Yes. It was as if a little black cloud had rolled over the sun.

The Book of Morwen

Richard Thorns

I pushed gently at a door. The wood squeaked slightly as it made a slight gap. I stopped, considering: if I shoved any further the door might collapse.

I edged myself carefully into the room, and looked around me.

'Hey, Beth', get in here!' I yelled in delight.

There was a muffled gasping as a side of Bethan squeezed through the gap. I heard a faint crunching sound under the dried slime as she walked towards me.

The room was dry, and littered with small chairs and tables. A long platform of wood shut off one end of the room. I looked at the shelves behind the obstruction.

'I don't believe it - *I* know what this is,' I murmured.

Bethan sat her small frame at the window and placed her hands on the sill. 'You can see the main street from in here,' she remarked, 'that sunny street and we've got the whole town all to ourselves! But it doesn't *feel* like a house in here, Morwen. Do you know what I mean?'

I smiled. I ducked under a hole in the obstruction, and popped up again. I reached up at the shelves.

'Hey, Bethan!'

Bethan looked at me; I was grinning from ear to ear.

'I can't serve you! You're not old enough!'

Bethan frowned at me: 'What are you on about?'

I took down a bottle from the shelves. 'We're in an *alehouse,* Bethan! This is a *pub!*'

The bottle in my hand had its ancient stopper pushed right in. I poured out dirty lake water which splashed on the floor. My heart pounding with excitement, I placed the bottle on the counter and looked up at the shelves; with all the filthy bottles in front of me *surely* there had to be at least one and - sure enough - I suddenly caught my breath.

I stretched up my arm and gently took a bottle down from the shelf. I held it like a first-born. The bottle was a rich, opaque golden brown, carrying the faint, raised rippling of a rose. I passed it gently across to Bethan.

'What you said on the train about burying things for five hundred years, Beth',' I said, and I was aware of the trembling in my voice. 'Try this. It's an unopened bottle of Tudor ale. Yours as a souvenir, Bethan! Greetings from Gravenhead.'

The Book of All

Mrs Lundy looked steadily at the old lady in the back garden.

'You look a little shocked, Mam. I think we'll just have to ask her what she's up to. Remember Morwen's best attribute? She'll always tell the truth; she'll never lie.'

The old lady took a sip of tea and forced a smile. 'I suppose what's only a story to kids is someone else's idea of wasting police time. But it's funny the police are so interested in *Morwen?*'

Richard Thorns

Mrs Lundy hesitated. 'He said he was interested *personally* Mam. He said Morwen shouldn't worry; he just wants to know why she hasn't gone running off to the papers or a museum or whatever. You know, Mam, I think that policeman might actually *believe* that story of theirs!'

Suddenly Mrs Lundy looked very serious, 'He said they'd tried to find the missing man - how they'd asked at all the local clubs, the reservoirs, even the coastlines. He was a local historian. And he was a *diver,* Mam.

The Book of Morwen

'You know, it's funny,' I said thoughtfully.

We had wandered through the sunny streets, the tangle of hedges high on either side. We had crossed the village green. Ahead of us lay spartan graves and the door of Gravenhead church.

'Have a look around you,' I said. 'Do you notice anything?'

'Quite a bit, actually.'

'No... I mean, look at all the houses we've passed. What did you think of them, Bethan, drowned for nearly five hundred years?'

Seeing Bethan's expression, I went on, 'When we first arrived here we even made out a *vegetable* garden, Beth'. *That's* how well preserved everything is. Remember I said on the train about how the steeple was in wonderful condition? Well... generally, it *is. Everything* is!'

'You got that right,' said Bethan, unnerved and slightly irritated by my tone.

'Then why,' I said slowly, 'do all those other houses, past the church on the other side of the village... look like *that?*'

Bethan followed my gaze past the church and I saw her shiver as if an icy shadow had run down her back. On the furthest side of the village, the houses seemed to grow directly out of the drying earth. Maybe it was the sheer *ugliness* of the houses that had shaken her - the teeth of the jagged timbers poked up from the crumbled walls. Only a single wall remained of one house, its chimney breast the only sign there had ever been a house there at all.

Bethan looked at me, her grey eyes full of fear.

'They're all, wrecked,' she whispered. 'Morwen, they're *ruined!* What *happened* here?'

'Look at that one!' I pointed at splayed fingers of timber stretching up like a starburst. 'That must have been a true timber-framed house - wooden from the bottom. There aren't even any walls! Something's blasted the hell out of it, Beth'.'

'Let's go, Morwen,' Bethan said to me fearfully, 'you're scaring me! Look, you've got the media camera. Let's just take some pictures and - *Morwen!*'

I was walking through the graveyard. Bethan caught up with me and tugged at my sleeve. 'What do you think you're *doing?* We can-'

'Are you coming in or not?'

Richard Thorns

Bethan walked gingerly over to the church door, and peered in through the timbers. She leaned against the door, and it swung open a little. I joined her, looking over her shoulder. Inside, the interior was gloomy, but not as dark as I'd expected, lit as it was by rays of sunlight streaming in through lost, hidden gaps. I could make out pews sitting in silence. The church was very quiet, but I could hear the faint gurgling of water caught somewhere in the interior.

'No, I'm not,' Bethan said, edging away.

'Oh, come on! There might be the village records in there! They'll make your ale bottle seem like a piece of...' I looked at Bethan.

'Come on Beth',' I said again. 'I don't want to go in by myself.'

Looking at me, Bethan shook her head silently.

I stared at her for a moment longer, moistened my lips, and shrugged.

'Alright. Wait out here, then. I'll only be a minute or so. I only wanted to go and take a quick peek around, anyway.'

I hesitated.

'Really, Beth',' I said. 'No big explorations - we'd be out in under a minute.'

Bethan shook her head again.

I shrugged. I backed away from the door and placed my hand on one of the gravestones. It felt surprisingly cool in the sun.

I walked forward, gently pushed at the church door, and went inside.

Chapter Ten

The paintings in the church (part 1).

The Book of Morwen (cont'd)

MY FIRST thought was how... *cool* the air in the church felt, out of the searing heat of the day. I looked back at the door, as if in longing and wanting Bethan to be spooked in the graveyard, and to change her mind and come running in to me.

But why be spooked by just a churchyard, though, when this whole village is one great big boneyard?

Long seconds passed. No Bethan.

Richard Thorns

So I walked silently to the aisle, the flagstones muffled by the lake slime under my trainers. *I'll have to watch my footing*, I thought. The deathly silence in the church ached in my ears, broken only by the faint gurgling and rushing of water from within.

And then I was turning left, the pews either side of me. At the end of them I could see the altar up its shallow steps, peeping through the ornate stone barrier that would be waist-high when I finally reached it.

I looked around for the door. It was still open, the sunshine flooding a lavender beam into the church, but not into its far reaches where I now stood. No, I was too far in now. I gasped slightly in fear. *A childhood night in a pear orchard.*

And that faint running water isn't helping! I allowed myself a grim smile. The aggression in my humour felt nice... yes, I thought, that was it: it would keep me from crying with fear and turning tail and running back to Bethan... this time I would *not* run away, with wet legs and crying!

To my gran's safe haven! Only to find when I got there-

(two jackdaws flapped up into the roof of the forgotten church and out, and a faint wind seemed to blow; it almost carried words....)

'Time to say goodbye for a while.'

And, even though my trainers made no sound, I found myself placing only the toes down as I advanced up the centre aisle. I passed pew line after pew line, and it was only as I passed the fifth that I realized that the pews were the same in one tiny little detail.

Yes! I can do this! I can see a tiny bump on every side, sticking out:

I knelt down, gently rubbed away at the slime, and recoiled.

The ghastly features of a tiny wooden face stared at me. Tiny details stood out in a rush: the nostrils flared, the lipless teeth exposed.

I jumped violently, moving on to the next pew, staring at the next tiny bump. A miniature line of three tiny, human faces. This carving also stared at me in silence and, even in my terror, I knew there was wisdom in those miniature wooden eyes-

'Beth'?' I said, but my own voice frightened me, and I knew then that I would not call out. I knew that a call that would reach Bethan would have to be a loud one, which I couldn't trust not to be a scream. I moved on.

Creature. Faces. *Creature.* Faces. All the same pattern. *End.* In my checking, I realized when I looked up that the pews had finished and I was at the barrier. The ornate carving still held. *It's still so beautiful,* I thought. I looked down the aisle. The church was empty and there was a clear run to safety. Faintly, I could still see the lavender-coloured sunbeam at the door.

Richard Thorns

I took my fingers away from the barrier. The pulpit lay to my right. As if in a trance I climbed the steps of it, and then I allowed myself a view of the church for the very first time...

Like Gravenhead itself, it was best viewed from above. The empty pews stared at me, as if waiting for something. On the wall to my left, my eyes slowly drew out the details of ancient paint. Above raging, world-drowning waters Noah challenged the Flood. The next picture was ruined, no more than a splash of ancient colour and all *faded, faded* towards and over the door and *faded, faded*, back again until... Ah! Lazarus walked forth from the chill depths of his tomb.

More ruined pictures, and then three painted beams of light hesitated at the barrier, and soared over it. They landed, bathing their white beams around the thin outline of a great heart. The gurgling of the water was much louder now. I turned my head.

Above me, the last of the lake ran shining down the church wall, freed from some ancient obstruction or catch-hole. It welled silently on stone carving and then fell, spattering on the flagstones and marching on to disappear down a small crack in the stones. A tiny breath of mist rose in the cool silence.

I pulled my eyes away from the water, preparing to leave. My feet banged against something, and I peered down.

In the darkness, I could make out a small shape.

Kneeling down, I gently touched it. It was a tiny box, the size of a shoebox. It was slippery beneath my fingers, but I knew in my heart that it wasn't wet. There was no seal or lock. It was as if the box was... *grown*. I tapped it gently, and a tiny piece of the surface fell into my hand. I turned it over in my fingers. It was slippery. But it was dry.

'It's... *wax*,' I murmured.

I tapped the box harder, and a great piece of wax fell away, revealing a thin line. I placed my fingers into the line and, trembling, tugged hard. I felt my fingernails bend and the wax cracked, and then I realized my mistake...

No! I'm tucked down in this pulpit and I can't keep an eye on things! I don't like it'

I ducked up again and looked down the church and I screamed loudly as I saw that the beam of lavender light *was broken.*

A figure was standing, silently watching me.

'Bethan!' I screamed.

And then the light beam was suddenly whole again as Bethan tore her way down the centre aisle. She ran hard to the end of the pews, almost colliding with the barrier. She gazed up at me, her face ashen.

'Morwen, I've just realized... there's something's very wrong with that churchyard,' she panted.

'Later,' I said shortly. 'Help me with this, and don't *ever* scare me like that again!'

'What's up?' said Bethan, as she clambered up to join me in the pulpit.

In answer, I motioned towards the box at my feet. 'It's completely sealed in wax - and it opens!' I said. 'Do me a favour and keep watch for me.'

My fingers ached as I tugged hard at the box, and the wax finally broke and splintered away for good. As I straightened up, I gently lifted up the lid. Inside was a sheaf of papers, as yellow as the beams of sunlight that flooded through the roof of Gravenhead church. I caught my breath as I touched them. They crumbled, but only slightly. I gathered them in my hand. They were quite dry. Replacing them, I quickly took my jacket off and wrapped it around the box.

'Are you taking it?' Bethan's voice sounded slightly disapproving in my ear.

I nodded. 'Yes,' I said firmly. 'I don't *think* it's... stealing from a church or anything if the church is like this. Anyway, they ought to be in a museum if they're so important they belong in a sealed wax-'

I broke off. I could see something behind Bethan.

Bethan caught my eyes going past her head.

'Morwen.'

'There's a painting on the wall behind you, Bethan,' I said slowly, 'the only painting this side of the barrier! I thought it was a heart, but it's *not* a heart! *Look!*'

Bethan slowly turned her head. I could actually see the hairs on her neck prickling and rising slowly, as she stared at the painting. The dark outer lines of the "heart" were two dark, stick-like arms stretching out of the ground; the curved-over crest was formed of bent-over wrists and fingers.

'It's not… *human*, Bethan, is it,' I said quietly in her ear. It was not a question.

The back of Bethan's head shook faintly from side to side.

But her shoulders were heaving fast; she was hyperventilating.

'Okay, we're going, Beth', yeah?'

The back of Bethan's head nodded slowly as she edged carefully down the pulpit steps - and then she started to run. From up in the hidden arches of the lost roof came a single, dull thud - a skeletal remnant of a musical note. It was *old!* A shrill sound joined it, and I realized I had heard the bell for a second time and that the sound was my own scream. I saw Bethan turn towards the lavender beam and shoot Lazarus-like through the door. I joined her within a second, and after the chill depths of the church the sun was like a furnace on my skin.

The Book of All

It was a calming, almost sleepy afternoon in Rosengrave, the bright furnace of the sun bathing the tarmac of the central roundabout, and overheating the red-brick complex in the centre of the town. Perhaps in happier times the new, invested-in buildings would not be the central police station and the magistrates' court. But for now, there they were, propping up the local paper, the *Rosengrave Runner* (which occupied the top tier) both literally with their bricks and mortar, and commercially with news.

Within the *Runner's* offices, Louisa Caybourne sat alone at a desk. It was not her desk and she knew why she was alone: she herself had written her weather column for the following week, so she knew that the air temperature in both the room and that part of the building was way too hot. With a right-on ex-union rep' as the *Runner's* editor, the air conditioning broken and it being a Friday, most people were either in their gardens by now, or down the pub.

Except Louisa.

The *Runner* lacked the glamour of her local TV weather slot, and Louisa could, in theory, have e-mailed her column whenever she wanted, but she liked to see the friends she had left behind at the paper. Sunita Bayall was always keen to let Louisa share her computer, just like the old days.

She sat at Sunita's desk and chewed her bottom lip, as if trying to come to a decision. She reached out to Sunita's answer phone, and pressed the button again:

"Sunita, Jack Arnold here, just returning, er, your call. Just to say that the sighting of the frogman in the Olindale estuary was a seal. Just a thought, this next bit... we have an account of an area where someone would be bound to visit if it's true. But since it involves a lost town under a lake, it's probably just kids mucking about. Get back to me if you think you want to do something as I have a name for you. Okay. Bye."

Five minutes later, a soft "beep" sounded through the office. Louisa opened the door and walked into the corridor, her rope-soled deck shoes quiet on the linoleum. As the door swung shut, it closed on a soft metallic voice:

"All messages now deleted."

The Book of Morwen

'Hey, Morwen!'

I paused at the end of the churchyard, my hand on the remains of the iron gate, looking behind me. Bethan had stopped running and was walking towards me.

'Wait, I've got a stitch, I need to sit down a minute,' she panted.

I nodded, anxious to get out from the confines of the churchyard. Outside, we walked across the village green to the streets, and sank down onto the ground beside a house.

'Well,' said Bethan, after getting her breath back, 'now I know why I never wanted to go to Sunday school. What the hell was that on the wall?'

'Have you still got your bottle, or did you lose it in there?' I asked her anxiously. And then it occurred to me that Bethan might suddenly answer smartly: *like you did?* But she didn't; instead she simply patted her jacket pocket.

'Yeah, you still got all that stuff from... in there?'

I nodded, getting up. The sun was so hot and the air felt so calm I felt slightly woozy. I looked around me; the village basked in sunshine, serene and completely deserted.

We walked away from the church and past the tavern, each lost in our own thoughts. I thought maybe we were like a boy and a girl at the end of love because we were mostly silent, and when we talked it was like we were talking in miniature.

'Fancy a drink for the road?' I said lightly. Bethan grinned at me.

'It's long past time,' she said, 'like - five hundred years past time.'

We carried on walking and the sun was so high in the sky it seemed to blaze down like the heat from a kiln. So, I thought, as the ground began to incline upward, that was where the lake had gone - sucked up into the sky in the broiling Gravenhead summer, the one last summer of my childhood that I knew I would never forget.

I paused for breath and took out my water bottle. Twisting the cap off, I looked at the hill we had to climb. To our right, a section of the lake wall was sheer and completely vertical. *That* would have been the place to fish, I found myself thinking.

I offered my water bottle to Bethan. 'You're going to need this, and your breath,' I said. 'We've got a heck of a climb ahead of us.'

Bethan nodded, squinting in the sunshine.

'You okay, Bethan?'

'What? Oh, yeah. I was just taking a last look at the village before you hand it over. It's so cool, Morwen: that pub; all those little houses; that great big place over there. It's all amazing! Cheers for the project, Morwen, I'll always remember it.'

I followed Bethan's pointing finger. The house was bigger than all the others, and it stood slightly aloof from all the other houses.

'I think it must have been owned by someone really important,' I murmured, 'maybe like the Lord of the Manor, Bethan? Anyway, somebody really grand, I think.'

And then, in the bright sunshine, I felt the first tremblings of a dream I'd had during an earlier visit to the lake. Yes, I had been on a train, hadn't I? And hadn't my head lulled against a train window all slippery in the heat and... hadn't I had a call from Bethan about the camcorder and hadn't I lied?

The cool green water in the church and the fish were so pretty and the people in the church were all so silent.

'It's so hot, Beth',' I murmured.

But... so restless in the pews because of the wake of my swim.

I stared at the manor house and the empty windows returned my gaze. Why should the manor house make me think of skeletons? I thought.

Richard Thorns

The Book of Morwen (cont'd)

An hour later, I gladly stepped over the dividing line from clay to leaf litter. Ignoring the screaming muscles in my legs I went over to the tree and picked up the bag. Unzipping it, I pointed the camcorder at Bethan, who was rubbing her bare feet next to her discarded trainers and socks.

'The smell of Bethan's feet would seem the most likely reason for the desertion of the village!' I said loudly. 'Morwen Lundy, *Wales Today,* Gravenhead.'

'Oh, very funny,' muttered Bethan, picking *The Comely Flood* up from the ground and stuffing it into her jacket pocket. 'Are you filming me?'

'Fat chance,' I said mournfully, stuffing the camcorder back into its bag. 'The battery's knackered. That's what you get for leaving a camcorder out in the woods for nearly two weeks.'

I peered through the Perspex panel of the camcorder. 'I can't get the tape out because there's no power, but it *is* still in there,' I said thankfully. 'Come on then, Bethan. One last look?'

I walked down the slope and took Bethan's arm.

'Come on, Beth',' I said gently. 'It's over.'

But as we rattled the bikes over the potholes and the thick, crusted furrows of the track, I felt the last remnants of the dream soak away from my memory, like the last of the lake through the church flagstones.

Why should the manor house make me think of skeletons?
   Bethan had begun to pedal the bike quickly, eager to feel the cool wind in her hair. I could see her twisting her head in a breeze of her own making. I glanced over to my left. Through the trees, I could see the spire of the church flickering through the branches. And then I wanted to feel the breeze too so I speeded up and it was gone.

Richard Thorns

Chapter Eleven

The middle secret.

The Book of Morwen (cont'd)

BACK HOME, I slowly climbed the stairs, sipping from a mug of tea in one hand and hauling up the bag (which knocked slyly into my knees) with the other. I went into my bedroom, sat on the bed and unzipped the bag slowly. Tucked on top of the little Hi-8 camcorder was my jean jacket, neatly folded. I carefully unwrapped my jacket and removed the box. I grimaced and picked gently at the ancient wax where it was smeared into the denim. The wax was dirty and grey and it made me feel sick.

I wondered at that moment what Bethan was doing with her ale bottle.

'Morwen!'

I jerked my head up, startled, as I heard the back door slam shut. My Mam must have been in the back garden. I heard footsteps in the hall and then they were suddenly advancing up the stairs. I hurriedly wrapped the box back in my jacket and stuffed it under the bed.

I sat down on the bed again just in time. The door opened; Mam was standing in the doorway.

'You've had a long day. Out since nine you were. It's past six now.'

'I've been out with Bethan, just collecting some stuff for that media project,' I said truthfully. 'How was your day? You're really brown, Mam.'

Mam walked into my bedroom without asking. 'What is it you're up to, Morwen?'

I jumped. 'I... don't know what you're talking about,' I stammered.

Mam looked at me. It was a long, slow look that I knew of old. It was a look that defied me to lie. 'Maybe I'll tell you something *I* don't know about, then,' she said steadily, 'Rosengrave police on the phone to me this afternoon - asking after you. Have you something you want to tell me?'

I gazed fearfully at my Mam.

'No,' I said, going red.

Richard Thorns

'Oh, Morwen, come *on!*' snapped Mam in exasperation. 'I *know* about the project. That Arnold policeman wants to know all about what you've found under the lake! I want to know if it's true. Is it what you're doing for that project? And I want the *truth*, Morwen!'

I looked at the floor.

'How did *he* know?' I muttered to myself. Then I looked up with a smile.

'Oh, of course,' I said with a little laugh. 'Garreth.'

Mam was staring at me. I knew that whatever she'd been expecting, it was not that. Denials - perhaps even tears - that the police had been drawn into our children's games? *Well, I thought with satisfaction, it wasn't what you thought, Mam; you wanted the truth, and how do you like it now you've got it?*

There was a long silence. I could hear the tiny ticking of my bedside clock.

'You're telling me this is all *true*, Morwen?' Mam said in a low voice.

'Oh, whatever!' I snapped. 'Yes! It's true! Look!' Sitting on the bed I tried to lift the media bag beside me, but it was too heavy. 'I found a drowned village. I found it. We filmed it and I know where it is and Garreth promised,' I felt my eyes almost well with tears, 'he *promised* he wouldn't talk about it and he's ruined everything!'

I was silent, staring at the floor. Even in my anger at his betrayal of me, I knew I was being unreasonable; Garreth hadn't promised anything of the sort. I looked up; I couldn't be sure, but I thought I caught Mam looking at a little scar I had on my left elbow; it was a livid white over my brown skin. When I was six, I'd fallen out of an apple tree in the back garden. I had cried, but not out loud. My Da had tried to pick me up; I had pushed him away. I'd just looked at the ground silently, withdrawing into myself and subdued. The memory flashed painfully at me.

Mam just waited. A blackbird sang its heart out in the warm evening air through the window.

'It's alright,' she said gently. 'It's all out now.'

I'm *not* crying!'

Mam flinched. 'No, I meant your secret, Morwen. Where is it?'

'In the mountains,' I said dully. 'There's a lake there. Or rather, there *was* a lake because it's all gone now. Now there's just a village. We're so lucky, because it's really old; it was lost in the sixteenth century. It's *Tudor,* Mam!'

'And you mean this? You really are the first to find it, Morwen?'

I nodded. 'I've known about it for a long time, Mam, since February,' I said, and I lowered my eyes. I'd seen my deceit fall and I knew, deep down, I was no longer glad.

Mam sat on my bed, and took hold of my hands.

'Morwen, listen to me' she said gently, 'I think this is why the police are keen to speak to you. Somebody's missing and they think he might have gone there. Do you think he did?'

I stared at her, slowly shaking my head. 'No,' I said honestly. 'Mam, I *promise* you there's no-one there. It's in the mountains tucked away, all deserted and there's only me, Bethan and Garreth who know about it. I'm never speaking to him again!' I flashed angrily.

'Morwen, they'd discover it sooner or later.'

'Yes,' said I flatly. 'And they will! And then it'll be on the news and in all the newspapers. Everyone will swarm all over it, and nobody'll remember it was me who found it in the first place!'

I took my hands away and took the camcorder from the bag.

'There's still *time*, though, Mam!' I said to her, my eyes beginning to shine again, 'even though Garreth's been so skank to me, because this camera's got the first images of Gravenhead for five hundred years!' I was almost shocked at the fierce longing in my voice. '*Please*, Mam!' I went on, 'I just want to get there first! Please!'

Mam looked at that bag for what seemed like a long time.

A *very* long time...

And then...

'You're *sure* there's no link, Morwen?'

Staring at her, I shook my head.

'I can speak to that Sergeant Arnold tomorrow if he calls again, and I can tell him what you've just told me, Morwen,' said Mam, getting up from the bed, 'and whether or not he wants to ask you about what you've found... well, that's up to him, I suppose.'

She smiled suddenly. 'Maybe, though, it depends on what you want to tell him. After all, you're the one who knows where it is.'

I looked up gratefully.

'Mam, they can do what they *want* after tomorrow,' I said. 'They can have it; it's what I wanted! The tape will be dated, and then nobody can *ever* say I wasn't the first to find Gravenhead! I'll get into uni - they may as well graduate me before I start!'

Mam's hand was on the door, and she had her back turned, so I couldn't tell whether or not the simple blow-through-nostrils was a laugh. But I thought for a second I saw a slight tensing of her shoulders. Mam turned her head to look at me:

'You know, you've probably forgotten, Morwen, but you try so often to keep things to yourself. That time at school, for instance. When you finally told us at the hospital what was going on - we took care of it, didn't we?'

Beneath the hidden code of words, I knew what was being said.

'Yes,' I said. 'I'm sorry, Mam.'

Richard Thorns

The door closed. I sat on the bed, stunned. Now the moment had actually happened I realized how badly, how thoughtlessly I had planned for it all. I looked at the clock. The seconds ticked by. In twenty four hours I would have that dead camcorder restarted, its tape copied over for me to keep and the original footage removed from prying teachers' eyes. And *then*... I could relax; I could cherry-pick who I wanted to give it to, and it would all be over.

Just in time! I thought.

Arnold was getting suspicious of me, I knew that. One person was dead and one was missing and my name was in the mix both times. Arnold had smiled at me in Mr Hughes's office; I doubted he'd smile at me now.

One day to go!

I looked out of the open window at the sky: it was a rich shade of lilac with a deepening purple edge. I was glad my Mam hadn't pushed me about Gravenhead. The thought burned at me: what would I have said if she'd asked me the one question I had dreaded her to ask, with the look that defied me to lie...?

Is Gravenhead dangerous?

I looked at the purpling sky and the answer floated silkily in through the open window. Yes, Gravenhead was bigger than my Mam's teaching.

I knew I would have lied.

I looked around me, scanning my untidy bedroom until my attention was caught by a Sunday newspaper lying on the floor. There was a photograph of a drab, unshaven figure sitting glumly on a step.

I felt the Other Thing call me, softly. Clearer and nearer than before - I picked the paper up and studied it:

"Now an alcoholic and living alone, Walter Emerson says he would give anything to see his daughter again after so many years."

'I know she's now a star, but I'm not after her money. I just want her to be Daddy's little girl again.'

Yes, there *was* a new one. I had thought so. I took a pair of nail scissors and cut carefully around the edges of the article.

Then I reached under my bed; my fingers knocked gently against my wax-coated discovery.

No, at this moment I'm not interested in that!

My fingers instead found something hard and flat and I drew it out from beneath the bed. I rested a little cardboard folder on my knees and opened it carefully. Inside, the newspaper cuttings were very thick by now; a cut-out article I'd stuffed in there the last time stared up at me:

"THAT'S THE WAY THE COOKIE CRUMBLES"

"Tracey Whittaker, better known as newly bestselling author Simone Dearing, is currently signing books in New York, while her estranged love rat husband works in a biscuit factory."

My eyes scanned the text:

'I know people will say I'm only after her money now. But I *know* we had something special! I've made mistakes! But I want the chance to make it up to her!'

I rooted underneath it and pulled out the one below: WOTTO LOTTO CLOTTO!

"Dozy Mark Brannigan was left kicking himself last night when the estranged Missus he'd finalised divorce proceedings with less than a month before, won a £1m top prize on a scratchcard."

I smiled to myself as I placed my newly cut-out article carefully into the folder with all the others and pushed it back under the bed. I heard a BANG from downstairs in the kitchen as my fingers brushed against denim and wax.

The box joined my folder! Now, beneath the bed there were two secrets.

The Book of All

Mrs Lundy took a packet of fish fingers from out of the freezer and banged them hard against the kitchen worktop surface. She fetched a box of matches and lit the grill, watching the cheap blue flame spit sulkily into life. She arranged the fish fingers beneath the grill, went into the living room and sat down to watch the evening news:

'And now, before we re-join the BBC at ten to seven with the National and International news, here's the weather with

Louisa Caybourne. Louisa, is there *any* sign to the end of this incredible heatwave?'

'Well, Bill, there's a band of cloud that seems to be heading across the Atlantic but don't hold your breath! But... you never know - by the end of next week, I feel sure I'll be able to announce a big surprise for everybody!'

Sitting on the sofa and staring at the television, Mrs Lundy thought it seemed an odd thing for the weathergirl to say; maybe she was getting married, or perhaps it was going to rain after all. Marriage was something Mrs Lundy felt unable to recommend. Her eyes flitted over to the dresser that contained the hidden memories of the past. Not for the first time, she reflected, she'd discovered she didn't know a member of the Lundy family half as much as she thought she did.

The Book of Bethan

In my bedroom, I held my lovely ale bottle up against the lampshade. It was a lovely ancient opaque amber-brown, and I felt a shiver of excitement. I placed the bottle on my mantelpiece, and took out *The Comely Flood* from my jacket pocket. It looked good beside the bottle, I thought: tiny pieces of mystery. I couldn't help but look at my computer... No. No way!

Ebay was *not* getting its hands on *that!*

Richard Thorns

I smiled in delight at the thought of our treasure! I found myself wondering what Morwen had done with the priceless little box she'd taken from the pulpit. I couldn't help smiling at the memory of her fierce little bravery at the door of the church, even with those tiny grey clouds of fright behind her eyes.

But I'm hanging about in that quiet little churchyard, enjoying the sunshine and only mildly spooked. My attention being caught by the three adjacent graves, set apart from the rest on elevated ground. I wander over to them. I reach down and swing one of the iron loops of chain between the three graves. The graves are chained together! Why? Saved from the elements in this great crypt of water, the writing on the graves is clear. And then the ancient writing had sent me flying through the lavender beam and into the church...

...where I had found Morwen in the pulpit with the box and the lights and the nightmare painting on the wall. I frowned:

There were *three* of those graves. Just like those three lights in the painting.

I jumped, gasping, and instinctively glanced at the window. It was shut.

It was getting late: the purple sky had dulled finally to black, but the heat still hung in the air. The bedroom was stiflingly hot, as if it had stored up the sun's heat throughout the day and was now slowly releasing it.

I thought for a moment and then slowly, almost reluctantly, took *The Comely Flood* from the mantelpiece, sat back on my bed, and opened it. No, *not* opened it; the pages zipped under my thumb as I caught open the back cover. My scrawl from the graveyard stood out in blue biro starkly on the white:

Edward Morton. Born 6th December 1409. Died 24th July 1476. Peter Fletcher. Born of this parish. Cowminster. 18th March 1415. Died 24th July 1476. Lihsen Chen. A visitor to these shores. Born 8th January 1397. Died 24th July 1476.

Yes, I had been right: they had all died on the same day. Well, maybe that wasn't so unusual in those days. Maybe they'd been burned, or died of the plague.

Was there plague in Gravenhead?

I turned a couple of pages back in *The Comely Flood* to find the index:

parliament: 6, 15, 22-4, 67, 118
peasants: 28, 55, 59, 63
peasants revolt: 29, 58, 65
pestilence: *see* Black Death
ploughing...

Richard Thorns

My eyes flitted back, back, back.

Black Death, *the:* 8, 13; *effects of:* 9; *desertion of Cowminster:* 80-1

My heart seemed to slow. I could almost hear the blood roar faintly in my ears, as I slowly turned back the pages to page 80:

"The mystery of the indentation up on Fawkes's Hill in relation to Gravenhead will probably never be solved, but it will always remain a tantalizing challenge to the archaeologist. The activity - showing sixteenth-century Tudor building work - dates back to when the lost village was known to exist. Another lost Welsh village is, by comparison, a far more puzzling enigma, as..."

I bit my lip. The sweat seemed to well inside me:

..."Cowminster, earlier ravaged by plague, was known (from parish records preserved at Treffynydd's county records office), to have been abandoned in the springtime of 1476, at which time it promptly disappeared from the historical record."

Impulsively I folded the page over at the top corner for future reference. And then, the fear welling up inside me, I zipped my thumb to the end of the book, and I knew in my heart I was doing it far more slowly: my eyes widened; one word in my quick scrawl stared up at me in blue biro:

Cowminster.

'Then what the hell are you guys doing in Gravenhead?' I said softly to myself.

My mind drew back to the three pathetic graves. Carted off in death from a plague village to a neighbouring one, and then buried there? No, that didn't make any possible sense. Unless... my eyes flicked up to the passage I had just read and slowly I brought my hand up to my mouth.

"... was known to have been abandoned in the springtime of 1476."

'But you *didn't* leave in the springtime, did you?' I murmured from behind my fingers. 'I've just seen your graves! You died in the middle of the summer! The three of you stayed, didn't you, in the deserted village for three whole months. And you all died on the same day. '

I put down the book. I couldn't help the thoughts coming: just how hot had been that summer of 1476?

What did you do in that village for a quarter of a year?

I stared in fright at my closed window...

How did you die?

I looked at my mobile, my heart hammering. No, I could see no point in both of us staying awake all night, frightened to sleep. Morwen would be told the following morning, when we went to the school to copy and date her tape. When Morwen would give her discovery to the world!

Morwen would be told...

That Cowminster wasn't some lost sister-village to Gravenhead..

Cowminster *was* Gravenhead.

Chapter Twelve

Louisa Caybourne.

The Book of All

THE NEXT morning dawned warm and bright, and Bethan's gravel crunched under the boots of the milkman as he wandered up the drive. It was already hot, but the cloudless sky was a weaker blue than usual, and high up there seemed a slight haze in the air. In this early air the colours of Bethan's house were beautiful; the red brick of the high walls was stark against white gravel. The bright lawns that separated wall from gravel were very shallow, like tiny green beaches.

Richard Thorns

Birds sang strongly in the light. The milkman stopped at the front door and pulled out a couple of pints of milk. He placed them in the shade of the porch and turned to leave. His attention was caught by something glittering on the gravel.

Stooping, he picked up some tiny pieces of lead, turning them over in his fingers. He looked up at the window, frowning. Then, with a shrug he tossed them lazily away, and walked off whistling down the drive.

The Book of Morwen.

In *Pile-Upz*, a lorry suddenly roared past the cafe window, making the cutlery on the cheap vinyl tablecloth rattle gently. I jumped and looked around me. Men in T-shirts stained with cement and stinking of smoke squinted at the morning papers, silently filling their mouths with breakfast.

I dug out my mobile and held it beneath the table, frowning at the text message:

"Gt sumthng 2 tell U. CU Pile-Upz 9.30."

I bit my lip, and unconsciously reached out to touch the media bag next to me. Yes, the precious contents were still there. I tried Bethan's mobile again:

"The mobile you are dialling is currently switched off. Please try again later."

'Excuse me?'

Hearing the voice above me, I looked up. Standing over me was a businesswoman in her early thirties, I guessed. She seemed slightly familiar and very out-of-place in that ghastly little griddle house, smartly dressed as she was in a pinstripe trouser suit and a white blouse.

'May I leave my bag here?' the woman said to me, 'I just want to go and fetch a cup of tea.'

I shrugged, turning back to play a game on my mobile to pass the time. *Why* had Bethan decided to play silly so-and-so's just when she was needed on this day? My heart sang with all the joy of a summer trip to the beach and I knew that I was metaphorically parting the curtain of the window because Bethan, metaphorically, had the car! But she *didn't* have the bag, I thought with satisfaction. I would give it ten more minutes, and then...

The woman settled into her seat and took a sip of tea, staring at the menu:

'I think I'll have the filet mignon with port wine sauce, served with mustard mash, and a carrot and butternut compote,' she announced.

I found myself grinning.

'Or I could have the main breakfast, followed by the house cardiac,' the woman went on, 'but I have to be at work soon. Unlike you, you lucky thing! Are you enjoying this fabulous summer, Morwen?'

I nearly jumped out of my skin. 'How did you know my name?' I stammered.

The woman smiled easily. She held up a hand.

'Sorry,' she said, 'But please don't worry - I come in peace. The thing is, Morwen, I do quite a bit of work for *Wales Today:* You may have seen me on the television from time to time. My name is Louisa Caybourne. I do the weather?'

The palm turned around, and I looked blankly at the woman.

She wants to shake my hand!

I felt terrified; the woman's first words suddenly seemed very false; no natural conversation there. No - that quip about the menu... *had been rehearsed!*

The woman withdrew her hand. 'So, it *is* you,' she said softly. 'I thought as much - you seem the sort of girl who would make a discovery just like the one you have. And you *have*, haven't you. It's true, isn't it, Morwen?'

I got up in a panic.

'No,' I stammered. 'I don't know what you're talking about! I'm just here waiting for my friend.'

'Would that be Garreth?' asked Louisa gently.

'Bethan,' I said in a fluster, still standing up. 'She'll be here in a moment! Go away! Go and sit somewhere else - there are plenty of other tables!'

Louisa Caybourne sighed, and then smiled up at me. 'Okay,' she said. 'I'll go and sit somewhere else. But, Morwen, think on this - I can go over there and read what's happening in the news while I eat my breakfast, but I'll still *know*. I can help you, Morwen.'

Still standing, I stared down at Louisa; Louise stared up at me, still smiling. After what seemed a long moment I felt myself slowly, dejectedly, sitting down again.

'How did you find out?' I said eventually.

There was a silence. I thought Louisa seemed to be choosing her words very carefully.

'I was doing my weather column in the *Rosengrave Runner*'s offices,' she said at last, 'and while I was there I took a call from a PC Arnold, who's keen to track down a missing person. I think he's been trying to contact you?'

I nodded.

'Well, I guess I shouldn't really have taken the call, but I did,' said Louisa blandly. 'But you see, the thing is, Morwen, I don't really think that's *all* he wants to find, if you see what I mean.'

I stared miserably at Louisa.

'Well, that's not what my Mam says,' I said at last, 'she said he was a police officer - not interested in anything to do with lost villages, just lost *people.*'

Louisa stirred her tea, wearing a rather wry smile.

'Morwen,' she said heavily. 'PC Arnold is *Old Bill!* With his uniform on he wants to find a missing person; when the uniform's *off* he's just a simple guy in a nice old woolly jumper, sitting by the fire and dreaming of finding just the sort of thing you've found. Either way, he's got a bizzie's nose for trouble.

'But I think I can give you what you want, Morwen,' she said.

'You don't know what I want,' I answered back.

There was a long silence. I couldn't bring myself to look at Louisa, so I cast my gaze around the cafe. A builder blew his nose and began to roll a cigarette while someone guffawed with laughter. The door opened and a face looked around the cafe and then thought better of it. The door closed again. Louisa waited patiently.

My eyes eventually settled back on Louisa.

'It seems so unfair,' I murmured, 'who else has he told? How many other people know now?'

Louisa took a sip of tea. 'Morwen, I'm going to be quite honest with you,' she said. 'What you've discovered is news. But I'm afraid you can't copyright news; you can't even own it. In fact, you could argue it's only after other people own it, it *becomes* news. Before then, it's only a secret.'

I thought for an instant of me and Bethan, running down our once-secret basin to Gravenhead in the hot sunshine. I grieved for it. I felt like an old lady remembering her youth.

I felt her hand on mine.

'In answer to your question,' Louisa was saying, 'about anyone else knowing, I don't think you need worry; if anyone knew, I think you'd know by now. Because,' she added, 'as I told you earlier, what you've discovered is news!

'I'll cut to the chase, Morwen: let us deal with it! We aren't the police - we don't care about missing people. Not this time, anyway. Look, you'll get all the credit and an interview and a *really* long piece about the village. *Hey!*' she said brightly, as if the thought had only just occurred to her, 'how do you fancy everyone at school calling you *The Lady of the Lake?*'

I stared at her. 'I'd rather set fire to myself,' I said, 'and anyway, why are you doing all this for me; what are *you* getting out of it?'

Louisa looked surprised, 'exclusivity, of course,' she said, 'and you should know about that! Look, nobody's going to steal this off you, Morwen; we're not explorers or adventurers, we've all got jobs! We just want to be the first to broadcast it. So you see, Morwen, we're really both on the same side, can you understand that?'

I said nothing.

'You're still not convinced,' Louisa said, staring at me. She dropped her voice, leaning closely into me as she spoke: 'Okay, does *this* make sense? Morwen, you go to a museum and they'll run straight to the National networks; your discovery will disappear from you much faster than it appeared, believe me. You think you'll feature high in their priorities?

'But *we* can look after you on a regional basis, and *then* we'll show it to the Nationals, but by then, of course, everyone will know you found it. I think you'll find, on this occasion, you *can* copyright news.'

After a while, I nodded.

Richard Thorns

'Yes, I suppose so,' I said in relief, 'maybe that does make sense! But I still can't believe I'm having this conversation! Alright! So, now what?'

Louisa was thoughtful. 'We'll want to do the interview... beside the lake, I think. Just with the steeple poking through the water. Can that be done, do you think?'

I was about to object, and then the thought hit me... *she thinks Gravenhead is still flooded.*

'I gather you did this once before - with Garreth,' Louisa was saying, 'do you still have the footage? I can look at it at the studio if you like, so the writers can prepare a juicy voiceover for your interview.'

Something in that voice was too pure. I resisted - just in time - to stretch out a protective hand to my bag. I stared across the table at Louisa.

'No,' I said tonelessly. 'I don't have it. It's with Bethan, who's working on the project with me.'

'Oh,' said Louisa, pursing her lips in disappointment. 'Maybe you can email it to me, then; what have you got it on?'

I went scarlet with embarrassment, 'it's going onto VHS,' I said to her, 'you don't live around here; you haven't seen our school! I bet you don't know there's a betamax video machine in our I.T. room. It's been there for years; they won't throw it out!' I leaned forward to stare into Louisa's surprised face, 'I have to get out of here! Can you understand that? I can't stay here; I'll go mad!'

Louisa nodded, looking slightly shaken.

'I think we can help,' she said eventually, 'all right, then; go and get it off Bethan, and then give it over to me. Here's my card. Will you call me to arrange a chat?'

I took the card. It looked very flash.

'I'll see Bethan,' I said.

Louisa nodded. 'I have to cut along to work now,' she said. 'I hope we can talk again soon.'

I shook the hand held out in front of me, still unsure. 'It's not that I mind you having the tape,' I said hesitantly, 'just... not today. Maybe I can call you later, though. Maybe tomorrow we can do something.'

Louisa was smiling again. She slid her chair back, and gathered up her coat.

'I understand. It's been nice to meet you,' she said to me.

I watched her leave. Her tea was virtually untouched.

The Book of Morwen (cont'd)

Once I was sure Louisa was really gone, I drained my own mug and got up to leave. The bag was heavy on my shoulder, and the warm sun promised a niggling, heavy walk to the bus stop.

I felt pleased; I remembered my idea of bringing the Panasonic to the lake as backup, and with Garreth's phone going in the lake how right I'd been! Louisa *seemed* nice enough, but I thought about that sugar-smile of hers.

Richard Thorns

Just before I closed the door behind me I could hear Ricardo Silvinho, the owner of *Pile-Upz*, as he handed mug and cup over to the griddle-chef.

'You see,' he was saying, 'one white shirt and a lovely navy suit, and a smile to charm an angel's heart, and *still* they make two teas last all morning!'

The Book of Morwen (cont'd)

The school was drenched in mid-morning sun, and very quiet. There were a few cars parked in spaces, some with their soft tops down. I glanced around me: the prison-themed setting made the freedom of the holidays seem more real, like I could taste and touch escape.

It was very hot. A meeting point during my time at school now lay baked and abandoned, without a single blade of grass. I thought of our outdoor pool at the back, still going strong from around twenty years ago; built when Rosengrave seemed bursting with coal and the demand for it unlimited. I found myself wishing I'd brought a costume and a towel. Even with teachers in the pool, it sounded inviting. I sat on a low wall, filled instead with bark chippings and roses. Big windows stared emptily back at me. All silent and Formica and dust. Bricks and roses.

I smiled as the small frame of Bethan appeared around the corner of the Tennyson wing of the school: she looked as hot as hot, stopping to try to get the most out of her ice pop. She looked up and waved. I stood up, my doubts disappearing in a sudden burst of excitement. I dragged up the bag.

'Sorry I'm late,' said Bethan. 'I had to wait in, and then I missed the bus. Did you wait long for me in *Pile-Upz?*'

'Yeah,' I said, grinning. 'But guess what; we've got our footage sorted out! We might be on the telly, Beth'!'

Bethan looked at me, shocked.

'What do you mean? When?'

'Soon!' I announced, aware of the fierce joy in my voice, 'maybe in a few days, but I don't want it to be *today;* nothing's going over until it's dated and backed up! But it could happen soon, Beth'!'

Bethan's reaction was disappointing me. She stood still in front of me, running her fingers through her streaked hair.

'I don't understand. How did you get it sorted so quickly?'

'Oh, there was somebody in *Pile-Upz* from *Wales Today,*' I said impatiently. 'Her name's Louisa Caybourne and she knows about Gravenhead and she wants to run it on the local news. She's *really* nice, Beth' - she says the Nationals will just nick it from us. So, you know what she's going to do?'

'Uh, let me see now, *she'll* nick it from us?'

'No, she'll protect us and give us all the credit,' I answered a little hotly. 'What's the matter? Don't you want to-'

'Morwen,' interrupted Bethan. Her words began to tumble out in a rush. 'Morwen, *listen!* Gravenhead was built on the site of Cowminster and Cowminster was a *plague* village! *The Comely Flood* says it was abandoned in 1476, but three people never left. They stayed behind and then they died. All on the same day!'

There was a silence.

'So now we've found *two* villages,' I said a little tartly. 'We're doing well, aren't we?'

'Morwen, please listen. I think something bad happened back then.'

I was silent, looking at Bethan's face.

'You know, I don't understand you,' I said quietly. 'All the time we've been doing this thing you've *known*. And you never minded when you knew it was always in my mind. What's changed now, now it's all happening just as we planned?'

Bethan said slowly, 'Because somehow I feel things are different now. Something in me says to leave that village alone.'

'They *are* different now!' I pointed out, 'Louisa's going to look after us!'

Bethan looked at me, shaking her head.

'If you say so,' she said, 'she might, of course, just be out for what she can get! What does she owe you; you're only a kid.'

'Don't say that,' I said with a slight catch in my voice.

Bethan sat down on the sunny wall beside me. She placed a hand on my arm.

'Morwen, I see these people all the time,' she said to me, more gently, 'I see them at my own Mam's house! They don't think like you do; they'd never consider what difference they can make in the world; only what the world can give *them*, I reckon the least important bit in this video is you! I think my Mam would like this Louisa.'

But I had begun walking across the sunny courtyard towards the doors. Bethan had to pick away at the branch of a rose bush that had taken an interest in her T-shirt, and her words seemed to hang in the empty air between us.

The Book of Morwen (cont'd)

For once, walking the shady corridors could have been a pleasure, but we walked down the last of them all too soon. I frowned to myself: Bethan looked terribly uncomfortable. I pulled open the library doors. Inside, Ravel was at the media desk, a tiny screwdriver in one hand, holding half a camera up to the light.

He put it down as we both walked up to the counter. I had a pretty good idea what he was thinking as he looked at us: if it wasn't for my summer tan, my sensible navy T-shirt would've shown up my pale skin and brooding eyes just like my uniform always did. In contrast, Bethan looked a real summer child, only as tall as my shoulder and all cotton bracelets and a bright yellow top, cultivating that hip-pacifist look of hers she liked.

'Hey there,' Ravel said, grinning (his smile going straight over my shoulder to Bethan), 'how goes it with the project?'

'We're done,' I said, opening the bag and placing the camcorder on the media desk, 'but the Hi-8 tapes belong to the Media Department so please can we transfer what we've done over to VHS, Ravel?'

Ravel nodded, holding up the camcorder to the light. 'Tape nicely rewound back, I see,' he said. 'Bethan, what you do is: first you plug your red and white cables into the Panasonic and then out to the back of the VHS recorder. Red is pictures, white is sound. Then you...'

Their voices became a low murmur. I cast my gaze around the library: Mrs Jennall was taking books from a pile on a table, slowly walking the aisles. Then my eyes narrowed as I saw a boy sitting at one of the tables, reading. Unable to stop myself, I stormed over, snatching the book from his hands.

'You haven't the faintest idea what you've done!' I breathed quietly at Garreth. 'I've had the police ringing my house; I'm in trouble with my Mam. I've even got people finding out where I go for a cup of tea! All because of you!'

'I know,' stammered Garreth. 'Look, Morwen, I'm really sorry, but I had to say something. I-'

'But that was the *easy* bit... you *didn't,*' I said under my breath. 'All you had to do was keep your trap shut until today; that wasn't too much to ask! Don't you realize - you nearly blew the whole thing.'

I broke off. Bethan was coming towards the table.

'Ravel's in the viewing room doing it now,' she said. She looked down at Garreth, unable, despite herself, to suppress a grin.

'Hiya,' she said, 'having a nice quiet chat, I see?'

'Well, probably it isn't the best place for him to be,' I said, calming down a little. 'I just wanted you to know,' I continued, flinging a glare at Garreth, 'what it's like to have people in your face!'

'Morwen,' said Bethan heavily, sitting down, 'I *wasn't* late to meet you because I missed the bus; I was trying to get Garreth together to come here. If you won't pay any attention to me, at least listen to him.'

I nodded. 'Right. I'm wondering if I'll ever be able to tell him how I'm feeling, without having to say sorry afterwards

'It's *important,* Morwen,' said Garreth anxiously, 'I swear it on my little brother's life.'

I looked at him pityingly: 'Garreth, you *hate* your little brother!'

Feeling their eyes on me, I buried my face in my hands.

'Oh, whatever,' I said at last. 'Go on then.'

'Morwen,' said Garreth, 'that day we went to the lake for the very first time. You remember it was a Sunday? Well, I didn't get out of there for ages because of... well, you know. And by the time I got to Treffynydd station it was dark - around nine p.m., I think.

'You know,' said Garreth, 'all the time I was trying to get away I had this instinct in me, but it felt... *old,* like it had been hanging around for hundreds of years: I knew I had to get towards a light. I was aiming for this yellow orb that was the light of Treffynydd station...'

I nodded, my heart beginning to beat very quickly, because hadn't something *happened* at Treffynydd station that night? And–

'The train; it was waiting to leave,' said Garreth in a low whisper to me. That man at the station, just talking to the driver, and then the train revved and moved slightly out of the light, and it was then that I looked up from my seat, and away from the light from the station I could see *everything:* the moon was so bright that night. Those black fields.'

Trembling, I stared at him.

'That road to the mountains,' said Garreth, 'was just flooded with moonlight. *I looked straight over that old man's shoulder*, and there was something in the road, and I knew it was watching him. It looked like a person, but it *wasn't* a person.' Garreth stared at my stricken face. 'Morwen, if you looked at it out of the corner of your eye you could see it. But if you tried to look at it, it wasn't there. I did try to warn that old guy, you know.'

My throat was suddenly dry. I tried to swallow.

'You're telling me you saw death?' I said faintly, 'or a ghost?'

Garreth shook his head. 'No, *not* a ghost,' he said, 'because I think that ghosts come from people. I don't know what I saw, but it's why I dropped out of your project, Morwen, and why I'm staying dropped out.'

I looked at Garreth. There was no trace of humour in his face, and Bethan looked very grim. And then I saw what lay behind their eyes; it convinced me:

'Garreth,' I said weakly. 'I just... I didn't know.'

'I'm leaving a few books with Bethan to take out, because she wants to know more about something *she* saw,' said Garreth. 'Morwen, Bethan told me there was a mist on the ground in late morning. In *this* summer? I don't think so! And there's something else; do you really think a lake evaporates that quickly? Come on, Morwen, you're not stupid! So the sun can't burn off the mist, but it can boil a lake away to nothing, which it shouldn't.'

'Garreth's right, you know, Morwen,' pointed out Bethan.

'So be very careful with that village of yours, Morwen,' said Garreth, 'because there's a lot that's strange about it. I don't think you should go any further with it, but what do I know?'

'I'll get the books out,' said Bethan, 'otherwise I'll forget.'

I watched as Bethan walked up to the desk. Mrs Jenall tutted and put down the books, her work interrupted. Garreth walked out of the library without a backward glance. I suddenly felt very alone. I had a pretty good idea what he thought of me. I wanted to ask Bethan what *she* thought of me as well. Maybe it was best I didn't know. My fingers brushed Louisa's card in my pocket, and I turned it gently over in my fingers. It felt like the calling-card of a traitor. When Bethan returned to the table I was sitting there (appropriately quiet in the library), just staring into space.

Chapter Thirteen

Gravenhead: the Director's cut.

The Book of Bethan

A *mustn't shout* whisper echoed starkly across the room.
'Bethan!'

I looked behind me; Ravel was standing at the door of the I.T. room, beckoning me across the library. I could see him mouthing the words: *"get over here!"*

'Are you going to be okay for a bit, Morwen?' I said.

Morwen nodded at me. She seemed lost in the heavy air, and in her own thoughts.

I walked through the library's alarm barrier and into the I.T. room. Inside, Ravel was holding open the door of the tiny viewing room.

'Get in here a second, Bethan,' he said.

I went through the door and Ravel closed it behind us. It was terribly cramped and claustrophobic in the viewing room, with space for only two chairs. The Panasonic stood next to a television on the desk, coloured cables sticking out of the side, and disappearing into the back of a prehistoric-looking VHS recorder.

'Maybe you should see this,' said Ravel, 'because I really *don't* want to be the one who has to tell Morwen!'

I was puzzled: what was he was on about? But then I could see the glowing green light of the Panasonic Hi-8 and the red 'record' light on the VHS player, as it happily recorded away. The output TV was showing images on the screen: tipping, lurching film pictures and all uncut segments of…

A whooping child was pulling faces at the camera.

There was sound, too: *'Come on, you muppet!'*

Laughter filled the viewing room.

'It's copying over to VHS okay,' said Ravel. 'The only thing is… I don't know who was behind the camera?'

'Garreth was,' I said, surprised, 'he's just gone. Why?'

'Well, he never pressed: "Record" on the Hi-8 Panasonic,' said Ravel, 'because *that's* footage from the middle of last week!'

I put my hand to my mouth. Oh no. Poor Morwen!

'Are you sure?' I said at last.

Ravel nodded. 'I remember we had to send a note to that kid's Mam because he broke the strap,' he said. 'I'm really sorry, Bethan.'

I nodded slowly.

'Morwen will be too,' I said.

The Book of Morwen

Sitting at the table, I reached out and turned Bethan's books over lazily:

The Sweeping Blade: England 1300-1485.
The Golden Power: England 1485-1689.
British Churches through the Ages.

Feeling exasperated, I pushed the books away from me, got up from my seat and (unable to resist a glance at the I.T. room doorway) went out of the library. I walked quickly through the silent corridors and pushed open a door that led to the playground. Sitting on a shallow wall, I took out my mobile:

'Louisa,' I said in a low voice. 'I've been thinking about what you said in the café. There's no time and I'm being put upon; I'm getting a VHS tape sorted now!'

I waited, listening to the reply.

I shook my head slightly. 'No, it's getting too late,' I said. 'But I can definitely see you tomorrow afternoon at my house, if you like. I don't want to go to any studio with everyone looking at me. And my Mam is out tomorrow. Can we say two in the afternoon? I'll make you and the film crew some tea and play you the tape.'

I gave my address, knowing that Louisa had it anyway; how else could she have found me at *Pile-Up*? One of these days, I thought, I would complain about that PC Arnold....

Ending the call, I held my mobile in the palm of my hand and my thumb reached for the power button. *Bye-bye mobile for the time being. No offence, Bethan, but - you know...* My heart sang in the heat as I watched a sparrow in a dustbowl, fluttering its wings. The mobile winked and shut off. I smiled...

I would complain about him. But not today.

The Book of Bethan

'It *must* be there,' I said desperately.

'I'm telling you it's a no-no,' said Ravel. 'Remember the tape in the camcorder was right at the beginning? It hadn't even been used.'

I looked around at all the videos on the shelves, my teeth squeezing my lip. The whirring of both the Panasonic and the VHS recorder buzzed in my ears.

'She'll go mad,' I said at last.

Ravel shrugged. 'Well, she's known Garreth for quite a bit, hasn't she?' he said. 'And she could always do it again. The camcorder's booked out to you for two weeks anyway.'

'No!' I said quickly, thinking of the empty lake. 'I mean,' I went on, 'what she *thought* she'd recorded - well, things aren't really the same anymore.'

'But she won't mind too much? She and Garreth are friends, aren't they?'

'You don't know the half of it,' I said. 'Look, I'll go and tell her; you try to keep the roof on!'

I went out of the viewing room and looked around the library. Morwen's books still lay on the table, but of Morwen herself there was no sign.

So, there was an end to it. Thankfully, I felt my fear of Gravenhead evaporate like a lake in the sun. Because the truth was, I had that old feeling again I'd had on Mrs Lundy's run-down old landing. When I'd thought Morwen had abandoned her project I'd felt only relief then, and I felt it again now.

I walked out into the corridor, and then stopped. There was no-one about. But Morwen wouldn't have gone home? And then I felt the squeeze of the library door in the small of my back. I spun around.

Ravel's head was poking out of the doorway.

'If you've given Morwen the bad news, tell her she can come down off the ceiling now!' he said, grinning at my startled face. 'Come on, don't you want to view her masterpiece?'

The Book of Bethan (cont'd)

'It was typical of that skavvy kid who had it last; he didn't bother to rewind the tape,' said Ravel.

Suddenly I understood. 'So, what happened was...' I began.

'Yeah, when Morwen and Garreth started they were about ten minutes in,' finished Ravel. 'She's here, look!'

In my relieved mind's eye, I could imagine some stupid kid moving across the screen and a line of snowy pixels appearing, juvenile antics fuzzing downwards to be replaced with a forest. Now, on the television's output, it was a summer day: Morwen was walking around on dappled leaf litter, beside a lake that was flat in the sunshine, and as still as glass. I could see the excitement in Morwen's eyes as she paced the forest floor, her mouth silently forming speech.

'Is there no sound?' Ravel looked at me, puzzled.

'Yes. She's rehearsing her lines,' I said softly.

Morwen's face stared out from the television at me. It belonged to the past and looked so youthful all of a sudden, I thought a little sadly. It was as if Gravenhead had exhausted her and spat her out during the long summer. Then I jumped: for a second, I thought Morwen was asking *me* a question; her face was very large on the screen, staring at me:

'How about trying for a good close-up on the steeple?'
'The *steeple!* What the hell is *this?'* whispered Ravel.
'Can't, if I zoom in on the steeple I'*zoom in on you - you'll fill the shot.'*

Morwen was walking away from the camera. I smiled, as her fierce obsession seemed to nurture and protect me; as it almost reached out to me. I sensed it. I understood. My doubts fled away as, deep in the lake and hidden up to its spire, Gravenhead looked even more lost and found. What on *earth* had gone through Morwen's head when she'd first discovered it, I wondered. I found myself trembling with excitement.

'It's what they filmed. Just watch and enjoy, Ravel,' I said in a low voice.

The Book of Morwen

'Hello, Morwen! Are you enjoying the summer holidays?'

Richard Thorns

I jumped, realizing I was half-asleep in the sun. Mr Hughes was standing over me, a towel rolled up under his arm.

'Oh, hiya, sir,' I said. 'Have you been swimming?'

'I have,' said Mr Hughes, 'and very nice it was too, in this weather; delaying the evil hour of setting out the new term for you rotten lot.'

I smiled. 'We're not that bad,' I said.

'Well, what are you doing here, then, Miss Lundy, trespassing on school premises?'

'We're doing some film work,' I said. 'We're just finishing it now.'

'Any good?'

I smiled again. 'I think so,' I said. 'I think as head of History you might be quite interested.'

'Oh, *now* I'm intrigued,' said Mr Hughes, sitting down beside me.

There was a silence.

'I think the last time I saw *you*, we were in my office, trying to ascertain someone's murder, or accidental death as it turned out,' he said.

I said nothing.

'Well, I just wanted to pass on my relief that things turned out the way they did,' said Mr Hughes. 'I think you must have been quite worried, Morwen.'

'I was,' I said. I wanted to get back into the library, but didn't want Mr Hughes following me.

'Well, no doubt I'll see you in September. And, Morwen?'

'Yes, Mr Hughes?'

'I'm very much looking forward to seeing that completed project of yours. I imagine that anything that involves special notes to teachers for camcorders and police visits must be something worth seeing! I trust you'll show it to me?'

The reproach stung me. So Bethan and Garreth's ghosts were *still* hanging around, jabbing at me. I felt anger surge inside me.

'Don't worry, sir,' I said. 'It is! And I will!'

The Book of Morwen (cont'd)

I opened the door to the viewing room, and poked my head around.

'Is it all done?' I asked.

'There you go, there's your master-copy for media,' said Ravel, handing me a smart new VHS tape.

'Ravel stopped transferring after Garreth said the immortal words: *"cut!"*' said Bethan. 'It's dated and everything as well. Where did you disappear to? I thought you wanted to see this.'

'I had to ring my Mam,' I answered smoothly. 'Thanks, Ravel, I *soooo* appreciate you doing that!'

'No worries,' said Ravel. 'By the way, that's really something you've got there!'

'Yeah, well, you've got to promise to keep your mouth shut for a while,' I said. 'By the way,' I went on casually, 'can you do *me* a copy? I think Bethan wants one as well.'

Ravel nodded. 'I'll do you one each; there's some other stuff on it as well, Morwen, but I'll tidy that for you. I'll get it nice and-'

'Whatever you like!' I cut in quickly, 'just can you... please, I have to go!'

Ravel nodded, looking a little surprised. 'Okay,' he said, 'I'll bring them out to you.'

The Book of Bethan

We left Ravel (happily unwrapping two new VHS tapes) and we sat down in the library to wait. I found myself looking at Morwen sideways. Well, she *would* be jumpy, I supposed. It had all been done just as she'd insisted. *'It's over,'* she had said gently to me, as we'd stood at the rim of the basin, high over Gravenhead. So I would have expected joy, celebrations; even a trip to the shop that sometimes sold me alcopops and cider.

But there was nothing, only a grey, tired nervousness.

'Morwen, are you sure you're okay?' I said.

Morwen nodded. 'I think I want to go,' she said to me. 'I'm sorry, Beth', it's not you; I feel a bit sad at letting it go, if you must know. I hope you understand. I'll take this tape now, but after you've got your copies, can you keep one and hand the other in? But promise me you'll erase the Hi-8 before you leave, yeah, Beth'?' The submission form is in my bag; I've already put your name on it.

I nodded, taking the form. I watched Morwen go to find Ravel. And then after a while, she walked out of the library. She turned around and waved to me.

A slight smile on my face, I waved back. I walked over to Ravel, pretending not to see the questioning glance he shot me.

'Come on,' Ravel said to me, 'we'll get a fantastic take this time, Bethan! Let's go over the Panasonic Hi-8 again. But first… we stick the kettle on!'

The Book of Morwen

I walked past the sports cars and out of the gates. I felt as if I had lived in the past all summer, but for just one moment – this moment - it was as if I could see into the future! I was walking out of the school gates for the very last time, and the Year nine moments faded into memories and died. And my Gravenhead summer would make everything all right. It would always be all right. I could almost imagine what it would be like.

The Book of Bethan

'What is it?'

'Morwen, that weathercock just moved.'

My hand clasped to my mouth, I watched in horror at the television screen as the Panasonic whirred silently away. Ravel sat silently in the chair, his hand also at his face, squeezing his mouth in thought.

'I *gave* Morwen her tape after Garreth said: *"cut!"'* he said to me. 'What's *happening* here?'

'You gave her the tape all right,' I said grimly, 'but she hasn't got *everything*, because Garreth suddenly got distracted.' My eyes widened. 'He saw something in the lake!' I said, because the reality had hit me as I'd watched the ghastly weathercock rotate slowly on its ancient, weed-choked spindle. Morwen's high voice wavered out from the television speaker:

'It's probably just a high breeze. Which wouldn't show up on the water?'

The thoughts raced through my mind: *The battery was flat when Morwen picked up the Panasonic:* Garreth never stopped recording! *That's why the tape was at the beginning - because it recorded the whole three hours, ran out and rewound. And that means...*

A black shadow hopped over the screen.

Everything that happened to Garreth is all on the tape!

An enormous crow was standing on the leaf litter. I let out a low whimper of fright as I watched it tilt its head and look intently at Garreth who was completely unaware of it: he was simply flat out on his back, lolling in the sun. The crow hopped nearer, joined by two more. A slight breeze made the trees rustle and whisper. We both jumped as Garreth suddenly came to life, flinging a handful of leaf litter at the crow, which flew indignantly up into the trees. Then Garreth leapt to his feet and ran out of shot, and the flapping sound was horrendous ; the screen blurred with shadows until, eventually, they cleared. With a thrill of terror, I heard the distant sound of the bending and snapping of twigs. The fishing rod lay on the floor.

And then... there was nothing.

We sat in our chairs, unwilling to move or to turn away from the screen. Long seconds ticked by.

'That's that, then,' said Ravel at last. He sounded shaken. 'Well, that's the Director's cut finished! Somebody ought to let Morwen know, because she's-'

'There's something on the tape!' I said.

Ravel's finger flew out and pressed the "Pause" button on the Panasonic.

Look at those trees,' I said, 'those slender saplings. Follow your eyes right into them. It's as thin as the trees. There!'

Among the trees, something was standing.

'Go on,' I whispered.

Ravel reached out and hit the "Pause" button on the Panasonic again and the tape whirred. There was slight movement in the saplings, as whatever was caught on the tape blurred and blended with the thin shapes. And, was it

Richard Thorns

my imagination, or was the shape clearer whenever I took my eyes away and gazed across the surface of the lake, flattened into silence in the summer sun?

PART II

THE DRAGON CURRENT

In one hand bread; the other, a stone
The hunter enters the forest.

Rutherford/Banks. 1976.

Richard Thorns

Chapter Fourteen

A walk in the park.

The Book of Morwen

CAUGHT IN the traffic, the 144a bus edged past the Place of the Dead and then swung triumphantly out of the jam and off the High Street, drawing to a halt at the bus stop. I checked my watch.

It was 1.53pm. It would be a long day of staying out.

I joined the line of people waiting patiently to get off. A woman was struggling with a buggy and I felt suddenly desperate; without the inrush of cool air through the open windows, the air in the bus suddenly stank of sweat. I fled through the open doors, wincing in the bright heat as my feet hit the pavement. I looked around me, and my eyes alighted on dull green railings.

Of course, the park! It was as good a place as any.

The Book of Bethan

'Well, Morwen's really protective of her discovery, so maybe deep down she doesn't *want* to share it with anyone.'

'Oh, come on, Garreth, she was *always* going to do it,' I said despairingly into my mobile. 'She always said that as soon as the tape was dated, she was going to present it to the world.'

Sitting on the playground wall, out of the heat, my stare travelled around the empty spaces in the hope that Morwen would suddenly march around the corner of the sports hall clutching a drink. I knew in my heart it was a waste of time; I knew she'd gone.

'*When* did she say she was going to do this?' Garreth said.

'She said: soon, or in a few days, I think,' I said. 'You know what her Mam said to me when I went round to see her earlier this summer? "Morwen's trouble is she never knows when to let go of something." And she won't let go of *this* - not in a million years!'

'But have you tried calling her?'

'I can't even get her voice mail; she's switched her phone off.'

Garreth's voice floated into my ear.

'She looked really done in when I saw her in the library. Maybe she just wants some time to herself.'

I felt the panic in my voice. 'You're trying to reassure me, Garreth, will you stop it! Look! I'm telling you I *saw* it, partly hidden in the trees. It's caught on the tape!'

There was a silence.

'Garreth, are you still there?'

'You still haven't told me what it looked like?'

I felt suddenly panic-stricken. I sighed, trying to remember. 'Oh, it was *tall.* And it was so thin and dark, and I remember its head seemed to shine but it was blurred when I tried to look at it properly. Garreth, don't mess me about! It was what you saw at the station, you *know* it was! It killed that man.'

'Well, in that case, you know what *I* think you should do.'

Relief flooded over me.

'Go for it,' I said.

'I think you should tell the police, Bethan. If Morwen can help in some sort of inquiry, then it's pretty clear she ought to-'

'Oh, great, that's sorted then! Problem solved, but what about *you!*' I said, feeling slightly hysterical. 'You're dumping on her just like everyone else does, what's the *matter* with people around here!'

Trembling, I felt the pause in my ear:

'That's a bit harsh, Bethan, I'm not sure it's fair, either.'

'Yeah? You want to know what I think *you* should do? There's still a month of summer left. Go and - go and play on the beach!'

I snapped off my mobile, and then wished I hadn't. I remembered standing in Morwen's bedroom, staring at my CD's lying on her floor and reading her love-poem, because for the second time that summer I felt a sudden, inner wave of a terrible black rage welling inside me. And it was all directed at Morwen. I stared across the empty playground; the cars had all gone, I noticed. The leaves above me gently whispered in my ears. Was it my imagination, I thought, or was there something else: distant chuckling blowing faintly through the trees?

Are you trying to separate us? I thought.

I tried Morwen's number again, listening to the detached electronic message:

"The mobile you are calling has been switched off. Please try again later."

'Yes, I think you are,' I murmured.

The Book of Morwen

In the park, I sat alone on a park bench. Children were yelling and running around, pestering their parents for drinks and ice creams. My feet rested on tiny gravel, and beyond were ornate, low railings. Over the railings were tangles of scrub and low, scummy water. Muddy bread pieces floated, slowly falling apart.

Staring at the little lake, I murmured:

'Gravenhead.'

A mallard, irate, motored at a rival, splashing its way across the lake. I watched it go, a slight smile on my lips. The park lake was like a safe, tiny child against my much bigger one as my old thought came again, as if I were once more approaching the lake with Bethan: *Carnivorous plants with sweet gifts.* The lake I stared at seemed so public and known-about; Louisa Caybourne had been right, I thought, shooing away the terrible panic in my mind. Before something was news, first of all it had to be simply a secret.

You'll be right up there, Morwen, the thought dug slyly at me. *This is very big, just like the discovery of Troy.*

A little child broke free from its mother's hand, and wobbled towards a flock of sparrows:

How it was when the spring came early. How it was when you first stumbled down the bank to see the head of the bird. Away from pokey Rosengrave High with its stupefied, new-frontier dreams. When Louisa finishes up and you're famous, take it all to London! They'll graduate you before you even start.

My fear melted like ice-cream! I smiled in the sunshine, my world so full of such bright hope! My thoughts turned to the simple secret beneath my bed: the folder I treasured with all my newspaper clippings neatly tucked away inside that lay with the ancient wax box. The Other Thing called me gently.

The Book of Bethan

In the mid-afternoon sun, my leg was going to sleep.
I shifted my position as I sat under a tree overlooking the playground, searching through the books I had taken out:

"The fourteenth-century mass was a ceremony of colourful, elaborate drama and, most of all, one of mystery. It took place behind the 'rood-screen': both a barrier and no barrier, for the drama of the ceremony. Performed in secret by the priest and his assistants, few people were aware of the ceremony itself."

'Yes, I bet,' I said quietly.
A stabbing ringtone cut suddenly into my thoughts. Instantly, I snatched up my mobile.
'Morwen?'
'No, it's me,' said Garreth's voice in my ear.
'Where are you?'
'I'm on the beach.'
I winced.

'No, I'm at my house. Look, Bethan, you can shout and scream all you want but I can't get involved any more. I can't go back there, I'm sorry! At least I'm being honest with you - and Morwen as well.'

'Thanks. I understood you the last time,' I said coldly, 'If you-"

'But *listen!* If you can't reach Morwen, try her gran.'

'Her *gran?* What are you *talking* about?'

'I don't know! Me and Morwen had a fight on the phone once. She said she'd mentioned Gravenhead to her grandmother, and that her gran had said she didn't want to frighten her.'

Despite myself, I found myself actually smiling. 'And *that* was supposed to reassure you?'

'Well, yeah, if you think about it, it makes perfect sense. You know: "If- I-can-do-it-so-can-you."'

'Meaning?' I said slowly. But I had been in front of the church; I knew what Garreth was going to say next:

'I think Morwen was trying to say... that she was facing her own fears, so why couldn't I do the same?'

I nodded silently to myself, my heart beating strongly. From the long low wall overlooking the empty school, I saw Morwen's facade fall apart in front of me. The grey clouds of fright behind her dark eyes, as she had once stood in front of the church door.

'She knows,' I said in a low voice, feeling suddenly very cold in the heat, 'She's *always* known, deep down, that there's something very wrong with that village. It hasn't stopped her, Garreth.'

'She *is* a bit of a loose cannon at the moment.'

'Yeah, and you know what, Garreth? Before I really saw that tape of hers I got so… *tangled* in her way of thinking, and I'm still so sorry for her. Even more so, now.'

'How do you mean?'

I had to think for a moment.

'Oh well, Morwen's had just such a shit time of everything, and then she gets this *one break* and now she's got to give it up. She can't go ahead with it now, Garreth, can she?'

'Bethan, maybe some people just aren't meant to get the breaks.'

'I still don't want her to fail,' I said.

I thought of the past swellings on Morwen's face; those terrible grazes; Morwen's wishful love-poem to Garreth - *"I met a lady in the meads."* My pity for her, and my guilt at having seen her poem stabbed viciously at me like a knife.

I struggled to keep focussed.

'Something survives there, Garreth, and I've seen it. We both have! All except…'

'The one central person who discovered it: Morwen!'

'It *wants* Gravenhead to be found, Garreth.'

'Yes. Do you know where she lives? Morwen's gran, I mean?'

I felt a slight sting of memory in my head.

'I've... been there once before. I'll try to see her. It'll be okay; I think Morwen would have said something if she was going there. I'm sorry, Garreth, about screaming at you earlier.'

'Don't start that all over again!'

The affection was warm and clear in his voice. I could feel it. How could I ever have doubted him? Gratefully, I stepped back onto what felt like a tightrope of love, and calm. It wobbled. It seemed a long way down!

'I'll see you soon, Garreth. And thanks! Oh, wait! Garreth? What's a minster?'

'What's this: *Phone a friend?*'

I smiled grimly. 'If you want. You've got ten seconds.'

'A minster is another name for a church, I think, Bethan. It's probably where you get your "minister" from.

Cowminster was known by its church, then?

'Bye, Garreth,' I said.

I snapped off my mobile, and then stared at it; I had been on the phone a long time. I went to the menu and pressed until I came to *missed calls*.

The screen flashed back at me, almost patronising in its reproach:

No missed calls.

The Book of All

Richard Thorns

On the outskirts of Rosengrave, Louisa Caybourne sat in the sunny pub garden, and nibbled at a last piece of salad. She pushed her plate away from her and took a small sip of gin and tonic. The sun streamed down, making her squint across the table at her partner. Louisa's sunglasses were off because she wanted him to see the serious look in her eyes. Reaching across the table, she took his fingers in hers and squeezed them gently.

'Thanks for lunch, Giles,' she said.

'It was nice! When do you want to do it again?'

'Not until after tomorrow,' said Louisa, 'because I want to keep my head clear before picking up the tape from that girl. Speaking of which - the Sotheby's event you're going to this evening. Watch what you drink!'

Giles's voice was slightly defensive, 'Louisa, it's an *auctioneer's* do; there'll be cooking sherry if I'm lucky.'

Louisa tutted: 'I'm not bothered about drink driving; I just don't want any booze loosening your tongue! You *haven't* mentioned anything about that lost village to anyone?'

'Mum's the word.'

'Well, please keep it that way.' Louisa stretched her arms. 'I *don't* want to do any more stupid weather than necessary; I hate working for the Met Office now, it's boring!'

'Louisa, I don't understand why you're so obsessed about this! Instead of editing her out and claiming it, can't you just *tell* everyone? "Local girl stumbles across lost village" sounds a great story to me.'

Louisa groaned slightly and closed her eyes, and not through pleasure at the sunshine:

'Giles, if I worked directly for the BBC it might be different, but I'm paid for by the Met Office. It isn't actually such a good story, is it: "Contracted weathergirl doesn't find lost village!"'

She felt her fingers being stroked.

'Well, you won't have to do too many more. But shall I tell you something? Last month at the auction houses, a pendant from the seventeenth century went for twenty grand and... *ow!*'

Louisa thought she heard a faint, panting gasps of distress.

'Giles,' she was saying, '*please* don't go getting any ideas! You know what this is about: twice I've been turned down for the news desk. First when Chloe left, and then when Sophie went off to do her-'

She looked up: Giles had snatched his hand away, finally freeing himself. He was examining his scratched, bloodied fingers in dismay.

She looked across the table, for once mortified:

'I didn't do *that*, did I?'

The Book of Bethan

Richard Thorns

"Although during the reign of King Henry VIII many religious buildings lost their treasures, in more remote areas the ornate interiors of local churches still survived."

I sat at the bus stop, the book slowly dragging itself down. I placed it on the seat next to me. An ancient lady shifted on another seat, her jaws working on invisible chewing gum.

My lips worked, too. In silent speech.

I'm on to you! I don't know what the hell was there before Cowminster but I'll bet my life it was Middenwich, and by hell did they get rid of YOU way back in the fourteenth century! But when they did, the village was repopulated and the name was changed. And then you did something that the parish records said you did, although not in so many words...

I dug out *The Comely Flood* from my jacket (I seemed to be *wearing* that book these days!) and found a page folded over a little at the top corner:

"...Cowminster, earlier ravaged by plague, was known (from parish records preserved at Treffynydd's county records office), to have been abandoned in the springtime of 1476, at which time it promptly disappeared from the historical record."

You came back! In the springtime of 1476, and Cowminster was abandoned for good.

Someone spat onto the pavement.

And so it all happened all over again! Another empty treasure; an empty village just waiting to be built upon! And it became Gravenhead. But... from the fourteenth century, all the way up to the sixteenth, you were always there, weren't you...

A bus ambled around the corner and whined as it began to apply the brakes. People were getting up from the seat, and I stood up myself, feeling in my jeans pocket for some loose change, trying to control my breathing.

And – oh, God! - all the way through to the twenty-first century and me and Morwen! You've always been there!

Standing in the queue, I looked at the book I was reading as my foot drew up to the first step of the bus:

"Although by the beginnings of the seventeenth century the medieval altars, images, wall paintings and windows had been stripped and whitewashed over (the eager demonstrations of purity), time-honoured devotional customs still persisted."

'A child one way ticket to Fairwater, thanks,' I said to the driver. I heard the buzz of the ticket being printed and the door hissing shut behind me. They seemed the last things I would ever hear that were normal in this world:

"Well into 1539 at Ashford, Kent, there was a crucifix in the North Aisle which was an object of local veneration before which, the reformist of nearby Hothfield reported, 'There stands a box to receive offerings, and people daily blaspheme God by making reverence to it."

'Can you go and sit down quickly, love! I'm a bit late this afternoon.'

I felt the ticket pressed into my hand

'They blaspheme God by making reverence to... a *box,*' I stammered under my breath. People were craning their necks, staring at me.

'Don't know what you're on, sweetheart. But off you go.'

The driver revved the throttle. The great engine howled, and the bus began to move away.

You stole the wrong thing, Morwen! What the hell have you got in your house!

I ran down the aisle of the bus and felt my hand stabbing at the emergency button above the doors. They hissed open. Heads fell forwards, gasping, as the driver slammed on his brakes. Faintly, I heard a woman whisper: 'honestly!' to her friend.

'RIGHT! OFF MY BUS! NOW!'

I fled from the mouth of the bus; the pavement snatched at my legs and I nearly fell over. And I was running across the busy road and dodging the traffic. Towards a row of taxis.

The Book of Morwen

From my park bench, the treetops had begun to tickle the base of the sun. The lake water had cooled, leaving ducks gliding around in search of new bread.

"SLAM" went an ice cream van's doors. Its side lights flicked into life.

I got up from the bench, casting a glance over the dark grass. I walked slowly towards the main gates of the park, beyond which the yellow lights of Rosengrave had flickered on. I felt my day had begun from the first moment I had entered the park. And the first half of my day had worked. My thoughts turned to the silent village, far away from artificial light. Now would come the second part. It could be easy.

It would be.

The Book of Bethan.

'Here it is. I recognize this,' I said.

Shaking my purse out into my hand, I gave almost all of its contents to the driver and got out of the taxi. Yes, there had been a small grocery shop on the corner of the street, back in those Year nine days that Morwen had suffered in. The shop was still there; the only difference was the iron grid now lining the front door. I didn't remember that.

In that case, could I now trust my memory? Well, Morwen had been followed as she'd run down the street, and turned into that road on the right. Yes, that was where she'd gone, I was sure of it, towards her gran's safe haven, towards the house with the red door. It seemed to me that distant taunts, once shouted out, still hung in the dusk.

The Book of Morwen

My Mam pushed open my bedroom door with her foot, the tray nearly upsetting itself.

'How are you?' she asked me.

'I'm okay,' I said weakly from my bed. 'I think it must be just a summer cold.'

'Alright then, darling, just get some rest. Is it still alright for me to go off to Llanwyth tomorrow? You know I'll be gone a couple of days.'

I nodded. 'Don't worry about me. You go off and have a good time.'

I hesitated, and turned my face to the wall.

'Oh, and Mam?'

'Yes, love.'

'I don't *think* Bethan is going to call, but if she does, well, we had a bit of a fight today. It was about... well, she likes this boy at school and I do too. It's just a stupid fight. But if she *does* ring... just say I'm ill, will you? I'll make up with her tomorrow.'

The Book of Bethan

After ringing the bell, I waited on the step, my heart beating quickly. I heard footsteps in the hall, and the fumble of the chain put on the latch.

'Who is it?'

'Excuse me, are you Morwen's gran?'

'Who is it?'

'My name is Bethan. I'm doing Morwen's school project. I'm helping her... I think.'

The door slowly opened, and I saw the ancient face staring at me through the gap.

'What can I help you with? She's not here, you know.'

I took a deep breath; I knew my voice was about to tremble. I wasn't disappointed: it wavered in the dusk.

'I need to talk to you about Gravenhead.'

Maybe Morwen and her grandmother had skipped a generation, because they shared the same features, I noticed as I looked at the old lady's face. They both shared something else: those grey clouds of fear behind the eyes that I had seen at the church door.

Little pulses of silence.

'Has she found it?'

Richard Thorns

Yes, they definitely shared those clouds.
'Yes,' I said steadily. 'She has.'

Chapter Fifteen

Tales from the backyard.

The Book of Bethan (cont'd)

IN THE back garden, the old lady asked if I wanted *'orangeade or lemonade?'* I answered gratefully: *'lemonade!'* thinking of a long drink, chilled and clear and fizzing. The "lemonade" turned out to be lemon squash. I felt a pang of despair: *So* that's *how much of my world you know about.* The moment jabbed a finger slyly into my ribs.

'You'd better call me Nora,' she said, and then, for a while I just had this kind of vision: those repeats of Wimbledon again, but this time it was ghosts playing tennis in that back garden, because all we did for ages it seemed was just rally words backwards and forwards and it was all just so *avoiding;* it was just filling talk. Our conversation turned to Nora's plants, dying in the heat and my plans for Year twelve after the holidays. Plants and the summer break. I pounced: One thing in common that we had at last: the summer:

I said: 'It's nice to be here; out in your back garden after eight p.m., I mean. It's so warm this summer.'

'It's a freak summer, Bethan. You've never seen a summer like this one. If you had, you wouldn't be here.'

Carefully, I let the statement hang in the chirping air. Nora leaned forward slightly in her chair.

'Tell me when she first found it. I want to know.'

'In February, but I never knew about it then; nobody did,' I answered honestly. 'But you see; there was this school project-'

'I know about the school project.'

A little embarrassed, I ploughed on. 'Well, I was never really supposed to be in on it, you see? Except... then Garreth went missing, and somebody died and then the police got involved (my head spun - so much had happened already in the summer!), and so she *had* to tell me about it. We were in a little cafe and it all came out. I... kind of invited myself in.'

'How did she seem to you when she told you? Did she appear... *safe?*'

It was a curious question, but in the back garden my heart sank because I knew why she was asking me. I paused, trying hard to remember:

'Sort of, I think. She seemed excited, I know that, but at the same time she did seem very... *frightened,* back then. I don't know; maybe she was just worried for Garreth. But *safe?*' I sipped at the revolting warm squash. 'Yes, I think so. After all, she went back there again at Easter all by herself, I remember her saying that. She said she *always* used to wander alone in the mountains and in the valleys.'

Nora nodded. 'She stayed with me a lot during that time, when her parents were breaking up, and after. She was always going off alone even then; even if it was just along the railway cuttings and the lanes. Are your parents still together?'

'Yes,' I said. Nora leaned back once again in the chair.

'It's such a difficult subject these days, don't you think? One never knows whether or not to ask. So - she saw the steeple?'

'Yes.'

'In strange, freak summers...' Nora murmured, almost to herself. She left the statement unfinished.

'When were you born, Bethan?' she said suddenly.

I jumped. '1990,' I said without thinking.

Richard Thorns

'There was a summer, a fabulous summer fourteen years before you were even born, Bethan! 1976 was a freak summer, they said. Everyone was saying it was the hottest one ever. But it was *not* a summer like this one. *This* is hotter! We've probably skipped a generation, Morwen and I; it's not only Morwen who walks the mountains!'

I tried to interrupt, but Nora held a hand up.

'Bethan, drink your lemonade, please let me finish! You see, that 1976 summer was so bright and so strong it seemed to dry up the whole of the country! Huge great cracks began to appear in the earth and there were sunstroke cases, and people queued in the streets for their water. And then...'

I could almost see transparent waves of memory in the warm air:

'And then, there was great excitement in Rosengrave... it made all the papers... because, in that blistering summer, something nearby revealed itself...'

'Gravenhead!' I breathed.

'No, *not* Gravenhead! High on Fawkes's Hill, over the crescent on the right side, as the water evaporated in the heat, ancient building work slowly began to appear.' Nora shook her grey head silently. 'A great hole appeared in the right side of the hill, lined with ancient brickwork. It was Tudor! And, you know, it seemed that *everyone*, from the local papers to the British Museum itself came to Fawkes's Hill that summer.'

'But what did they *find?*' I asked, my eyes shining.

'I'll tell you,' Nora said bluntly. 'Nothing! The walls of the brickwork had collapsed long since: it was really just a brick-lined funnel. They thought that's all it was - a Tudor folly!'

'But you knew different?' I said gently.

Nora's eyes were hard in the dusk. 'No, but I remember the discovery on the hill made me wonder. You do have a kind of.... a spirit of adventure when you're younger, don't you. Even if you don't know quite what it is you might find.'

There was a long silence. I knew I had to say it... It was now or never:

'Will you tell me what you found... for Morwen?' I said.

'I was... like I said... *like* Morwen. I was in the mountains on my bike, all excited about the discoveries up on the hill. I found the old track that seemed almost extinct. I saw the steeple...'

Funny, I thought, how soft an old lady's hand can feel.

'In the summer of 1976, *all* the water levels were dropping, you see? I was on my bike and trying to cycle away, and I think I would have given anything to tell the world about my discovery in the lake. Something happened.'

'Yes. I think you saw something. What did you see, Nora?' I asked her as gently as I could.

Suddenly, Nora's old eyes widened. 'I could only ride my bike so fast without striking a rut and going over. And all the time it was through the trees to my left, keeping up with the bike in the corner of my left eye. I remember thinking: *It doesn't have to worry about the trees!* I screamed and it was such a loud scream because no birds ever sing there - have you noticed that?'

Feeling suddenly bloodless, I nodded. I squeezed the old hand gently

'I went faster and faster on my bike, leaving it behind and I felt myself winning! And then I hit a rut and the bike went over and so did I.'

The old hand carefully removed itself from mine. And Nora gently teased up a leg of her faded trouser suit. The pale flesh like a prisoner's skin, never seeing light and air and summers. I caught my breath: in the dusky garden, I could see the livid, red edge of a terrible scar on the kneecap.

'You've never seen blood like it,' said Nora simply, 'Pouring from both knees, and from my elbows. That rutted earth was like steel!'

'Go on,' I said faintly.

'I looked back and it was on the track, left behind. Watching me. It had its arms in the air... like *this!*' Nora held up her arms in front of me, the hands curved over to form the shape of a great "heart". The loose sleeves of her ivory blouse fell. More terrible scars.

'I call it the Melanchol,' Nora said. 'I picked up my bike, crying... yes, even in my thirties, I was crying; can you understand that?'

I've seen that shape before! On the walls of Gravenhead church... beyond the barrier!

'The Melanchol,' I said quietly.

'Yes. It carried an air of darkness around it, you see, but Bethan,' Nora shuddered in the darkening garden, 'Bethan, believe me, you never want to see its face! And then... it simply disappeared into the trees. I remember cycling fast, even downhill on the road, towards the safety of Treffynydd station!'

'But,' Nora shook her grey head, leaning forward in her chair. 'What do *you* know about Gravenhead?'

It sounded dismissive, but I knew it was a serious question. I opened my mouth to reply, and then stopped; what would it do to Nora - if she knew that both me and Morwen had not only walked Nora's track, but wandered around Gravenhead itself? I wasn't even sure what *I* felt, on the back of all Nora's memories?

I found myself shaking with fear and relief as my mind flew to our escape in the church. My thoughts turned to the bag at my feet. My copy of the Gravenhead tape was in it but instead I looked at Nora; she was sipping at her tea with old, trembling lips. I felt only pity.

Instead, I said simply: 'I've seen it. I'm on your side! Do you know what it is?'

'No, but I think I know where it's from,' said Nora. 'We have to go inside, Bethan. I have something I want to show you.'

The Book of Bethan (cont'd)

Nora closed the patio doors, firmly locking them. She motioned to the living room table, and then crossed to a dresser.

I watched silently as Nora spread a great map out on the table. I frowned to myself; it was unlike any map I had ever seen before for there were no roads. Great expanses of green, with grey areas for the mountains and tiny pools of blue (I wondered if those little pools of blue, after this summer, would have to go).

'Rosengrave, Treffynydd, Llancellwyn.' Nora's fingers stroked at the places. 'Now - look at *these.*'

I saw Nora's gnarled fingers tracing the pencilled-in lines that stretched over the map.

'Do you know what those are?' Nora asked. I looked up, shaking my head.

'They're ley lines, Bethan. In 1922, a man called Alfred Watkins noticed many ancient sites in this country, all linked by these lines.'

'Ancient sites,' I repeated slowly.

'Yes. Stone circles, prehistoric burial chambers and the like. Over the path of whole patterns of ancient lines, stretching across the entire landscape.'

I said helplessly: 'So? What about them?'

'You see, since their discovery, several theories have been suggested as to what they might be: *Watkins* thought they might have been prehistoric trading routes, linked to Hermes, the Roman god, as a guide to travellers on unknown paths. *Other* people, associated with the occult, suggested they might be lines of power.'

The room was very hot. Two words swam into my head. They stayed there.

The occult.

'Don't you *see*, Bethan? The presence of all these prehistoric sites *along* the lines means that the ley lines must have been known about *before* construction, when this country was very young. But what if the sites didn't just mark certain energy points in the lines? What if they tap into the energy source *itself?*'

I stared at the map. The words continued over my head. Dancing. Glittering.

'The most important prehistoric monuments occupy sites where the ley lines cross, Bethan. Ley lines can even be located through a divining rod; that's a simple hazel stick, which taps into the Earth's energy points.'

Like the hazel stick that Morwen destroyed in Gravenhead?

Now, Bethan, I want you to look... at *this!*'

I watched the pencil draw a straight line across the map, west of Treffynydd and nearby Llancellwyn. Two lines. The *second* line advanced slowly across the map. I saw its smudge. Slowly across the green. Over a tiny, tiny, spatter of blue. I saw them cross.

Richard Thorns

'Do you want to tell me *where* you think they cross, Bethan?'

Behind my cupped hands, I said: 'What does it mean, Nora?'

'I think... maybe some kind of a gateway, Bethan. I think you must not go home tonight. *Stay here!* Come with me on a little journey tomorrow.'

The Book of Morwen

In the darkness of my bedroom, I lay in bed, free from any summer cold and free from worry. I'd looked at my newspaper cuttings until late and they had soothed me as they always had. My thoughts turned to Gravenhead, and never mind my Mam's silly teachings: how silly *I'd* been to discuss it back then, but it was alright now. The air in the room was hot and thin, as thin as the whispering voice in my mind that seemed to charm me to sleep; a voice that was *skinny*, with no flesh on its bones...

Old riddles, to bring the veils of sleep, made up all by myself when younger:

What do you eat when you're cold in winter, and when you do, it's hot?

A chilli pepper!

I flinched: the voice seemed to flutter and billow in my mind, like a warm summer breeze drying sheets:

Don't fall out of the tree! I do know what you want. I can help you, Morwen.

And then I slept easily.

The Book of Bethan

In Nora's spare room, I slept uneasily.

My mind hated the paradoxes of dreams. My guilt drew me to Morwen at the cost of my own happiness. But then again, if I let Morwen go, then my guilt would remain and haunt me and never let me rest.

The paradoxes blew and fluttered in my mind... Morwen liked herself, she just didn't love herself enough; sometimes I loved myself a bit too much but I didn't like myself...

The anger and disgust I knew Garreth would one day feel for me drew ever closer, like the hunter of Morwen's story.

The hunter

(hunted?)

entered the forest.

I entered the forest and in my dream I stood among the trees at the shore of the lake. It was night and the lake looked like clear, polished glass. The moon hung in the sky, glaring and white, and illuminating everything but the dark trees. The squonk was hiding somewhere, I knew it; in the moonlight I could see silver tears sparkling on leaves. Behind me in the distance I could hear shrill voices and I felt a child's excitement at them, like a sudden awareness of ice-cream chimes in a distant street on the hottest of days. But here in the night, the lake looked sinister and smooth and I didn't like it, but to go back towards the voices would lead them to the hiding place of the squonk.

So *I* turned to hide as well, and my legs struck something in the bracken and heard a faint twang; a very high-pitched *bing!* I looked down and I saw a fishing rod lying abandoned on the ground. The line was tight, stretched out over the ground, and it disappeared into the lake.

I crouched down and plucked at the line; it felt like an over-wound guitar string, and it twanged gently and it *sounded* like one. And immediately I plucked it I felt a scurry in the water behind me. I looked behind; in the middle of the lake, a large ripple was expanding lazily in the moonlight.

My heart sank as I had one of those strange, all-knowing sensations; deep in the lake, perhaps even inside the drowned church, or inside a sunken house, I felt as if something was waiting at the very end of that line, with one finger resting very gently on it, waiting for the merest sensation of something blundering into the line, and then the vibrations would travel all the way down the line… and then as I stood there, white with fear the water surged, foaming and the voices grew suddenly louder in the woods and I knew that both my horrors had arrived at the very same time.

Chapter Sixteen

On Fawkes's Hill.

The Book of Bethan (cont'd)

HIGH UP ON Fawkes's Hill I looked around me, my heart lifting in the misty blue heat, but not as high as the skylark I could see climbing steadily, a tiny speck in the sky as big as a flea. Its sweet song dribbled into the air like water.

My neck aching, I looked behind me. It was half past ten in the morning and already the haze was beginning to burn off. Nora's parked Morris Traveller was a distant wink of chrome. I turned around; Nora, too, was fast becoming a dot in the haze as she tramped steadily away towards a ridge. I began to jog to keep up.

Nora was waiting for me at the crest of the ridge, working dried sheep droppings off her boots.

'Quite a view, isn't it.' she said to me as I joined her.

I nodded, my eyes following the patchwork of fields far below me. A warm breeze was blowing hard and my hair kept getting in my eyes.

'I wish Morwen was here,' I murmured. 'What did she say when you called this morning.'

'*She* didn't say anything; I got her Mam just as she was leaving for Llanwyth. She said she thought Morwen's summer cold was getting worse.'

'Well, I'm glad, in a way,' I said awkwardly, 'it means we needn't worry about her doing anything stupid for a day or so. But it's a shame.'

'Don't worry about her; those colds pass soon enough.'

'I meant,' I said, a little embarrassed, 'that it was a shame you got her Mam. I think... maybe Morwen might have wanted to speak to us?'

Nora looked at me, a little strangely, I thought.

'Maybe,' And Nora said no more.

The Book of Bethan (cont'd)

Over the ridge, walking downhill was easier, and as the great line rose behind us the wind disappeared. I was silent as I followed Nora, picking her way down quite a way ahead of me.

Below, perhaps fifty metres below me, the hill flattened out to a shallow basin. I could see a great plain of shallow, brackish water ahead of me. I saw Nora crouching beside a scrubby patch of trees at the water's edge.

'There's a newt in there,' she said absently, as I caught up.

'What about the *folly*, Nora?'

In answer, Nora straightened up and pointed simply past my head. I turned and gasped: in front of me a great hole stared, yawning at me, disappearing into brick-lined blackness. I shivered as a great chill swept over me.

'What do you think, Bethan? It's impressive, isn't it.'

'Is it always this exposed?'

Nora shook her head. 'The autumn showers and the winter rains always keep it well covered. This lake is usually fuller, you see. In very hot summers I'm told you can just see the tip of the folly, but it wouldn't have been *completely* uncovered like this since... oh, 1976, I should think. You understand I don't make a habit of coming up here, Bethan.'

'How do you know then?' I was aware I sounded rude.

'Because I don't make a habit of coming up here in *summer!* But I promise you, you never see it normally.'

I nodded, chewing my lower lip. I walked out of the sunshine into the shade cast by the hole, and as the sun disappeared I felt a blast of stale, cold air from the folly. Walking into the blackness, I wrinkled my nose at the smell of sheep's urine; there were a few small bones and feathers on the floor. A fox's kill?

'How deep is it?' My voice seemed very loud in the black silence.

'It goes in for about another ten metres, but then it stops; it just becomes a part of the hill.'

I jumped as Nora joined me. My smooth little fingers gently touched the rough sides of the folly.

'So this is Tudor brickwork, then? *Gravenhead's* Tudor!'

'An interesting coincidence, don't you think?'

Infuriated, I turned to face the darkened features beside me. 'Well, hasn't anyone tried digging it out? Maybe it's collapsed.'

Nora snorted. 'What with? How would you get a mechanical digger up onto the hill? And even if you tried the rains would come soon enough! Bethan, face it - nobody can be bothered with it. It's a folly.'

I smiled to myself. 'In more ways than-'

I screamed loudly as ahead of me in the darkness, something white and shining reared up. I caught sight of yellow, baleful eyes.

I clutched at Nora's coat as a sheep scrabbled past us and galloped out into the light, its hooves scraping loudly on the stones. I looked at my hand. It was trembling hard. Then I looked at Nora, whose face was white with sudden shock.

'Nora,' I said, 'did you think, just for a moment, that it was-'

'Yes. That's the folly of Fawkes's Hill, no more, no less,' Nora said to me, almost brutally.

The Book of Bethan (cont'd)

As we walked out of the folly, I was very glad to be out in the sunlight. Silently we both trudged up the hill towards the great horizon line (I resisted the temptation to give the sheep a kick). A pang of hunger hit me and I checked my watch: it was twenty past twelve; I made a mental note to ask Nora about some lunch. My mind moved much faster than my feet: there *must* be a link between the Fawkes's Hill folly and Gravenhead, I thought - both were Tudor, after all. Morwen's naive questioning from the early part of the summer seemed to hang in the air.

But why would they just... dig? Back in the sixteenth century, I mean? I don't understand.

'No, Morwen, neither do I,' I murmured.

The Book of Bethan (cont'd)

'Did you ever read *The Comely Flood?*' I asked Nora, as we sank down on the crest of the ridge.

Nora nodded, unsurprised at the reference. 'Clarke? Professor P.N? Yes, I read it when it first came out in the late-seventies, Bethan. What did *you* make of it?'

'He seemed to know his history,' I ventured.

Nora snorted, 'That's as maybe, but he doesn't know his Welsh!'

'What do you mean, Nora?'

Nora smiled faintly: '"Treffynydd" in Welsh, roughly translated, means: "the town in the mountains,"' she said.

'Oh,' I said, a little lamely.

'I mean,' I went on, 'he didn't really have the first idea where Gravenhead was, or even if it ever existed in the first place.'

'*I* did.'

'Yes,' I said thoughtfully, 'but you never thought to say anything?'

'Would you?'

I shuddered at the memory of what was caught on the tape. 'No,' I said honestly, 'I don't think I would.' I gazed over the crest of the hill towards the thick, silent forest that hid the village. A sweet singing filled my ears; the skylark was back. I gazed upward, trying to find it. The soft, warm wind gently blew my streaked hair all around my face. It was idyllic up here.

'Morwen would,' I murmured into the blue sky. Then the thought brutally hit me.

'*She's going to!*' I said suddenly, clutching at Nora's arm. 'That's why she wouldn't answer the phone. This is no summer cold, Nora: *She wants to be out of the way!*' I broke away from Nora, beginning to pace the ridge of the hill. Nora crossed over to me and grabbed me.

'Has she said anything about telling anyone?'

'Yes! Hold on for a second; let me think for a moment,' I said. I turned away from Nora and walked quickly in the direction of the car. I could hear Nora panting and grumbling a little as she followed me. The wind blew my hair hard into my eyes *let me think!*

Morwen, alone with her plans and her dreams; unaware of the Melanchol.

'But *we* are!' I murmured, 'because I've felt its terrible anger twice this summer. And Garreth abandons his friends to blow-dry in the wind!' I smiled balefully to myself; it would *like* that, I thought.

'But *you* found Gravenhead again this summer, Morwen,' I said quietly to myself as I tramped across the ridge, 'and yet you're blissfully unaware of it. Because it's staying away from you; it knows you can help it, just like it kept away from Nora.

'It *let* you go,' I said, turning back to the startled old lady. 'Has it ever occurred to you *why?* Because it was back in 1976, and back then there were no satellites or e-mail or YouTube or Facebook, or *anything!*'

The old lady stared at me.

'Do you mean to say-'

Richard Thorns

'Yes, I said bluntly, tugging my mobile from my jeans and checking for a signal, 'you found it too soon! It wants a wider audience, Nora. And so does Morwen!'

The Book of Morwen

I sat at the living room table, ignoring the ringing telephone, and glanced up at the clock yet again: it was a quarter to two in the afternoon, and through the opened kitchen door distant screams floated in over the fence from next door's paddling pool. My heart thumping with nerves, I cast a look towards the forbidden dresser. Yes, today I seemed surrounded by relics of the past...

Because...

On the living room table (which I had newly-polished) sat the box I had stolen from Gravenhead. I looked at it one more time: it was stomach-churningly rutted with grey wax, another ugly relic, I thought to myself, from a time that was long lost and long dead. This time, however, my videocassette sat next to it, a bright hope seeming to burst outwards from its interior.

Smiling, despite my nerves, I listened to the telephone, ringing and ringing and ringing, as I waited for it to stop.

The Book of All

Louisa sat in the car at the end of the street and ended the call. She turned to the driver:

'Giles, she's not going to answer it,' she said. 'I'm going round there. She told me 2pm anyway.'

'Good luck! Just remember, you can't do anything without the tape.'

Louisa nodded, and opened the door of the car. She walked around the corner and looked down the street. It was a very long one, but she already knew what she had to look for; she knew that if she walked the street for long enough, she would eventually see a poster of a lost cat staring out, drawing-pinned, from a gatepost.

The Book of Morwen

In the kitchen of the now-silent house, I carefully placed four mugs containing teabags on a tray, together with a plate of biscuits. I didn't know, but I thought a camera crew probably liked tea. I pushed a note pad to one side (containing an old shopping list - victorious in Lundy failure) and switched on the kettle; no harm in letting the water warm, I thought to myself.

Suddenly, the shrill sound of the doorbell filled the hall.

Despite myself, I jumped. I paused in the hallway, dragging a brush once more through my hair and checking myself in the mirror. Yes, I was nicely made-up and I knew for once I looked good. And no need to worry about the mobile –

switched off since yesterday. *One more thing!* I darted into the living room and took the telephone receiver off its cradle, placing it gently down on the dresser.

That was it! Beaming, my heart thudding, I pulled open the front door.

'Gran!' I stammered.

From behind my Grandmother, a small figure stepped out to show herself.

Behind me, I heard a sharp "SNAP" as the kettle switched itself off.

'Hello, Morwen,' Bethan commented grimly, 'you look nice!'

Chapter Seventeen

In the last days...

The Book of Bethan

'WELL, YOUR COLD SEEMS a bit better now,' I said bitterly to Morwen, 'I can't *believe* you; what have we been saying to you?'

Tears sprang suddenly to Morwen's eyes. 'I don't want to discuss this out here on the street with you,' she said. 'Please go away!'

'Watch the mascara!' I said bitchily. 'Let us in, then.'

Morwen's eyes were going past me, looking over my shoulder. Just like, I thought with a sudden stab of fear, when we'd been together in the pulpit of Gravenhead's church. I shook my head at her.

'Morwen, how could you?' I said, 'it's that Louisa Caybourne, isn't it.'

'Did you really think I wouldn't?' whispered Morwen.

'You're a bloody idiot!' I snarled, 'she'll edit you out!'

But I knew my anger was fighting - and losing - against what I now saw in front of me: Morwen's mouth was open, and her lower jaw was trembling. She looked so tired all of a sudden. I felt desperately sorry for her.

Oh, Morwen, I suddenly thought, *I do so want you to win, but not like this. Not this way!*

'Morwen,' I said to her a little more gently, 'it's okay, you know. It really is! But two people have already been killed this summer. You mustn't give that tape over to Louisa. She doesn't care about you.'

I turned my head unwillingly around: a distant figure was walking slowly along the street, glancing carefully at the gateposts.

Morwen looked at me uncertainly.

'Beth'...' she said to me.

'Oh, get in!' she suddenly. She bundled me and Nora into the hallway and through the kitchen (I caught a fleeting glimpse of tea mugs set up, and a note pad). And then we were suddenly in the back garden.

'You *have* to stay out here!' Morwen whispered to us urgently. 'Don't say anything. And *don't* let Louisa know you're here!'

There came the faint ringing of the doorbell from inside the house.

Morwen sighed. 'I have to go now,' she said. 'Please understand, Bethan, Gran. I'm serious - I *have* to go; you have to let me do this. There'll be a day one day when you understand. *You* will, especially, Gran!'

Morwen turned around and began to walk into the house. I darted after her, only to find my favourite denim jacket held in a claw-like grip. I twisted around: Nora was simply standing there - shaking her head slowly from side to side. I wriggled like a child.

'Let me - *go!*'

'Don't,' said Nora.

The Book of Morwen

'Hi, Morwen,' said Louisa brightly. 'You look nicely made-up. Boyfriend?'

There was a terrible pause.

'Where *is* everyone?'

'I'm sorry? What do you mean, Morwen?'

'The film crews, or cameramen, or whatever,' I said shakily.

Richard Thorns

'Oh! Well we weren't going to - you *can't* think we were just going to do it *here,* do you, Morwen? No, I thought I could just take a quick look at the tape, and then I could take it away to show to the guys to prepare a good, juicy voiceover, just for you,' she ended coaxingly. 'Wasn't that what I said to you in the cafe?'

'What about... *me?*' I said slowly.

'Oh, don't *worry;* we'll have you in the studio soon, I promise!' Louisa motioned towards the hallway, raising her eyebrows. I walked into the hallway and into the living room, aware of Louisa's soft footsteps.

Behind me all the way?

The Book of Bethan

Nora pulled me towards the stone coal bunker to the side of the back garden. I craned my neck around: I could see two figures in the living room. I could see Morwen wandering the room, almost afraid to sit down. The thought rushed through my head. *It's a good sign! If she sits down, she commits. Don't sit down, Morwen!*

'Trust her,' Nora's old voice croaked in my ear. 'You think she doesn't know there's a problem with Gravenhead? She knows!'

The Book of Morwen

'So,' said Louisa, her own note pad on her knees, 'I suppose the one question that's going to be first on everyone's lips will be: *"Where is it?"* How did you find it, Morwen?'

I went red. 'I... like walking in the mountains all by myself, you see,' I said nervously, watching Louisa scribble frantically away. 'A lot of people find it strange because I'm young, or whatever. But, well, from Year nine onwards I didn't enjoy school very much, and after my Da left my Mam, I-'

Louisa held up a hand with a little smile. 'Morwen, this is all very interesting but it's not the Jeremy Kyle Show,' she said, 'can we just stick to this village of yours?'

'Yes. I'm sorry. Well... if you go to Treffynydd railway station and get off-'

Louisa scribbled very briefly into her notebook, and then tapped it with her pencil.

'Treffynydd. Lovely, There was a death there, wasn't there, during the early part of the summer?'

I nodded a little miserably. I felt so alone. I heard Louisa's tinkling little laugh:

'Isn't that funny? I *thought* I'd heard that name before. We're a good team, aren't we, Morwen! So, are you saying that Gravenhead's near Treffynydd station, then? And what about that lake of yours; is the church still poking up through the water, just like your friend told that policeman? What did you think when you saw it, Morwen?'

Richard Thorns

I took a deep breath.

'There's something I think you should know,' I said.

The Book of Bethan

'Nora, she's got her doubts,' I whispered. I was thinking about that note pad I'd seen in the kitchen: an idea had come to me. 'I'm going to try to get in the house.'

I took off my jacket; less bulky. I edged my way past the coal bunker; my back scratched against the fence.

The Book of Morwen

'Gravenhead is no longer just a steeple in the water,' I said tonelessly. 'There's no more lake there at all, and we went there and we walked all around the village. Everywhere you look, there are all these houses lying empty and deserted, without a soul in them. It's so quiet. There's a Tudor pub and a church. And all these houses. I've been in the church.'

I stopped. Louisa was looking hard at me, a dawning of suspicion in her eyes.

'*You've*, been in the *church?*' she said slowly.

'*Yes!*' I said. The summer heat was rising balefully in my head. 'It's *true!* Look, I'll put on the tape and then you can see for yourself! I have to get some air. I'm *sorry!* It's so hot in this room!'

The Book of Bethan

I sat against the fence, the note pad on my lap, writing frantically away. I finished just as a figure walked slowly out of the kitchen and into the back garden. Morwen stopped at the side of the coal bunker.

'I can't do it,' she said quietly. 'Bethan, you said there were two deaths this summer. Did you mean it?'

I nodded. 'The old man at the station - and the man who's missing,' I said, 'and it will never stop killing,' I went on, 'I know it still frightens you, Morwen. *Look* at me! Can you tell me you've never felt its hatred this summer? *Can* you?'

Morwen stared, stricken at me. And then she flinched, as if in pain; as if all the thoughts she'd had in our summer had suddenly struck out at her in a rage in that garden, as if in fury at being found out.

(Stories would later be told of sweet, flowering nettle-smells through a taxi's opened window: a taxi that had sped through empty roads amongst black, towering slag-heaps at night. A fever-night. Night-thoughts and first thoughts... *if I could have killed you that night, Bethan, I would have).*

And then Morwen flinched and cocked her ear slightly, as if she could hear her gran's voice floating as if from a long way off.

Richard Thorns

'*When* is Gravenhead in your mind, Morwen?' Nora was asking her, 'does it ever let you rest? When is it in your mind?'

'All the time, Gran!' groaned Morwen, as she suddenly turned to face us; ashen-faced and running her fingers through her black hair. 'I can't un-find it - I can't even wish for it!'

'But, darling, you can do something about it,' said Nora gently. 'Morwen, give us a little while and we'll all do it together. We can help you.'

Morwen ran her hands through her hair again.

'I don't know,' she said helplessly. 'I don't know.'

I ripped off a page from the note pad I had been scribbling on.

'Then *read* what I've written on this page, Morwen,' I said urgently, 'and then you have to show it to Louisa. And if you need backup...' my voice trembled slightly; I knew the shock I was about to give her, 'Morwen, you have to play her your Gravenhead video *from the very beginning!*'

Morwen stood beside the coal bunker, reading the note. One side of her mouth twitched, as if it didn't know whether to go up or down.

And then she turned her back on us, and went back into the house.

The Book of Morwen

I stood in the kitchen, reading Bethan's piece of paper and my eyes filled suddenly with tears; at once I knew that it was the end of everything, and that the kitchen and my house would all go on exactly as it always had, forever! I tore off a piece of kitchen roll and wiped at my eyes. There was a black smudge of mascara on the tissue. And then I placed my shoulders back, adjusted the summer dress I had saved for, and walked into the living room.

The Book of Bethan

In the garden, time passed. And then I heard a raised voice, first of all. The voice was *not* Morwen's. Straining, I leaned out from the coal bunker (and was just as smartly pulled back again):

'Better things... do than... STUPIDITY! I've... good mind to... SCHOOL!

I heard a door SLAM! Loudly!

Morwen did not come out. I looked around at Nora.

'I was once told by my daughter, much earlier this summer in this very back garden,' she said to me a little sadly, 'that Morwen never lied; she always told the truth. That friend of yours is growing up.'

The Book of Bethan (cont'd)

Richard Thorns

We found her defeated on the couch, clutching at a piece of kitchen roll in one hand, the remote to the video recorder in the other. Her thumb gently stroked the remote. Instead of the Gravenhead footage, a whooping child was pulling faces directly at Morwen, it seemed. I heard the laughter:

'*You muppet!*'

'Morwen?' Nora said gently.

'After I showed her the note you wrote, I played her the tape to prove it,' Morwen said dully. 'I didn't actually *need* the video to back up what you wrote, Beth',' she continued, 'but I put it on anyway.' Without taking her eyes from the screen, Morwen passed the note pad over her shoulder. Nora took it gently from her fingers.

'And when she viewed the tape I think she wanted to kill me,' Morwen continued, still in that strange, bald voice. Nora sank into a chair, and began to read what I had written. I could recite the words in my mind:

Morwen, you know this project? What if we told everyone we'd found a village under a lake? We can get out into the valleys and have a laugh! We could really wind a few people up, as well!

If Morwen's Mam had been in the room at that moment, perhaps she would have remembered a scene that Morwen told me about later. Morwen - aged six - falling out of an apple tree in the back garden, and collecting what would later turn out to be a tiny white scar on her arm. And crying, but not out loud: just looking at the ground silently and withdrawing into herself. It was different now; suddenly there was the need for kitchen roll again, collecting more mascara smears. I hastily complied, feeling monstrous and unable to look at those tears.

'And you know what?' Morwen was saying, 'you know what? You never even had to try so hard with me, because it was all just such a failure anyway.' Her mouth turned down as she looked at the stupid clowning on the tape; all that remained of her beautiful discovery. 'Just... *look* at it!' She burst into fresh tears.

'No, *you* look at it,' I said gently, glad at last to be able to help her. I squeezed the remote from Morwen's fingers and pressed: "picture search". After a while, a line of snowy pixels marched down the screen, to be replaced with a forest.

Morwen watched herself pacing across the screen. I pressed my thumb hard on the remote, and then released the button:

"*- here in this peaceful countryside, twenty miles from the town of Rosengrave, something very peculiar is happening:*

"*The lost village of Gravenhead, long thought to have vanished in the sixteenth century...*"

After a few moments, Morwen dragged one of her hands across her eyes and attempted a smile.

'I'm a natural,' she commented, through one or two gulps and shakes. 'It was good, wasn't it?'

I was about to spoil things again. 'I've got a better one!' I said grimly, reaching into my bag.

The Book of All

You damned little brat!

Louisa stood in the street, leaving the gate open. It swung sulkily in the heat. The sun beat down and she felt the heat rising chokingly in her head. On impulse, she stretched out and ripped the photograph of Morris from the gatepost. It fluttered in the still air onto the pavement.

You'll admit it for a second time won't you! When you're expelled! You'll be working the fitting rooms at Primark or turning hot wings for a career in September! And then I'll make you admit it again!

She walked down the hot street, wincing in the searing sunlight. She rounded the street and then stopped: Giles's car was gone.

Louisa looked about the street. There was no-one about. She checked her watch: it was three twenty. *Well, people have to work, and kids on holiday wouldn't stay in this armpit of a place.* But, as she stared at the empty place where the car had been, she felt a little shadow of cold fear; Morwen's words haunted her like a child's ghost:

Everywhere you look, there are all these houses lying empty and deserted, without a soul in them. It's so quiet.

Yes, post-plague quiet.

In the empty street Louisa bit her lip, and actually tasted a little coppery smell of blood. The silent houses stared back at her. Screwing up her eyes in the sunshine, she looked around her once again.

It's a strange ghost town.

She took out her mobile, and it was then that she heard it... a faint *hiss;* was there someone near after all, and had they slowly opened a bottle of something? Or was someone crouching beside a car where she couldn't see, letting air from a tyre? Ahead of her, a long way off, she could just make out the terminal of the bus station, brightly-coloured vehicles edging slowly in and out of the building. With relief, she began to walk.

And it was then that she saw him.

Why is it that old fossils like him wear tweed coats and hats, even in this damned freak summer? He was crouching on the pavement; Louisa could hear low groans from where she was standing. Walking quickly now, she caught him up:

'Are you alright?' she managed to say.

The croaking voice seemed to flutter inside her skull. Was she now going to get heatstroke in this damned summer?

'I have angina.'

'Oh, look,' said Louisa impatiently, 'I have to get going soon.' She could see the buses moving in the distance and, more than that, now she could faintly see people crossing the road. 'Where do you live? I've got my mobile.'

'Just around the corner,' whispered the old man. 'I would be...'

Again, that muttering voice seemed to billow inside her head. Louisa pursed her lips. Taking hold of an old, tweedy arm she walked him quickly down the street towards the next turning on the left: it was an alleyway. She stared: it was deserted except for a cat rummaging in a dustbin. It scampered off the moment it saw them. The light left them both behind.

'It's cooler here,' said Louisa. 'You should take off some of what you're wearing. You'll be...'

She stopped, aware of her voice trailing away in dismay because perhaps the old man had moved suddenly: she could feel the tweedy cloth beneath her hand gently collapsing beneath her touch. The arm she clutched was still there...

But only just... it felt like a broomstick.

'You're so kind, my dear,'

Her heart beating strongly, Louisa reached out on impulse and snatched at the old man's hat. Had she imagined a hat? She knew she was panicking. *The summer light was very strong in the street, so, yes, I probably imagined it.* There was no hat.

And then the old man turned around and she saw his face. And he smiled at her.

Chapter Eighteen

The dragon current.

The Book of Bethan

MORWEN WAS SITTING ON the floor away from us, her eyes on the television; her battered video recorder had been set on "Pause". The lake lay full and placid on the screen and the Melanchol stood there in the saplings, its shoulders hideously shaking (thanks to Morwen's prehistoric video heads) as if in awful, grisly laughter.

'Are you okay now, Morwen?' I asked her.

For myself, I thought I was destined to spend the rest of my life flitting from place to place. It seemed to me that Fawkes's Hill would be the last day I would ever spend in open space: I thought of the velvet dark of Nora's back garden; the shady scratchiness of Morwen's coal bunker. Now, another summer evening was drawing in once again.

I perched on the couch, sipped at a mug of tea and watched Morwen's gran. At the table, the ghastly wax box had been prised open once more, and the table was littered with the crumbling Tudor papers, plus scribbled sketches we'd supplied as best we could remember. So Nora sat there, beadily staring through a large magnifying glass. Through the hatchway, I saw supper plates lying forgotten in the kitchen sink.

Morwen turned around and nodded in answer to my question.

'Whether or not you deserve to be is another matter,' butted in Nora sharply. 'You both took an appalling risk.'

Morwen sighed. 'Gran, we've *been* through this already.'

We had! Nora's words had stung my ears and now jabbed at my memory in my shame; told off by someone I'd regarded as an ally without conditions. Or not, as it had turned out.

"You two go into that church another time – and then see if you ever come out again!"

'Bethan, Morwen? I think you should look at this,' said Nora suddenly.

I got up and went over to the table.

'I've checked these papers through and they're *definitely* in reading order. They're terribly crumbled, dear, so do handle them carefully if you're going to look at them.' She tutted: 'This writing is so ancient it's almost a code. But look at this.'

Craning my neck, I began to read aloud with Nora correcting my mistakes, and I have to admit I made a lot. Our voices droned away and Morwen got up from the floor and settled into Nora's sofa; I think she was enjoying the new feelings of warmth from our new-found companionship:

Richard Thorns

In the yeare of our LORD fifteen hundred and thirty five, the deſtruction of Gravenhead waſ decryd by King Henry, for word had finally reached Richmond that thiſ creyture that ſtepſ from ayre who brought ſutch bitter deathe and miſerys to Cowminſter, waſ known to be with life once agayne withyn the King's paryſh of Gravenhead.

Gravenhead

It was confidered fitting that thif deftruction should be vifited upon Gravenhead by way of itf bequefted BAPTIfM. Alfo, within thif inheritance may yet be the great Binding Maff of CHRIST'f dragon, or futch that remaynd of it.

It fhould alwayf be conidered neceffary to note that thif deftruction fhould remind each of uf of the Divine Prefence of GOD and Hif judgement upon our nature, alfo to be found in the wider Nature of thingf. Af the wyked landf of Noah were drown'd and Platof kyngdom waf deftroyd through watre, fo too did Gravenhead peryfh beneathe wavef.

'You're having a little trouble with the letter "S" Bethan, dear,' Nora said to me with a smile. 'It's a Tudor "S", I'm afraid, and it looks so much like an "F".'

'What about it, Nora, any ideas?' I asked.

Nora cupped her hands, and pecked at her index fingers. 'The Biblical Flood... Plato wrote about Atlantis. Great civilisations destroyed through water. God's destruction, and Nature's wrath. And Gravenhead... I wonder?'

'Gran?' said Morwen timidly.

Without looking up, Nora said: 'I spoke to you before about those ley lines, Bethan, do you remember? Atlantis! I wonder... could geomancy be involved here? Gravenhead could be more important than you realize. Atlantis.... Atlantis.'

'That's a lost drowned continent, Nora,' I said helpfully.

'Thank you, Bethan,' said Nora with a smile.

'And Geo-what is it?'

'Geomancy. I've *studied* the ley lines, Bethan. John Mitchel took up the subject in 1969 in his book: *The View over Atlantis.* I'll try to explain: Geomancy involves the scattering of earth or other materials on the ground to generate a range of dot configurations, which could then be "read" by a seer.'

'Fine so far, Nora, I think,' I said, but Morwen frowned at me.

'Go on, Gran,' she said.

'Well, the geomancer could then use a sort of a circular magnetic compass to detect these earth currents, bringing them into harmony before the building of important religious sites. And those lines of magnetic force,' Nora ended thoughtfully, 'were known in ancient China as the "dragon current".'

'This is *Wales*, Gran!'

'We've got a Welsh dragon, haven't we? The dragon current was thought to exist in two forms - and that's where you get your *yin* and your *yang* from: positive and negative energies in the earth. Complete harmony of *both*... was where you built your temple.'

'But, China!' Morwen said helplessly. 'That's *thousands* of miles away.'

'But images of dragons survive in human culture the world over, darling. You see, the slaying of the dragon in *China* formed a symbolic re-fertilisation of the land; all the elements combined in harmony, you see? But in Britain, it's different. What do *you* think, Bethan? Name me a dragon-killer.'

I sighed. 'Oh, I don't know... St George?' I was tired and didn't see where the conversation was going.

'It's getting really late,' I murmured. I got up and walked over to the big window that looked over Morwen's darkened back garden. The moon was waxing, I thought; tomorrow it would be full. High clouds hung in the warm air, their heat flush gone: the colour of sour milk. I heard Nora behind me, fussing like some old hound worrying a bone.

Richard Thorns

'*Or* St Margaret, Bethan, or St Michael; you can take your pick; there are plenty of them around! And these sites of dragon killings took on great sanctity, Bethan: dragon-slayers became saints. Sites of sanctity became Christianised. What do you do when you have a site of great Christian importance on your hands, Bethan?'

And, suddenly, I understood! Looking out of the window at the blackness of the garden I whispered, without turning around-

'You build a church.'

The Book of Morwen

As Rosengrave slumbered through the night I lay in my bed, my thick hair spilling all over the pillow. I was staring at a streetlamp's glow through the curtains. My thoughts were with my silent village, far away from artificial light:

'Beth'?' I said softly, 'are you awake?'

'Uh-huh?'

'What do you think those papers in the box are *really* saying?'

'I don't know. A warning of some kind?'

'You know, Bethan, I've been thinking. You know in the old days there were paintings on the walls of the church, because people couldn't read or write? Well, all those sermons must have been delivered from the pulpit - and that's where we found the box.'

'Mmmm,' Bethan was almost asleep.
'Beth', do you mind if I ask you something?'
'Mm?'
'You said you stayed at Gran's last night. And tonight you're staying here with me, but you never called your Mam and Da. Don't you ever think they'll worry?'

Silence. Was there... *envy* in the answer, when it came?

'I don't think having one parent's quite so bad. Goodnight, Morwen,' murmured Bethan.

The Book of All

Rosengrave hospital is as non-sleeping as any airport, with golden neon, sparkling sodium lamps; the occasional white flash of car headlights. It's almost a friendly place if you're a frightened child who can't sleep: it tells you other people are still there in the world.

The ambulance was stationary, parked clumsily at the Accident and Emergency entrance, its rear doors open. Doctor Maxwell sighed a little to himself; it was just after 2am, and his evening of patching up drunks (accompanied by indignant stories and a hope not to be declared their friends) had gone on for too long tonight! Now, he took hold of a handrail and pulled himself up, standing on the steps and peering in. He could see the chromium bed inside, on which a figure lay. He turned around to speak down to the crew on the tarmac. White stripes shining on yellow plastic uniform, in neon light.

'I can't get paged every time there's an admission,' he said slightly irritably, 'didn't you think it best to simply bring her in?'

'We thought not to,' the driver said. 'Maybe you'd better see her in here.'

Doctor Maxwell sighed and swung himself up into the rear of the ambulance. He leaned forwards and gently pulled down the sheet of the bed.

He stared down at the patient, in an instant taking in the accelerated black inflammation of the lymph-glands and the skull-like face staring up at him. He stared, and the thought crossed his mind that somehow he knew this figure on the bed; that he had seen her before, perhaps on the television and that she had once been very pretty.

'The patient's murmuring outside consciousness,' the paramedic said to him in a low voice, 'she's complaining about her limbs; she says they ache. She has a high fever. If those swellings break we could lose her, due to shock'.

Maxwell nodded, moving towards the patient. He had seen something, a miniscule little sigh from her that only a trained eye could see; a slight relaxation of the lungs…

A fine puff, a tiny spray of perhaps two, maybe three droplets of red on the sheet.

'Sputum,' Maxwell said, 'containing red blood cells, exacted through the respiratory system into the air.

He turned to look at the paramedic. Maxwell's pragmatic approach had been forever set by others' parameters: his upbringing and personality; his training and experience. But this was something he'd never seen before. And as he looked back to the patient, a wave of goosebumps suddenly blew across the lady on the bed. Maxwell shuddered; suddenly it reminded him of a childhood wonder once seen on a long-forgotten holiday; a gust of wind blowing over a lake, a moving blast of silver leaves.

'OK, get her inside,' he said, 'I want to see antibiotics inside her: Tetracycline, a.s.a.p. And in isolation!'

The Book of All (cont'd)

In the dim, late wake of the house, Nora caught her breath:

Richard Thorns

The Prayer as in that time
it was publiſhed.

Decreed that the great Binding Maſſ of CHRIST'ſ dragon ſhould not fayſ by the Bleſſed wyſ of GOD. But it fayled Auguſt fifteen hundred and thirty four. It waſ thene knowne that thiſ creyture that ſtepſ from ayre could not peryſh but indeyd had eternal lyf. That dyſmal afflictyn that playged Cowminſter would not peryſh with itſ hoſt, but inſteade brynge eternal deathe.

The authority of the King therefore ſent the diggerſ to the hill and prepared the Cowminſter furviverſ for thyre ſacrifice if it pleaſeſ GOD.

'Well,' Nora murmured, 'it's out now.'

As if in confirmation, her old eyes flitted to the last of the passage; the words stared out at her from the yellowing parchment:

This creature that steps from air...
Down...
Eternal death.

The Book of All (cont'd)

Nora looked up from the last page and rubbed at her eyes. Rosengrave slumbered on through the long night. Upstairs, she heard the faint sound of snoring. She knew Morwen never snored, so it must be Bethan. She smiled: the moment felt good.

Morwen's face would be relaxed in sleep, before the new day demanded that fierce little determination in her face, even before breakfast.

She remembered Morwen for a fraction of that moment, then: defiant in defeat, when she was alone with only her mother in the house. Defeated, and *not* defiant (and a lot of the time in tears), when her Year nine was battled through, from September to July:

A THANKES·GIVING

Forsakynge Gravenhead, the diggers appoynted by King Henry will compleat their worke and alle wyll indeyd soone be watyr. These pages shall be entombed with Gravenhead, in wood, and wax, and therein much watyr.

But thankſ be to GOD for Hiſ Bleſſed wyl, for it iſ decreed that all ſhall be prepared for dry ſtreetſ once agayn, in whatever yeare it may be that the evil one in hiſ miſchief ſhould viſit upon uſ in fiuture tymeſ.

Nowe iſ there iſ no more drownyg we invoke the ſeconde Booke of Actſ for another trap awaytſ thiſ creyture that ſtepſ from ayre. Go to the manor houſe with a feare of fire and watyr. There, the Cowmynſter ſurvivorſ awayt.

Nora nodded, almost to herself. She added to the page of notes she had been scribbling. She picked up Morwen's sketch: three beams of light illuminating the thing creeping out of the earth.

'But... not waiting wait for *you*, Morwen,' she murmured. 'Not for you.'

She put down the sketch, drew a deep breath and took a sip of tea. She cast a glance out into the darkened back garden. Her skin prickled on the back of her neck:

She could see something walking silently through the garden towards her. And as Nora watched it, she felt her old fears of recognition beat strongly inside her. She thought: *It doesn't have to worry about the roses.* Her thoughts flickered upstairs to the bedroom, with the made-up bed for Bethan as well.

No! She would *not* cry out!

The thing in the garden recognised her too, then, and it ran in a shambles to the light of the window. Nora ran quickly to the wall and snapped off the light switch. It was the last light left on: the room and house itself plunged into treacle-thick darkness.

Her arms stretched in front of her, Nora felt her way back to the window. Yes, it was still there. She took its features in once more, this time only inches away from her. And then its jaws seemed to stretch slightly in a grin of final recognition.

So now I know! Nora thought. *I* will *see it again. I'm seeing it!*

'Hello,' she murmured. 'It's been a long time.'

Ancient fingers scratched at the double-glazing, squealing quietly on the glass, like bush-twigs.

'Not by the hair of my chinny-chin-chin,' Nora said softly, 'yes, you tried that once before, didn't you? On our first day you picked away at the lead that surrounded my window, before you let me be. But *FastSeal* has seen to that now. We've moved on.'

The voice in her head was so scratchy – yes, just like bush-twigs on glass. It seemed to whisper coaxingly at her.

You alone will be spared

'Like... before?' murmured Nora. 'Look what you left me with!' She lifted the arms of her blouse; the terrible red marks on her arms seemed to shine in the poorly-lit room. A little breeze seemed suddenly to blow across the garden, rattling the tree leaves, as if in excitement.

The scars have healed, crooned the voice. *What really happened in the forest?*

She whispered: 'Go back to that old town, because you won't win, and you can't come back! Oh, I know,' she continued, her old eyes fixed on the window, 'Gravenhead will still be found. But by then you will be dead.'

Her reflection in the glass seemed to match up exactly with the face staring in at her, and her lie died in her throat: the being slowly inclined its head upward.

Richard Thorns

It was looking directly up at Morwen's bedroom.

'What about my Grand-daughter?' whispered Nora fiercely. Panic-stricken, she pushed down the cry that welled in her throat.

As if in answer, it raised a pointing finger and in the half-light, the head lowered itself to look at her. Nora caught her breath: surely it was not a trick of the moonlight? That rippling of a reflection that makes you think you can see someone behind a front door, when really it's *you* who's moved? She thought she could see two reflections blending together on each side of the glass: there were dark swellings on the neck like pestilence-marks from a dark past, or a black mark on someone's character. The glass seemed to create caverns for eyes, and a deep, dark hole for a mouth that seemed to change its shape and leer at her when she moved.

Nora could see stick-like lines hiding in the very heart of the reflection and, as they grew steadily stronger, she realized they were her daughter's rose bushes, becoming clearer in the moonlight. She stretched out an arm and pushed at a nearby lamp switch. The room flooded suddenly with yellow light and Nora wiped the hand across her eyes and looked once again into the darkened back garden, but the Melanchol had gone.

Chapter Nineteen

Signs on the Earth below...

The Book of All (cont'd)

THE SKY was beginning to lighten. Inside an empty bedroom within a house on a smart road, somewhere between Rosengrave and Conwy, a telephone began to ring, joining two alarm clocks that had already been bleating a mechanical chorus for some time; the clocks now read 04:10 as they chirped beside the bed; a bed with a thrown-over duvet and a slightly buckled sheet.

Richard Thorns

After six rings, the telephone fell silent, and an answer phone clicked into life:

"You're through to Louisa Caybourne. I'm sorry I can't come to the phone right now..."

Moments passed, and then...

...your early morning call... This is your early morning call... This is...

The message endlessly repeated itself, blending with the alarm clocks. The sound carried across the room with no-one listening, and out of the still-open bedroom door to nowhere.

The Book of All (cont'd)

Nora stood in the hallway, and gazed silently at the front door. No, she had no key; that door would click loudly if she pulled it shut, unless she left it ajar. She smiled grimly to herself. *No, don't do that!*

But there was another way! She went into the kitchen and removed a key from on top of the refrigerator. Slowly, she turned it in the lock of the back door and let herself out. She locked it firmly behind her, and tested it.

A first, solitary blackbird had begun to sing. The back garden was very warm and clouds puffed high in the sky; lilac-bruised yet edged with a golden, caramel light. It was going to be a lovely day! She heard the faint whine of a milk float from the front of the house as she walked quietly around the side, towards her waiting vehicle parked on the street.

As Nora's battered Morris Traveller snorted into life the trees blew and shivered as if in faint excitement. The car slipped away as Nora left the street to begin her last journey to meet the Cowminster survivors. The street was silent, everything just waiting for the dawn.

The Book of Morwen

I gasped and jumped out of my sleep, wincing. The sound that came from the ghastly mouth in my vanishing dream, was Bethan's simple snoring.

Sunlight flooded my bedroom. For a moment I lay in bed, listening to the birds and making pictures from the patterns in the bright curtains. Then... I didn't like the faces my mind was beginning to form. I threw back my duvet, getting up.

I padded down the stairs and into the kitchen. I switched on the kettle and almost immediately it began to roar softly. Then I picked up the piece of paper lying next to the kettle:

"Morwen darling, please let me sleep in this morning because I was up all night with the papers from the box. Please try not to wake me. Love gran xx"

I smiled to myself. Bless her heart then, and all right! I placed a mug back into the cupboard and fished around in a tin for some teabags, and then jumped at a bleary-sounding: 'Good morning.' Turning, I saw Bethan's small frame in the doorway dressed in a bathrobe, rubbing her eyes.

'Morning,' I answered back. 'Tea?'

Bethan nodded, and yawned. 'It's a lovely day again.'

'You snore, by the way.'

Bethan picked up the note and read through it.

'We'll have to be quiet,' I said. 'Switch on the TV and I'll bring the tea in.'

Bethan nodded and went into the living room. Through the hatchway I saw her sink into the sofa, her streaked blonde hair in a real mess: a tired crumple not yet in the shower, but lazing in the bright morning:

A morning so bright I couldn't see the face on the television.

But I could *hear* it...

'Well, Trefor, as we've heard earlier in the bulletin, no member of staff at Rosengrave hospital seems prepared to talk to us further, but it would appear that this unknown strain of superbug - and some hospitals do seem to experience this from time to time - is pretty much raging within the building, with cases including an ambulance driver, paramedics and at least one doctor. Not to mention of course the many nurses within this building.'

'Rys, what *is* the latest on Louisa Caybourne?'

'Morwen,' Bethan called out to me desperately.

'Trefor, Louisa is... stable right now; the treatment she's been given is - and I quote -: "a cocktail of strong antibiotics." Quite what these administrative drugs *are* we're not being told, but if there's any news I'll let you know back at the studio.'

'Rys, thank you.' Turning back to the camera, the presenter continued...

'He looks shaken,' I whispered as I joined Bethan, blood beginning to drain from my own face.

'...the moment we get them. Now, with something of a surprise appearance for the very worst of reasons, we've got a stand-in for Louisa and Gwen Cannell brings us the regional weather for this morning:'

'*Thank* you Trefor! Well, this morning *does* bring that high pressure once again over Wales for the umpteenth time today bringing *glorious* temperatures of around 31° for most of the region, and...'

'Just listen to her, and there's something in her eyes,' I whispered. 'Can you see it, Beth', that glint of triumph? She's got a break; she's glad this has happened. She's *glad!*

Bethan nodded.

'That Louisa Caybourne woman, the one who's sick; she was here yesterday. It's *started,* Bethan, hasn't it?'

Bethan nodded again.

'I'm getting gran up,' I said decisively. I got up from the sofa and made a new mug of tea. Taking it, I paced slowly up the stairs to the shut bedroom door.

I tapped on the door…

'Gran,' I whispered softly. There was no reply. Squeezing the door handle, I opened the door and tiptoed in; my thoughts seemed like a dropped jigsaw:

She wanted to sleep in but there's light all over the place so what's with that unmade bed is she in the bathroom no I would have seen her

Then I saw the note on the pillow…

I picked it up:

My scream seemed to fall heavily down the stairs.

In a second Bethan was at the doorway, taking in the sight of me standing in the empty bedroom. Gran's mug of tea lay on the floor and a dark swamp of tea was soaking into the carpet. Silently, I held out the piece of paper. Bethan's eyes quickly went over the letter:

"Morwen, Bethan, darlings, please try not to be angry with me, but if the lake is dry now things can happen to protect you! Morwen, you especially must not leave this house today! Do you understand this? Do NOT !

Love, your gran. xxxx"

The Book of Bethan

'It's obviously trying to get her back,' Morwen said to me on our way down the stairs, tears springing up in her eyes. 'It wants to finish what it started with her in 1976, all those years ago!'

Or it's trying to get you back there, Morwen! I think you'll find it's pissed off with you; you've let it down big time!

But I kept my thoughts to myself as I went quickly into the living room. Going over to the table I snatched up Nora's scribbled notes, lying abandoned on the table:

"The sketch Morwen made of that painting; the only painting the wrong side of the barrier! Three lights are shining on something coming out of the ground. Or are they?"

"The diggers have finished. Is this a reference to Fawkes's Hill??"

"The Cowminster survivors will invoke the second chapter of the Book of Acts. This has to be a Biblical reference. Is this creature an angel???!!"

"The Great Binding Mass. Very strong, then?"

I quickly gathered the notes together as Morwen walked into the room. The last line Nora had written seemed to mock me:

"Not strong enough!!!"

The Book of Morwen

Richard Thorns

The train rumbled through the valleys, the carriage growling and lurching from side to side, but alone in the carriage with Bethan there was to be no hot sleep for me this time; no dreams of tiger-striped perch as they skittered through the gloomy, drowned ruin of the church.

I shook my head slightly, for a moment still in the ancient dreams of early summer when I had first brought Garreth to the lake. It seemed fantastic that I could once have thrown bread towards the steeple, and that the sunny water would then have surely flickered, as fish pushed the bread around with their heads:

Was it really so very changed, then, my summer?

'But then I wanted it so much,' I said quietly to myself, biting my lip. 'I wanted it more than anything.' I dug in my pockets for my mobile.

Down the other end of the carriage (and wincing as sunlight flashed in the carriage), Bethan had her shoulders up on baggage rails with her feet off the ground, and as the diesel train purred and swung, so too did her whole body.

'Bethan,' I called. 'Can I borrow your phone?'

Dropping to the carriage floor, Bethan tossed it down the corridor to me and then jumped up for the baggage rails once again.

'Hi, Bethan,' came Garreth's voice through the phone.

'No, it's Morwen here, Garreth,' I said, 'I'm using her mobile. Listen, do you think you might have a Bible somewhere in your house? Good! Well, will you look up "Acts" for us, the Book of Acts, and call us straight back?

Chapter two is what we're looking for, can you do that? Chapter two?'

I paused, letting him speak.

'Gravenhead. But it's okay Garreth; we're okay.'

A particular lurch of the train swung Bethan wildly, so she dropped to the floor. She walked a little unsteadily down the carriage gangway.

'Look,' she said, sitting down beside me, 'we'll go and get Nora back and then we'll just... *leave it alone!* We won't go there, or talk about it or anything. It's nothing to do with us.'

I shook my head. 'It doesn't matter anymore,' I answered simply, 'even if we *did* just leave it be. Do you remember when I said I couldn't un-find it or even wish for it? The lake's *gone,* Beth'! Gravenhead will still be found.'

'Genies and bottles,' murmured Bethan.

'Pandora's Box,' I said.

'It can't be closed, so that's why she's gone there,' I said flatly. 'She thinks she can kill it.'

The Book of Morwen (cont'd)

We found gran's car parked carefully in front of the foliage shielding the track. The ivory paintwork was half-cool, half-very hot in the heat of the morning. I noticed sorrel and hogweed buds littering the bonnet where gran had tried to mount the verge, and push away at the hawthorns to get off the road; there was a small scratch on the wing from a branch.

My eyes stung: had Nora noticed that?

The Book of Bethan

The track, deep rutted, led on and on; the gorse buds cracked in the blazing heat. I think Morwen was worried about Nora's car; maybe if a car took off its wing mirror, or maybe if the paint was scratched? Anyway, I had *my* own thoughts as I sucked in the hot air, following Morwen along the track. As it led through the shade of the trees I realized I'd begun to notice the birdsong when it occurred, no longer taking it for granted.

Yes, we must be very near now, I thought. To my right I saw the distant flicker of the church spire through the trees, and my stomach tightened suddenly. Ahead of me, Morwen was parking her bike and making her way through the fronds that hid the basin.

'Bethan!' she called. 'Come and take a look at this!'

Hurrying slightly, I caught up to Morwen, staring down into the basin...

The scene that lay below us was just like it was before: the church, the ugly houses at the far end of the village smashed into pieces. Everything was the same but for one horrible little changed detail: the mist now lay heavily in the streets, wisping gently in the undulating breeze.

I frowned to myself. Yes, I *remembered* this mist. At least, in much smaller detail as it had curled from the gaps in the church flagstones as I'd run towards Morwen in the pulpit. But Gravenhead's *streets* had been fairly clear of mist. It was all very different now.

'It doesn't look right, Beth', does it?' Morwen murmured to me.

'No!' I rubbed at my forehead with my wrist, and felt the sting of salt. 'It's so *hot* - why isn't the sun burning it off?'

'GRAN?' screamed Morwen. Her voice seemed to float straight across the basin, too high in the air to be heard.

There was nothing, only the birdless, aching silence.

Shaking her head, Morwen picked her way down the bank, grabbing at roots to stop herself from falling. I watched her walk over the dividing line of leaf litter and pine needles to set foot on the beginnings of the lake's now-dry floor. I saw Morwen's dark hair disappearing over the basin edge and pop smartly up again:

'Come *on!*' she called up to me.

And then, standing on the dividing line I trembled slightly as I gazed down into the basin. I knew in my heart that I was very frightened of Gravenhead now. I looked at Morwen, picking her way down the deep slide of the basin and exclaiming to herself, as she examined the scratched palms of her hands.

How have you changed? I thought. I felt a brief stab of memory, very painful now as I remembered hearing all about Morwen: frozen in silent fear in a pear orchard, her head filled with false stories of gunshot.

But... *here,* Morwen was walking down the parts of the basin she was able to, her brown shoulders up in the sun. Little dusty whirlwinds spun gently around her in the heat. Grimly, tremblingly, I followed Morwen's distant shape as it descended.

I sat down heavily on a rock and pulled out my mobile. I selected a number from the menu, rang it, and waited:

'Hi, Garreth,' I said nervously.

'Oh, hiya, Bethan, you got your phone back. How's it going?'

'Not bad, but I was hoping you'd call us,' I said in a small voice. 'We can't... just chase after you like this! You said you'd *call* us, you said-.'

'Are you at Gravenhead yet?'

I nodded. 'Garreth,' I began, 'there's something about Gravenhead today that's really scaring me. There's a mist in the streets like before, only it's much thicker now.'

'It's not in any shadow, though?'

'Garreth, it's *sweltering* here!' I whispered.

'Bethan, I couldn't find the Bible Morwen was asking for, so I looked it up on the internet. Do you want me to read it out?'

Something deep inside me wanted to scream at him in despair: *You got the information but you didn't call us? You didn't call* me?

I took a deep breath. 'Go for it,' I said to him.

'Okay, here we go: to begin with there's a bit about dreaming dreams and seeing visions. And then it goes: "Yes, even on my servants, both men and women, I will pour out my spirit in the last days... they will proclaim my message. I will perform miracles in the sky above and wonders on the earth below. Blood, fire and billows of smoke." And that's pretty much it, Bethan.'

I nodded silently, still sitting on my rock and watching Morwen. She was ahead of me and walking easily now in the shallowest part of the basin, exclaiming as she stepped in marshy areas still sodden with lake water. She looked up at me and waved me down.

'Bethan, you know I'll help you. I just want to do a bit of digging around. Will you tell Morwen what it says in the Bible?'

I nodded, hoping I could remember it all, 'what sort of digging around?' I asked him, my mouth turning down.

'Oh, well, there's a lot that's weird about it. Remember I tried to warn you in the library? Coal so near the surface and the lake evaporating so fast; mist that won't burn off in the sun? I *said* I'd help you if you-.'

'Garreth, do you still want to go out with me?' I said suddenly.

'What?' There followed a very pregnant silence on the other end of the phone because I didn't ask the question again.

Yes, of course I do! What's brought this on?'

Because Morwen's chasing the ugliest thing in the world! The hunters are in the forest!

'You just won't, soon, Garreth,' I said, 'that's all.'

'Oh, shut it, I think you're gorgeous! Just… be *careful!* I'll get back to you, Bethan, if I think I can help.'

Sadly, I ended the call, severing all links with the modern world, it seemed.

'If you will, you will,' I whispered.

The Book of Morwen

I felt my stride lose its tightness; my leg muscles relaxing. I walked onto the still-marshy ground in the shade of the first house and looked around me.

'GRAN?' I screamed.

After a while, I felt Bethan at my shoulder, clutching her mobile as if her life depended on it.

'We've got to search the whole village,' I said bleakly. 'We *know* she's here - maybe she's lying injured somewhere, or even… *look,* I'll go down the main street to the church and all those little houses; you go round the area of the manor house and follow the street right round. I'll meet up with you.'

I saw Bethan hesitate.

'Beth', I'm not trying to get rid of you. Do you want us to stay together?'

After a moment, Bethan shook her head. 'No, you're right. I know you're right! I think we'd better...'

Bethan let her voice trail off, allowing the sentence to go unfinished. She gave me a tight little smile and walked over to the empty gateway of the manor house. She watched me walk off alone.

Something bumped against my feet and I looked down at the humps and tussocks of weed. There was a crusted iron band, balefully sharp with something shining beside it. I looked behind me at Bethan as I bent to pick that shining thing up; she was staring at the manor house and then over at me: the sun seemed to be bouncing off the walls, baking the weed on the garden terraces, and even the shadows seemed hot.

Richard Thorns

PART III

HOW TO CATCH A SQUONK

All are not huntsmen who can blow the huntsman's horn.

> Rutherford/Banks. 1976.

Richard Thorns

Chapter Twenty

Blood and fire. And billows of smoke.

The Book of Bethan

I STOOD IN the manor house's empty gateway, watching Morwen as she tramped away down the main street, kicking away at the mist. At least, down what had once *been* a street, for now there was simply a mass of pale waterweed (lying dry and dead now). I could still see the faint outline of the road. I saw Morwen pause for a moment, turning over the crusted band of a half-buried cartwheel in a clump of weed, as if she had found something.

Richard Thorns

She *had* found something; I could see it winking in the sunshine as Morwen held it up to the sky. In the distance, I saw her walk over to a house as if sheltering from the sun beneath the great Tudor overhang, with its still-steaming frame.

I saw her lean her face tenderly against the wood.

Stretching out my arm, I looked at my hand. It was shaking hard. I turned away from Morwen and began walking slowly down the manor house path. Images from the grand ruined garden lay to my right and to my left: high walls; a baked and cracked stone fountain. The tiny corpse of a dead fish lay ahead of me on the stone path, dried in the sun.

Ahead of me, the great wooden doorway.

With my foot on a stone step, I pushed gently at the door and it swung open easily

(how easy was that? Should it have opened like that?).

I recoiled at the stench of must and baked weed and peered into the cavernous silence.

I saw a great room. At the end were patterned windows through which a sickly olive light gleamed. There was enough light to see by, I thought. Slowly, my eyes adjusted to the gloom and I tiptoed just inside.

'Nora?' I called softly.

The room was full of rotted oak panelling, and against a very few hung once-rich tapestries, now enormous rags that hung almost from the ceiling. It was a scene of utter devastation: the dark ramp of an oak table lay on its side, surrounded by overturned chairs. Here and there, darker pools of black told me the wooden floor had collapsed in places during the centuries spent beneath the lake. I went further into the room; my arms stretched out in front of me for obstacles, treading carefully on the floor, my eyes hard with terror.

'Morwen, come back!' I almost whimpered, as I moved towards a great casket shape at the back of the room. It was lying inanely half-in, half-out of splintered wooden floor panels. A faint wisp of mist curled lazily from the black gashes in the floor.

Moving forwards, my foot kicked a little golden cup which whirled around and banged against my other foot. A little scream escaped me, and I placed my hand against the ornate bannister of a staircase.

As if in answer to my scream I sensed a shuffle of movement from upstairs.

'Bethan,' whispered a voice from above.

Terrified, I turned my face upward, and almost cried with sheer relief.

'Nora!'

'You had absolutely *no* right to come here!' Nora hissed down the stairs at me. 'Where's Morwen?'

In Gravenhead, looking for you!' I stammered. 'Nora, I'm *so* glad to see you!'

'I can hardly say the same thing! Come on up, then, if you must. But DON'T step on the seventh stair: there isn't one!'

'Okay.' Trembling, I climbed the stairs, feeling the weight carefully under my feet, but the rest of the stairs held firm. Reaching the top, I wanted desperately to collapse into Nora's earthy same-ness, but something told me Nora was in no mood to hug me in return. I held back.

But then I felt Nora's arms suddenly around me, pulling me, nestling my head against a cotton cardigan that was spun in my modern and safe world. I felt my eyes prickle.

'Tears, Bethan?' came Nora's whispering voice in my ear, 'from my little heroine of the folly? Surely not!'

'You said in your note you might be able to help,' I said, wiping my eyes.

'Yes,' said Nora. She pointed down over the bannister to a large stone box that hung on the lip of shattered timbers below.

'You know what *that* is?'

I shook my head and said automatically: 'What's inside it?'

'Nothing - now. There *was* another wax-covered box inside it, though. Bethan, did you notice a rather large hole in the ceiling above you, when you were downstairs?'

I shook my head again.

'Well, the stone box must have fallen through the ceiling at some point and ended up down there. Hardly surprising, really; it must be incredibly heavy! And these floors and ceilings are all so rotten.'

'Where's the little wax box now?' I asked in a small voice.

Nora hesitated. 'There's a room along the corridor - it's the lightest in the manor house because there's a bay window with no weed on the glass. I think I'll be able to read the papers by the sunlight, you see. The thing is...'

'*What,* Nora,'

'You see, Bethan, I don't think you ought to come in there with me. But you understand there are things I - *we* - need to know. You see, there *is* another trap.'

I shook my head in the finality of terror, at the only thought relevant to me: 'No, Nora! I'm *not* staying out here on my own! Don't you *dare* abandon me!'

Nora hesitated again. 'Bethan… the Cowminster survivors are in there.'

'I don't care! I'll shut my eyes!'

'*No,* Bethan!' Nora was edging away from me, faint after only five steps in the gloom. I looked around the empty manor house and a terrible rush of panic seized me. I darted after her and seized one of her hands in both of mine.

'Nora, you don't understand; I can help you, you *need* me! You left the house early in the morning, didn't you, before the news came on. Do you know what's happening back in Rosengrave?'

I suddenly realized I had Nora's full attention.

'*What's* happening?'

'Louisa Caybourne's really sick,' I babbled, 'and so are lots of other people. Louisa's in hospital and they say there's something terrible happening there. And it all started with Louisa. They say it's some kind of a modern superbug.'

Richard Thorns

I stood shaking in the ruined manor house, all awash with dirty light, almost watching my words as they hit Nora. They *had* hit her... hard.

'No, it's not a superbug...' Nora was shaking her grey head silently in the gloomy manor house.

'Maybe it's a *pestilence,* a very old one,' Nora said softly, almost to herself.

Nora hesitated on the great Tudor landing for a moment and then, in the gloom, I saw her unwillingly pull her arm - and me – along the corridor.

'You shut your eyes then, Bethan, but *don't* shut them yet; this floor is full of holes!'

The Book of Morwen

In Gravenhead's deserted streets I leaned my face against warm wood. Tenderly, as if against the cheek of my only love.

Reluctantly, I drew my face away. There was not a breath of wind now, I noticed, as I began walking the forgotten village, not knowing quite what it was I might find. All around me, there was only the *then,* as opposed to the *now.* Behind me the basin sloped gently upward: it was where I had first run down to Gravenhead in my bright excitement with Bethan. I remembered us giggling like children in the sunshine. To my left lay the ruined tavern where I had once presented Bethan with her ale bottle.

Everywhere was old. Even my memories.

Turning away from the centre of the village, I wandered down a street that was new to me; tight with ruined shops on either side, with overhangs so close together that even the sun felt distant and cold and the timbers were still damp, stinking faintly of the lake. Signs for coopers and carp-mongers hung silently above my head, rusted and still. *Everywhere* was the litter of Gravenhead's abandonment: collapsed against a house was a tangle of old wood, just identifiable as the remains of a Tudor cart.

'Gran?' I whispered.

Behind me, I heard a voice, calling softly in reply. My heart seemed to soar.

In my mind, the Other Thing, the thing in the bathroom and in the park; that lurked in the part of my brain that had once known happiness, no longer said simply: *stay away!* It no longer hid behind my ambition; it was ambition and happiness itself.

'Morwen.'

It was not my grandmother's voice; I *remembered* that voice. My eyes filled suddenly with tears. It had been so long.

I nestled in the cool doorway of the carp-monger's shop. I felt almost cold in the street, as if everything I had ever wanted from Gravenhead would soon flood back to me; every sweet gift of fortune that Gravenhead had ever offered me winged in on the still, breeze-less air. At that moment, with my T-shirt getting wet from the wood and cooling me, and the lazy air circulating through the holes in the frame with my movement. In life, I arrived.

In the cool shade of the doorway, I murmured:

'Da?'

The Book of Bethan

Blinded by my shut eyes, I was fearful. I allowed myself to open them a tiny crack and immediately breathed deeply and fast. I could see the colour of Nora's cardigan, and I wanted to focus *only* on that as I finally, slowly, opened my eyes.

In the centre of the room, around a great hole in the floor sprawled the piled bones of two ancient, crumbling skeletons, still dressed in their dried rags. The yellow-brown bones looked like they'd been stained with weak gravy. I saw the remains of an ornate armchair, almost rotted away and within it sat a third; this one was barely more than a heap of bones. It was leaning forward to stare at me, as if in interest.

'Try not to be frightened, Bethan,' said Nora gently, 'they've been dead for hundreds of years: they can't hurt you.'

The room seemed to be held in a web of reverence. I nodded bleakly. 'I know who they are,' I said quietly. It was the last thing I wanted to do, but I tiptoed hesitantly, lightly up to the tumbled bones and reached between them. I already knew what I would find, and I was right: they were chained together.

'Chained, so nobody could run away,' I said, and I could feel emotion overwhelming me. 'Nora, these people aren't Cowminster's survivors as we know them, I'm sure of it; they're *descendants!*' I went over to the window, wondering if I could see the graves from this high up. I tugged *The Comely Flood* from my pocket and found my scrawls in blue at the back of the book.

I looked up at Nora, 'they're all out there, Nora: Edward Morton and Peter Fletcher,' *The Comely Flood* danced slightly in my hand, 'born of this parish. Cowminster.' I read on, my voice trembling as the truth of the room hit me gently. 'Lihsen Chen, "a visitor to these shores!" the final piece of the great harmonious Binding Mass. All dead, on 24th July 1476.'

'Christian doctrine meets Chinese geomancy,' said Nora softly. 'The great Binding Mass of Christ's dragon. What a very powerful Binding Mass it must have been.'

I nodded. 'And when that very powerful great Binding Mass… failed?'

'Some sixty years down the line? Gravenhead was buried here beneath waves, of course! Although Heaven alone knows how!'

'Well, we have to do what's right by them!' I said fiercely, wiping my face with the sleeve of my denim jacket, 'we *can't* let them down now!'

Richard Thorns

'Not for Morwen,' agreed Nora, tugging open the box. Pieces of ancient wax broke away and fell on the floor. She joined me at the bay window. The sunlight shone strongly through the glass, bathing Nora's old features and making them suddenly golden. I sat at the window, gazing over the basking village where every timbered outline met the sky; sharp lines against cloudless blue.

There was a single page in the box. Just one.

Nora placed her thumb firmly on the page and meant to scrabble, I think but then she stopped, as if she was saying to herself *No! It will break!* She looked at her hand. There was a tiny sheen of sweat on her palm. Smoothly, she placed the palm of her hand on the parchment. Her hand lifted.

It lifted:

Gravenhead

Nowe the Geomancere wille caſt hiſ ſtaffe over the Earthe to defyn the Dragon,. And Nowe the Earthe muſt be broken to bryng forth the united propheſy of Actſ throgh the Bleſſed wyſ of GOD. Yewe wille be ſhowne miracleſ in the Heavenſ above. And wonderſ on the Earthe below: Bloode and fyre and billoweſ of ſmoke. A tyme to dreame dreameſ, and ſee viſionſ.

Set out by the authority of the Kingſ Majeſty.
Richmond.

LONDON.

309

Richard Thorns

'*And...?*' I demanded.

'Bethan - I hate to say this, darling. That's it.'

'What do you mean? *No!* There *must* be more! Are those pages stuck together, Nora? Look in that box - just one more time!'

Nora shook her head silently and gazed out of the window. From the wooden bones of roof timbers the air shimmered, as if wet with heat haze, into the sky.

'It's so hot out there,' she murmured, almost to herself, 'but the sun's travelling fast overhead, Bethan. It's mid-afternoon; in a few hours it will be twilight. I think we're in very deep now. Maybe we should live to fight another day; do you want to go?'

I hesitated, looking around the room; the yellowed, ragged skeletons grinned silently back at me. I heard Nora studying the last page, muttering the words aloud to herself:

'The Earth must be broken. A time to dream dreams, and see visions.'

Stricken, I turned my face to the window. Beneath me, the village basked in the mid-afternoon sunshine. I gazed deep into the deserted, misty streets. My gaze travelled up the church walls. And then I saw something that made me catch my breath wordless in my throat!

The Book of Morwen

It was a voice that I'd almost forgotten, from secret drawers in forbidden dressers:

'Morwen!'

Alone, I gently replaced the churchyard gate. I looked at the deserted graves: nothing stirred or moved in the broiling heat.

Milk-and-nutmeg! Get a wriggle on!'

Well, that was reasonable enough, I thought: after all, the other time I'd remembered such detail (the old, long-lost name for myself) had been when I'd pushed my bike up the hill in early summer, ready to share my secret with Garreth. Yes, my Da had called me *milk-and-nutmeg* for my pale skin and faint scatter of freckles (and berry-brown now, I smiled a little at the memory). Had he always been here? After all, I remembered, *"Get a wriggle on!"* was his favourite expression for hurrying up.

'It's alright, Da,' I murmured.

Daughter barked the voice, *dream dreams!*

I frowned: *that* didn't sound like my Da. But then again, wasn't there a time when I thought that fathers knew... *everything!* So maybe he knew how I'd felt this summer when I'd dreamed: I'd been happy in brightness, observing as the sunlight had seared silver through the water. I frowned again: *had* he always been here? The dream in its glittering brightness; the figure I'd seen swimming steadily, so far down in the streets. I had so longingly wished it would look up, so I could only see its face.

I shook my head. Not the *then!* Only the *now!*

Richard Thorns

My shoulder pushed against the wooden door; my hands twisted the great iron ring.

The cool shade of the church was almost as I'd remembered it from before but there were *differences* this time: the faint gurgling of lake water from its ancient catch-hole had now stopped, I noticed, and the mist was now thick on the floor. I knelt down and the mist curled in my nostrils. It smelled of something in my memories: had there been carousels, or something? Anyway, it had been a nice day out, where faint hissing had filled the summer air; air that in patches where I had walked had smelled of chestnuts, and rain.

At my end of the aisle was the empty shaft room, where once bell ropes would have hung to the floor. It was very misty there and I moved away from it up the aisle...

(... I think it was a dream, because some dreams you know you'll never forget; still others come back in your memories much later when you've almost forgotten them, and this was both...)

...in my dream, music played as I walked shyly up the aisle of the ruined church clutching a posy of waterweed. The posy dripped lake water that ran over my hands and splashed over the floor; puffs of mist instantly spurted from between the stones. The church was packed full to bursting, and the skeletons in the pews nodded their approval and bobbed as if to get a better view of me; they nudged against one another as if in comment on my beauty as I now swam up the aisle (not walking), making my own current in the church; all Gravenhead, it seemed, had turned out for my reunion. One skeleton lolled back in a pew, its face upturned to the ceiling, its jaws agape, so I smiled at it.

It vanished in a plume of bubbles...

Every skeleton I looked at disappeared in front of my eyes, vanishing in a puff of bubbles. My first dream flowed into this one like lake water; for I had swum up the aisle, then, and I had turned and faced down those grinning horrors in my past as I knew I always would. They had vanished as, on the train back to Rosengrave, I woke up...

I woke up.

And I was walking (not swimming) up the aisle towards the altar and the forbidden barrier, and the church was empty as it had always been; my hand gently caressed a lump on the side of a pew. The three graven heads; three faces staring out from the wood, if I cared to look...

Instead, I kept my eyes on the shape that was now at my side of the barrier, motionless in the front pew.

The Book of Bethan

I gave a shrill cry of distress: 'The weathercock's moving!'

There had been no wind; I *knew* there was no wind! And, as if to prove it to me in the most ghastly way, the weathercock swung one way, and then the other. Sometimes flat and invisible it stared me out and then, slowly moving, formed the shape of the bird once again.

Richard Thorns

'Look at it go!' said Nora, 'how can it swing so easily on that ancient spindle in this terrible, still heat?' Then she jumped, wincing at the sudden pain in her arm: my fingernails were very sharp!

'Nora, *I* know why it's doing it,' I whispered, 'it's searching the earth for signs of negativity. It's trying to detect the earth currents and bring them into harmony. *It's trying to find the Melanchol!*' I turned from the window to look at Nora, my eyes wide with fear: 'don't you understand, Nora: *the weathercock is the Geomancer's compass!*'

'Well, it's been... successful,' said Nora slowly, 'because it's stopped moving.'

I followed Nora's pointing finger, almost begging myself to *please, please let me see the shape of the bird!* But then with dread I saw a single, thin line at the crest of the church. And when - my heart sinking - I heard a sound coming from just outside the room, it confirmed to me what I already knew; that the weathercock was pointing directly at the manor house.

Chapter Twenty one

A time to dream dreams, and see visions.

The Book of Morwen

IN THE church, the voice sounded very hollow in the church silence. It seemed to flutter and billow in my head.
My, Morwen! But you're all grown up now!
The figure in the front pew shifted slightly to its right, but did not as yet turn to greet me. I didn't need it to; there was all the time in the world now. I was rewarded by a tiny gesture of recognition made ahead of me; the fingers were

pale and so very long, I noticed, much longer than I remembered them.

I felt very calm, and smiled to myself, feeling pleased. I *was* grown up; my Da had just said so.

'But then you shouldn't really be so surprised,' I said. 'After all, I was only thirteen when you first left us. What are you doing here in Gravenhead?'

Well, but I'm here to say "well done" for being such a clever girl! I can't imagine how you managed to find Gravenhead all by yourself like this.

'Well, I did!' I said evenly. 'I'm still at Mam's; are you coming back with me today, Da?' I asked, 'I mean, I don't mind; I'd *like* you to.'

The dark shape in the pew gave a great sigh. It blew coldly through my mind.

I closed my eyes in sudden despair

(Da, what's wrong?)

and when I opened them, my Da was in the pulpit

(what's he doing there?)

holding up papers in his fingers, but *not* those old, esoteric sermons I'd stolen; Instead, I saw a newspaper headline:
"THAT'S THE WAY THE COOKIE CRUMBLES!"

Morwen, Gravenhead is so very old, and so precious. You'll be well rewarded for your discovery! You'll be rich! If I were to come back, perhaps people will think it's only because of the money.

'Oh, Da, is that *all?*' I exclaimed, my eyes shining, *'please* don't worry; you see, I *knew* it would be like this!

'You see,' I said, trembling with sudden joy, 'you read about it in the papers all the time: about people who are abandoned and then they go on to really, *really* make something of their lives and get rich! And then - I began to notice - the person who left always wants to get back in touch. And they *always* say the money doesn't matter! I know this because I kept the cuttings underneath my bed,' I ended in triumph, my heart singing. I spoke with finality, and wisdom.

'I was *right,* you see, Da,' I said firmly, 'it's going to be alright!'

So if you close your eyes, will our future together… be like this?

I did as I was told, and then smiled as the blackness behind my eyes turned steadily to orange. I opened my eyes, and gasped with joy:

All around me was… *colour!* I looked at the backs of my hands; Dancing pieces of mauve, green and red; rich shades of blue. They seemed to move as I moved my hands. *Motionless* colour, then; not moving in itself. And then I saw that the colour was coming from the beautiful, completed stained glass of the great window. I smelled the cool scent of flowers around the church; my hands caressed the rich, shining wood of the pews.

Richard Thorns

Gravenhead was... new again. No, not just new *again;* it was as if it had never been old in the first place...

All around me there was only the *now,* not the *then.*

Like my memories.

The Book of Bethan

In the manor house, I tore my gaze away from the window. The thin, iron line of the weathercock hung in the heat. I heard the noise increasing - a scrabbling, shuffling, almost dragging sound outside the door. And then... a *tapping.*

'It's *found* us, it's outside the door!' I whimpered.

Nora nodded in agreement. 'Try to keep calm, Bethan,' she said quietly. She kept her eyes firmly on the closed door, waiting for the moment it would swing idly open, and what lay on the other side...

'This may well be very awful, darling,' she whispered to me, 'when the door opens and it comes in, I want you to dodge around it and run, do you understand?'

'No,' I said in a tiny voice, 'What about *you,* Nora?' I felt Nora's old hands gripping my own very tightly.

'*Listen!* If that Gravenhead creature is here it means it's not with Morwen and she's safe! Now, do as I say! I'm an old lady. You have to leave me and find her, Bethan! You have to run away from here and never come back again. *Do you understand!*'

'No! What about *you?*' I squeaked again. 'We can - *Nora!*'

Nora had crossed the room and was edging past the skeletons. She turned around and looked at my terrified face, placing an old finger to her lips.

'It's not coming in' she mouthed to me.

The door was closed, but the scuffling, tapping sound continued.

'What do we do?' I mouthed.

Nora mouthed back: *'We wait!'*

The Book of Morwen

We talked and talked. There was such a lot to remember, and to plan for. It didn't matter. In the church, I felt so very safe now.

'It's beautiful,' I murmured, glancing around me. What a pity, I thought, that there was so much mist around. And on such a lovely day like today!

'But, Da,' I said, puzzled, 'I don't understand: when the *Titanic* was found it was just a heap of iron and rust, and Gravenhead's five times older but... it's perfect! Gravenhead's just... it shouldn't *be* like this!'

Da nodded, grinning down at me from the pulpit; lake water welled up from beneath the collar of his shirt.

Richard Thorns

Ask away, darling. After all, in the Book of Books, on the road to Emmaus in answer to the questioning of Cleopas…did not our saviour (I thought I heard contempt in his voice) *beginning at Moses and all the prophets, expound all the mysteries of the Scriptures?*

'Well…' I said, trembling, 'the water, just evaporating in the sunshine like that,' But Da was beginning to talk fast (just like he'd done when I'd once dropped a chocolate milkshake in the car).

You have heard it said that the teachings of the Son of Man lead the way to the New Life. I tell you the truth; condemned shall be the meek, for the Earth shall not be their inheritance; condemned shall be the peacemakers; they shall know the true meaning of darkness

'Da… the way the water went, and the *mist* here!' I stammered, 'it should be all burned off by nine.'

But my Da was lost to me: *Condemned shall be those who mourn; condemned shall be those who are pure in spirit*

'Da, please… the mist?' I whispered.

All shall be cond-

Da had stopped abruptly and was gazing down at me from the pulpit. It was true that my mouth had turned down in disappointment and my smile had gone, but surely it was what I'd *said*, I thought. Da was staring at me, as if he didn't understand me. He flicked smoothly out of my vision and was standing at the foot of the pulpit and holding out his arms to embrace me. The voice in my head was very cold. But *that* didn't matter.

Morwen! This is the end of all mystery; this *is the road to Emmaus! Come and give your old man a hug*

The Book of Bethan

'*Don't... think* about doing that, Bethan!' Nora whispered fiercely.

I drew my eyes away from the shattered hole in the floor. The stone box lay beneath me. How far down was it? Maybe five or ten metres? If I aimed for it, maybe it could break my fall, but it wasn't the drop that frightened me: all around the stone casket I could see shattered timbers around a great dark hole, which meant I could *fall into the manor house's great dark cellars.*

I shuddered. 'I wasn't going to,' I said, drawing away.

And as I did so, my eyes drew back to something far below. It was gone in an instant but it was so fast, and so very black. I had seen it before, on Morwen's little innocent summer project. Camcorder footage.

And that tapping on the door sounded like

Pecking.

I inched the door open a fraction. Outside on the ruined landing, the very floor itself seemed to moving with black shapes. Beady yellow eyes, lots of them, staring at me in the gloom.

Crows! The rotted floor was a black feathered carpet. Moving.

Slamming the door, I turned to Nora as I tugged up a piece of wood, placed it firmly at the foot of the door and kicked hard.

'Oh, that thing's so sharp!' I said grimly. 'It isn't interested in us; it's not even here! It wants *Morwen!*'

I ran across the room to the bay window, and peered out. The drop was high. *That rutted earth was like steel!* Nora had once told me. And didn't she say that this summer was even hotter? Well, the manor house was surrounded by the shade of its own high walls. Did that mean the ground was still soft?

Pushing open the window, I edged my way out and sat trembling on the rim. There was only one way to find out, I thought. And if the earth *was* rock hard? Well, I couldn't run very fast - or far - with broken legs. It would be over soon enough then.

I hesitated, and then launched myself out of the great bay window into blue, open space.

The Book of Morwen

I felt myself take a slow, single step forwards, towards Da, as he simply waited for me at the barrier.

I couldn't understand why I wasn't running; was there something there in my head saying: *don't be so silly?* But then the warmth of that caring, watchful thought that I'd found for myself drained as I walked towards my Da for my reunion hug, like lake water that starts off warm and then goes cool as you start your dive, and then it just ends up cold. Yes. It was cold now:

Get a wriggle on!

'I thought I'd lost you,' I murmured. 'After I lied to Louisa I thought everything would always carry on at the house as normal, only it hasn't been normal with you gone.'

I laughed a little, suddenly. 'It's been such a long time, you see,' I said as if by way of explaining, 'I'd forgotten how *tall* you were.'

The Book of Bethan

I landed heavily on the marshy ground and rolled quickly over so my legs wouldn't take the full force of my drop. I scrambled up, holding my aching ribs. I'd dropped my mobile and I stuffed it quickly back into my jacket. I then allowed myself a brief look up at the window, and I shuddered: Nora's face, staring down at me, was horribly high up.

Then I turned and bolted through the ruined garden, shooting through the gateless entrance to the manor house. I paused in the main street, looking around the deserted village. To my left, the basin reared up towards green, leafy trees. I turned to my right and began running - and then fell heavily in the weedy street.

This hurts more than the jump from the window, I thought. My *leg* hurt! I sat down and tugged up the right leg of my jeans, wiping at a huge smear of blood from a long, welling graze almost cut out of my shin.

Could I see the bone? Possibly! My eyes filled with tears.

I had run straight into the iron cartwheel band, hidden in the mist and half-buried by clumps of weed. I wiped quickly at the ghastly flap of skin and blood, and instantly it welled again. Faintly, I remembered Nora's words:

'You've never seen blood like it.'

Tugging at the cartwheel band, I teased and worried it desperately in my hands, and suddenly the iron SNAPPED, leaving me with a sliver of sharp, slightly crumbling iron in my hand.

It would do! Rubbing at my eyes, I dragged myself up on my feet and began half-running, half-limping down the main street, my glance darting down side streets drifting with heavy mist. All ruined. *Worse!* All empty.

I reached the outskirts of the village green and then collapsed, gasping for breath against a dry stone wall. Desperately, my gaze searched the village. *Nothing!* I realized my hair was heavy and matted and I smeared it out of my eyes.

'MORWEN!' I screamed. My voice seemed to bounce back from the empty sockets of houses:

'MORWEN!'

A faint ringing sound, from inside my jacket. Snatching out my mobile, I stabbed at a button:

'Morwen, where are you?' I said. And then I remembered: Morwen didn't *have* a phone; she had borrowed mine on the train:

'Bethan, it's *Garreth!* Listen, are you out of that village yet?'

'What do *you* think?' I said, my mouth turning down, 'the mist's making it so hard to look for anything! And I can't find Morwen!'

'Bethan-'

(Morwen! This is the last thing I can give you!)

'I've met someone else,' I gabbled, 'I've been seeing someone else! You have to go out with Morwen instead; she loves you!'

'Bethan! Shut up and get the hell out of there!'

Shocked out of my hysteria, I began: 'What do you-"

'*Listen!* Remember the Llancellwyn fire? *It never went out,* Bethan - they just let it burn. Those coal seams have been smouldering under the ground for years!'

Tearfully, I asked: 'Why are you telling me this?'

'Because this summer must've cracked open the earth and opened up the seams, Bethan! That lake never evaporated this summer, it *drained!* It's in the burning galleries!'

Richard Thorns

In an instant, I understood. I remembered Garreth's tale of coal so strangely near the surface; the fast, unnatural "evaporation" of the lake even in this slow, unnatural summer. And - worst of all - the mist which even the sun couldn't burn off...

The Earth must be broken...

'*No!*' I whimpered, as I realized what Garreth was going to say next - even as he almost yelled it at me through the mobile:

'Bethan! You have to get out of there *now!* Gravenhead's going to blow itself to pieces! That's *not* mist, it's-'

I whispered:

'Steam.'

Chapter Twenty two

The death of the squonk.

The Book of Bethan (cont'd)

I FLUNG my arm against the rotted wooden door and ran headlong into the church. At a single glance I took in the scene: the stinking, ruinous decay of the interior; steam billowing from the bell room. Morwen in the aisle facing the shambling horror so near to her.

Running down the church's centre aisle, I grabbed Morwen's arm and half-pulled, half-dragged her back towards the door.

Richard Thorns

'*Morwen!*' I screamed in her ear. 'Get away from it!'

'You're *here,* then, Bethan?' Morwen murmured, squirming in my grip, 'Beth', the summer project's nearly finished. And my Da's here again after all this time and just look at the church! *It's* finished! Isn't it all just wonderful?'

'Morwen,' I panted hoarsely, pulling at her, 'whatever it is you think you're looking at - it's not your Da!'

Morwen, sighing and frowning a little in irritation, as she tried to get away. I heard a terrible hiss echo around the church. Was it from the steam or from the mouth of the being? I didn't know.

I looked down at my fingernails.

'Oh, hell,' I muttered under my breath.

Wincing, I drew a long, raking line down Morwen's bare arm.

'OW! You BITCH! What did you do *that* for?'

Morwen was standing looking at me in dismay, her face twisted in pain and rubbing at livid red stripes on her forearm. But I saw a slight warm flush appearing on her face.

'*Look*, Morwen!' I snapped, spinning her around.

I thought Morwen was going to drop dead on the spot, such was her scream at what she could now see. Standing directly in front of us, I thought I could make out rags fluttering slightly as if it truly had *stepped from air.* I sensed for the first time the spaces between the dimensions, where black winds from the past howled...

Morwen looked swiftly at me as I dully slashed my piece of cartwheel band.

'Bethan!' breathed Morwen, 'Get yourself out of here! *Run!*'

Child! You place yourself in the hands of such a one as this, the cold voice sneered. A thin arm stretched slowly outwards; a ghastly finger pointed directly at me. *One whose only loyalty was to herself and to the friends she hoped to win. It was* she *who made you flee the school... She was there!*

I glanced at her in utter terror; Morwen's mouth was forming a hard, flat line:

A pear orchard! In which the first screams of laughter and first-born names begin to be borne onto the wind to fly after her. And Morwen's face rushing, rushing *away from the orchard to be found, cowering and battered in front of a grocer's shop, staring to the very fringes of the crowd. Then fleeing towards the house with the door as red as blood.*

I felt pinned like a moth; the finger pointed unwaveringly at me:

She was there!

Found out at last, I stared at the shambling ruin. And what made my eyes fill with tears so much was how alike, how un-beautiful we both were!

Richard Thorns

And this time there were no summer-child cotton bracelets to hide behind; no crowd to stand at the back of; no place even in the forest to hide in anymore! There was only the three of us now: Morwen, me, and my monster. So I parted my arms in a gesture as, in my mind I parted the bracken of my hiding-place, and I at last stepped out to face Morwen, the hunter who was always going to find me. So her story was true, I thought: a squonk *is* the ugliest thing in the world; squonks do go to pieces, they *do* collapse in a pool of tears when faced with their own ugliness; cornered, and caught.

'Morwen,' I found myself sobbing desperately, 'it was because I was friends with Cathy Searle! They should all have been expelled!'

I remembered Morwen handing over a magazine to me, such a long time ago in the summer:

'Something to say thanks for being my friend, Bethan… just so you know I appreciated it.'

(My eyes filling with sudden tears as I sat beside her on her bed)

Bethan, are you okay?

Dear God, they're going to fracture her skull.

There's something on the tape!

Filmed on mobiles; posted on the internet, the monster caught on film and the bright celluloid of film shone straight back at me. It illuminated my ugliness like a mirror.

But Morwen by contrast was facing that ugly shape right down! And at last - at long, *long* last I could see that *wretched* dark determination fade, for she at last seemed without fear. Her lips triumphantly moved silently: I could... *see* her words going back, calm and reasoning:

'Yes! She was there! And this meant that later, much later, she knew how to find my Grandmother!'

Morwen turned around to face me.

'Beth',' she said to me gently, 'you can let it go now.'

I heard my own voice in the gloom of the church. It was the voice of an unnatural stranger to me; thick, my throat drying and closing with shame.

'You knew all along?' I blinked. 'You saw me there... in that crowd?'

Morwen nodded. 'I always knew you weren't really involved, Bethan,' she said a little quietly. 'It's alright.'

She tugged me back, preparing to run. And then she stopped.

Morwen smiled at me.

'Listen ' she said suddenly.

Muffled music beginning to ring, but without tone and colour. So old, the very music fossilized; the ghastly notes pealing and ringing out all over Gravenhead; as if smothered in earth instead of sky.

'The bell's ringing properly at last, Beth',' Morwen said. She smiled at me again.

'Now we have to leave,' she said.

She held out her hand to me, and I took it. Morwen tugged me along the aisle. I clutched her hand tightly as we ran harder.

I heard Morwen moan, 'Oh, no!'

Why is the lavender-light getting smaller it should be getting bigger it-

'The door's closing!' Morwen screamed back at me. She stopped abruptly and flung herself back into me. My feet skidded on the slime beneath my trainers and I nearly fell.

'*Quickly,* Beth'!' Morwen whispered to me.

She darted to her left in between the pews and settled down on the floor. I retched at the weed and slime beneath me as I joined her. I felt trapped in a living bad dream; the stink of decay in my nose and my mouth, and steam hissing in my ears. And the sight of something standing by the barrier, looking intently into the steam.

The overall light in the church seemed to be fading slightly, and I wondered why…

But, I thought later, it was obvious, really; there was a muffled BANG in my ears, as the door of the church finally closed.

PART IV

THE SCARS OF PRIVATE VICTORY

Here I am, I'm very fierce and frightening
I've come to match my skill to yours

Rutherford/Banks. 1976.

Richard Thorns

Chapter Twenty three

The Paintings in the Church (part 2)

The Book of Morwen

'LOOK WHAT you did to my arm,' I whispered to Bethan. I showed it to her, and Bethan had the tact to wince when she saw the red stripes of her handiwork.

'Sorry,' she whispered, 'but what did you expect! You were nearly toast!'

I nodded. 'Yeah, and thanks, Beth'. I guess that makes us quits.'

But Bethan's big grey eyes were widening and I followed her gaze to the front of the church; the Melanchol was staring into the steam, half-hidden, and beginning to pace and shuffle. It was moving slowly, as if the last pieces of the crumbling Great Binding Mass still remained; still holding it in its grip.

I frowned. My mind, that lyrical, objective mind of mine that I had; that had worked out that a *mead* was really a *meadow*, unlocking the mysteries of Keats (so long ago it seemed now); it could be my own saving weapon. It couldn't desert me now.

'Gran was on to something with those sermons,' I whispered to Bethan.

'I know, but you'd better think of something soon, because we're sitting on the biggest kettle in Wales! And that thing's beginning to move!'

I nodded, my eyes fixing on it as it stood in front of the barrier. Behind it, I saw the last of those paintings on the wall; the three beams of light illuminating the arms and hands of the being, as it came out of the ground.

'Any luck with that Bible?' I whispered to Bethan.

She nodded.

'Garreth called me,' she said, and for some reason this made her look very upset and her mouth turned down. She took a deep, shuddering breath:

'He said the Book of Acts was pretty clear in the Bible. "In the last days there will be… blood, fire and plumes of smoke, or something…"' She frowned at me, trying to remember, 'dreaming dreams and seeing visions; something about miracles in the sky above, and wonders on the earth below *hang* on a minute!'

'What is it?' I whispered.

'Nora found another sermon, Morwen. She found it in a stone box in the manor house.'

'As you do,' I whispered to her.

'Morwen, the sermon said the earth must be broken and the summer's already done that. But this smoky, fiery blood-thing in Acts Morwen, there *is* a fire under us: it's in the old coal seams where the lake went, and it's steam now!' Her eyes widened. 'Well, Morwen, steam's a kind of smoke isn't it? *I* know why the Llancellwyn fire started all those years ago; I think it started… *to prepare for this summer!*

Slowly, I nodded, and sat there in the filth and decay with Bethan beside me, staring at the Melanchol.

The Book of Morwen (cont'd)

The deafening roar of an escaping gust of steam behind me made me look quickly, and what I saw gave me my answer, although not immediately. Instead, the truth hit me gently as if in slow-motion, like eyes getting accustomed to gloom. I stared at the steam escaping from weakened flagstones and rotted wooden floors that seemed to be bending with pressure; the steam curled skywards towards… *miracles?*

Straight ahead of me, the carvings on the end of the pew opposite me stared me out; three tiny wooden faces, with their wisdom captured in their miniature wooden eyes.

Behind the being, the three white beams of light bathing the thing creeping out of the ground.

'Except it's *not* coming out of the ground,' I said. Morwen?'

Awkwardly, I said: 'it's going *in!* The Earth must be broken!'

Nora had come so close to working it out! I could almost see those notes of hers staring up at me! What was it she'd written?

"Three lights are shining on something coming out of the ground. Or are they?"

'It isn't coming *out* of the ground, Bethan, the three lights are killing it and *ow!* Will you stop *doing* that!'

'Sorry,' Bethan said excitedly, drawing in her fingernails, 'but there were three skeletons in the manor house. *Three!*'

'Three,' I repeated slowly, nodding and thinking of Nora making up our number, everything falling into place and confirming, 'three graves, and listen to that bell trying to ring! The Earth must be broken. Beth"

She stared at me.

'It's *already* broken! What can-'

'It's not properly broken *yet*, Beth',' I said to her, as I pointed over her head towards the belfry.

'Miracles in the heavens above,' I continued. 'Wonders on the earth below! We have to get into that belfry, Bethan, and climb!'

The Book of Bethan

Morwen tugged me towards the billows of steam from the bell room. And then we were standing there in the tiny square room, Morwen gently holding my face and turning it skywards. Through the shattered timbers, way up, I could see the flickering shadow of the weathercock against blue, as it began to tremble on the spindle.

'*It knows us,*' Morwen said simply to me. She shook her head suddenly.

'*Help me,* Beth'!' she commanded, as she ran to the side of the bell room, and stood beneath rotted, wooden stairs; the bottom step arched above our heads.

I watched as Morwen jumped and swung on the bottom stair and, gasping, hauled herself up. Crouching on the steps she stretched down a hand to me imploringly:

'There's no *time*, Beth',' she pleaded. 'Come on up!'

I knew I was smaller than Morwen, and the thought of jumping and clawing and grabbing nothing but air swam in my mind. But then the flicker of a ragged shape at the entrance to the bell room made me scream in sudden terror, and I leapt skywards with a strength that *surely*, I thought almost dreamily, I should never have had.

Hauling myself up onto the stairs, I looked up at Morwen and scrambled upwards to join her. We both began kicking at the wood and stamping hard.

The wood cracked and splintered. And... *dropped.*

I *heard* it roar as it fell - a great chunk of steps as the wood parted from the main staircase and dropped under our feet. It landed with a dull BANG on the floor, hidden by the Gravenhead mist.

We're safe I thought, squatting on the steps and gazing at the drop beneath us: *We're safe we're safe we're stuck we're STUCK! We're TRAPPED!*

I looked at Morwen. She was looking up the staircase. Upwards, to the sky...

The Book of Bethan (cont'd)

At the top of the stairs the belfry was as hot and as dusty as a corn attic. I was first to pass the still-vibrating bell. And then, what hit me the *most* as I leaned out of the belfry window was the warmth - the great blueness of the summer sky.

We seemed almost a part *of* the sky! I drew a deep, shuddering breath; we were sickeningly high up. Even the manor house seemed small below me. Craning my neck upward I saw the steeple above me, its weathercock much nearer to me now. I instantly took in its ugliness - the weedy iron, the scowling beak in the shape of a great letter "C".

Morwen had known what to do all along, I thought thankfully: the sloping church roof descended almost to the ground. But it was going to be very hard to get down because in places there was *nothing at all,* only the remains of slates and timbers stretching over precarious gaps. But it was possible-

'*Bethan!* Don't just stand there admiring the view!'

This isn't what you had in mind! I pulled my head in from the window and looked behind me.

Morwen was standing in the middle of the belfry, level with the dome of the great iron bell and staring thoughtfully at it. She reached above it and, stretching as far as she could without falling down the giant shaft, she touched the enormous black rope from which the bell was still suspended; her fingers could just brush it. The thick, black plait seemed as hard as iron.

'We can get down the roof to the ground,' I said. 'Aren't you coming?'

Morwen shook her head as she turned around. 'No, you go, Bethan,' she said to me. 'You can help me if you like, or you can leave, but I'm staying. The earth must be broken.'

'Morwen, how can you-?'

But Morwen was looking steadily at me, raising her eyebrows. Silently, I handed over my rusted piece of cartwheel band into Morwen's outstretched hand.

'If you're staying too, just hang on to me then, Beth',' she warned, 'I'm far away from the bell and the rope in this shaft; I don't want to fall!'

Leaning over the chasm of the shaft, and sensing my tight grip on her and almost blinded by the rising steam, Morwen slowly, carefully, began to saw away at the rope.

The Book of Morwen

Leaning over to help me, I think it was Bethan who saw it first...

The steam gapped and rolled, billowing in the shaft. Below us, a faint figure appeared on the far side of the belfry shaft, directly opposite us both. Slowly placing one hand above the other, it wasn't clinging or holding on. Just slowly ascending and... *sticking!*

'It's climbing up the wall!' yelled Bethan in my ear.

'I can see it,' I said grimly. 'I'm almost through.'

I was! The black, iron-like rope was fraying badly and the bell was sagging at a strange angle. Surely soon its weight would help us... *surely!*

Bethan screamed over my shoulder as, about a metre below us we saw one hand leave the wall *and then the other hand!* The shape was stuck to the wall and looking up at us.

It moved out from the dark shadow of the belfry wall and I stared clearly into its face at last. It matched the face in the photo by my bedside, and those in the drawer downstairs, but I thought instantly of Dickens's horrific depictions of Ignorance and Want, but this was far, far worse because this was a face that I *knew*, but Need had hardened the eyes, and Guilt had hollowed the cheeks, and Greed had narrowed the eyelids, and Weakness had turned down the mouth, and Stupidity had slackened the jaw, and stick-like arms and hands like claws were stretched upwards towards me, waving in the thin air:

'Don't fall out of the tree,' it gibbered up at me. *'I'll catch you if you do!'*

A hand, almost hidden by steam gripped the side of the bell and my vision filled up with black iron as it swung towards my face, hitting my protective arms. I fell back, gasping, knowing that the cartwheel-band had left my fingers: it was spiralling down into the shaft, and lost forever.

It's the end!

I knew it was the end, because that one single hand that gripped the bell tugged, and the face was now at my level, staring at us both. I felt its gaze on me as I decided my last thought: I would be remembered by my camcorder footage;

shown living in the world and known-about, working on my project beside a lake as flat as glass.

I felt a fluster next to me:

Barging past me, Bethan leaned forwards and took hold of the great black rope above the bell. Stupidly, a rhyme floated into my mind: *you're small; you'll fall!* Instinctively I hung tightly onto her legs as I watched her hands find the frayed, ultra-thin part of the rope.

She pulled... *hard!*

The ancient rope shattered like pitch as it parted. I think Bethan forgot to let go with her huge recoil forwards, so I tugged at her with all my strength. I heard her land in a heap on the floor behind me, but there were terrible crashes coming from inside the shaft, so I steadied my balance and gazed below:

The bell bounced off the walls before slamming into the wooden boards with a shattering roar. And suddenly it seemed that all the steam there had ever been in Gravenhead, billowing up from the tavern, the shops and the starburst, had instantly darted *backwards* into the crumbled stones and rotted floors; earth-fissures and holes, and was fleeing gleefully towards the great pressurised chimney. I saw the dull red flash of fire. Forcing myself to look, I stared far below...

In the steam, *something* was scrabbling for life. It looked briefly up at me, and the face I knew had disappeared. I felt only its great age overwhelming me. It felt older than the mines and the first origins of Rosengrave, and far older than Gravenhead. Its past travelled backwards inside of me, way past Cowminster and even beyond Middenwich; it felt as old as Neolithic ley lines and dynastic Chinese dragon currents. But I knew that it was dying. A thin arm was locked at the very edge of the chasm and then… was it the heat and the steam spinning my head, or was there something else there with it in the church? I surely could *not* see three gorgeous, beautiful white bolts of light suddenly lunge at the wooden floor (although I would later swear I saw boards and flagstones break, and rotted timbers fly up). The arm disappeared from my sight as the Llancellwyn fire *pounced*, firing a bright scarlet before my eyes, before fading slowly to grey...

After nearly seventy years, it's burning itself out...

And then to a deeper grey...

Burning out!

The roaring *whoosh* of escaping steam around my head began to fade...

Burned out!

To black. Blackness in the depths of the shaft. And then silence.

There was complete silence.

Trembling, I felt a hand gently placed on my shoulder, and I turned around: Bethan was standing there, her bright orange *Miss Behave* top and her favourite jacket filthy and ruined; her blonde hair still matted from her run.

Bethan, for her part would have seen *my* face, filthy and grimed with grit and steamed coal-smoke staring right back at her. I felt my face break suddenly into a smile... *almost.* My teeth probably seemed so white to her.

'It is... *over*, then?' Bethan asked me hopefully, her voice small.

She watched me cross the belfry floor to stare out of the window. I held up a hand in the sudden, aching silence as if to say: *don't say anything!*

I stared out over Gravenhead, as if listening for something. Suddenly seemingly afraid of the silence, Bethan joined me but *her* eyes travelled upward: the weathercock was just above her head on its spindle. For the first time we could see every detail: the rusted, silt-caked feathers and its scowling beak... Bethan flinched in the warm afternoon air. And then she realized I was speaking to her. She turned to look at me:

'Don't be afraid of the weathercock, Bethan. After all...' I was saying gravely to her at the window. The last wisps of steam billowed and gapped around us.

'After all, you *knew* you'd be shown miracles in the heavens above,' I said simply.

Reaching out, I snatched at Bethan's hand and held it up. There were reddish-brown smears on her fingers that were still a little sticky from the deep, bloody graze on her shin.

'And wonders on the earth below, Beth',' I continued, turning back to the window. 'Blood and fire, and billows of smoke.'

I remembered next door's barbecue, spitting out its fire and drifting its smoke all over our back garden: my mosquito collecting its *found you out* slap, leaving far too much blood for its own body. It seemed an age of summers ago that I'd sensed innocence, then, and sunlight, but also an ancient evolution to be respected and somehow feared. A little memory of the future, it had seemed.

My teeth squeezed my lip suddenly. The pain made me come back.

It's only a tiny little passage in Acts, but it killed it! Oh, wow! How many more are there?

'Yes,' I said after a moment, turning to look at Bethan. 'I think it *is* over, Beth'!'

I smiled broadly, suddenly: 'How do you think I know? *Listen!*'

Gravenhead basked serenely below us in the basin. Far off, in the warmth of the late afternoon sun, indistinctly, perhaps even hesitantly, a blackbird had begun to sing.

The Book of Morwen (cont'd)

We stood in the remains of the manor house garden, Bethan lazily stroking the bowl of the cracked fountain (still a little warm from the day's sunshine), imagining water. I waited patiently in front of the great wooden door, expecting gran at any moment.

Suddenly, we heard a terrible scream from inside the manor house.

I dashed inside, my eyes taking in the ruined interior for the first time: the great stone box at the rear of the enormous room, the huge rags of tapestries hanging in the gloom, all the way from the ceiling:

'GRAN!' I screamed.

I heard a dull picking from beneath the staircase as Bethan joined me in the room. Helplessly, I watched in dismay as two filthy arms with clawed-over hands reached out from the darkness, and then a shape hauled itself painfully into what light there was:

'I forgot about the seventh stair,' gran said to me. 'Bethan knows what I'm talking about, don't you, Bethan!'

The Book of Morwen (cont'd)

A starling scooted fast over Gravenhead, winging its way through the silent streets. The village was taking on the golden hue of a russet apple as the sun began to arch and sink towards the trees, as if marking the end of summer itself.

Marking the end of summer itself! I noticed Bethan was limping badly, trying to remove the weight from her right leg. And then I felt a gentle pull on my arm as gran let Bethan totter unknowingly on towards the incline.

Gran took me gently to one side, in front of the tavern.

'The book of Revelation tells of deathly angels cast into a lake of fire,' she said quietly to me. 'Morwen, you have many thousands of years of history - not just Christian history - to look after you now.

'Try not to dream of it,' she said, 'if that's possible. It's dead, Morwen.'

'Gran,' I answered earnestly, 'do you remember when I first played the video of my discovery? When I thought it hadn't even come out and that I'd failed even at that? I feel the same now.'

'That you've *failed*, Morwen?'

'Yes,' I said, 'I do feel like that.'

I felt her eyes resting on the tiny scar on my elbow, for it was a livid white over my brown skin. I thought of Gran's elbows, and of Bethan's lacerated shin: the scars of private victory. *But what have I done?* I thought, faintly surprising myself by even thinking about it now: *All I did was fall out of an apple tree in the back garden, when I was six.*

(I'll catch you if you do)

Yes, gran's old eyes were *definitely* looking at my little scar.

"That fierce determination of yours, Morwen," she murmured, as if to herself even though she had used my name, "did you somehow know, even back then, how useless he was going to be to you?

'You know your Da is never going to come back, don't you, Morwen,' she said, suddenly.

I nodded.

Nora tramped off. 'Then go to university! Make your Mam as happy for you as I am!'

The Book of Morwen (cont'd)

They were walking ahead of me. Gran (a little guiltily, I thought) was clutching an ale bottle just like Bethan's one. Bethan paused in the shadows of the last house, staring at the rearing slide of the basin. She *phlumphed* herself down, sitting on the dry earth - as if to put off her climb, and seemed grateful for my slow steps.

'Get a wriggle on, Morwen,' she called out to me.

I caught her up.

'Beth',' I said, 'will you do something for me; as a favour?'

Bethan raised her eyebrows at me (gran took a sudden interest in the walls of a nearby house).

I said: 'I may not be too good to be with for a while. Just, please don't use that phrase on me again because it reminds me… don't think I'm having a go at you because I'm not! I'd just like it, that's all.'

Bethan nodded, wondering if she'd-

'No, you haven't upset me, Beth'. I think… maybe just the opposite, if you only had the slightest idea. But you haven't.'

Bethan shrugged (a little chastened by my words), and hauled herself up, ready to climb the basin. I watched as she promptly tore the knee out of her jeans on a rock. An unknown thought – oh, it felt so *old!* - floated gently into my mind:

He tried to pick me up; I pushed him away.

I turned my back so that Bethan, mourning her torn jeans, wouldn't get the wrong idea from my smile. The village wallowed in the late afternoon sunshine, the heat haze quite gone now. Leaving something behind in its wake... I didn't know *quite* what it was, as I examined that tiny, white scar on my elbow. All I knew was that, for the first time in centuries it seemed, the poison of the past had been drawn. I felt my village at peace.

Richard Thorns

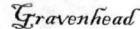

PART V

DELICIOUS AND VAGABOND

Listen here, you listen to me don't you run away now.

Rutherford/Banks. 1976.

Richard Thorns

Epilogue

The last secret

August – two years later.

The Book of the Squonk

P.N. CLARKE'S Visitor Centre seems very out of place in the shady forest with its leaf litter and acorn cases. Anyone who goes there is greeted by revolving plastic slide-holders (illuminated from the rear), books and postcards. And guides, glossy and neatly folded.

The guide tells you that the steep basin slope of gritty clay has now been smartly cut away into steps, but it warns that the climb is not suitable for everyone.

In Gravenhead itself, the route marked in RED indicates the areas restored to Tudor glory: the church, the manor house and the tavern, whereas the routes marked in BLUE shows you what Gravenhead must have been like before its discovery, because the village lies silent and ruined there. In fact, most of the areas are on blue routes; Gravenhead in the raw, but the visitor feels the wonder of its discovery this way.

I *like* it this way.

I was sitting on the edge of the village green with Bethan; her eyes were scanning the guide. It was a bleak, scudding August day, promising rain:

"'Gravenhead's Visitor Centre is named after Professor P.N.Clarke, an amateur diver, historian, and author of: *The Comely Flood,* who first discovered Gravenhead in the summer of 2006,'" I read aloud over Bethan's shoulder, "'we know this from the discovery of a watch inscribed with his initials, in Gravenhead's main street.

"'Unfortunately, Professor Clarke did not survive to see his magnificent example of Tudor life resurrected in the modern world, or witness Gravenhead awarded UNESCO status as a site of world historical importance.'"

'Fair enough, but I *still* think you were mad,' Bethan said to me, 'why did you just give it away like that?'

I shrugged.

'And you're off to London in only three weeks,' coaxed Bethan without much tact, 'just think, you could've really taken a part of Gravenhead away *with* you!'

'*You* did,' I pointed out to her, 'you nicked that ale bottle! Gran did, as well!'

Bethan nodded and shrugged, shivering, as it began to rain.

'In any case,' I said suddenly, 'I *have* got something!

'Somebody told me, that summer, Beth',' I said earnestly (avoiding Louisa Caybourne by name), 'that before something was news, first of all it had to be a secret. With me, it's different: for something to be a secret, first of all it has to be news!'

I smiled, a little hesitantly.

'Come with me,' I said.

I got up and walked around the outskirts of the village green to the very rear of the village. Trippers and tourists became faint in the distance as we walked.

And I stopped against a great starburst of a house, its timbers splayed out in a grotesque wooden fan, surrounded by another ugly ruin of a house which was simply a chimney stack poking out from the earth; the only sign there had ever been a house there at all.

Richard Thorns

'Do you remember when we first came here?' I whispered to Bethan. 'We looked at this part of the village and we wondered why *these* houses were so wrecked and ruined, like something had blasted the hell out of them?'

Bethan nodded. 'I remember,' she said.

I went around the back of the house, and began pushing my way into the undergrowth, scratching my legs on the briars as I crashed slowly through. Ahead of me, the ground had begun to incline upward: it was the first beginnings of Fawkes's Hill.

I gestured to Bethan to follow me. Bethan cursed as she waded chest-high through the stinging nettles.

'This had *better* be good, Morwen,' she said to me, rubbing her arms.

I took hold of Bethan's arm (white with nettle blotch) and guided it into the undergrowth with my hand. I could see Bethan curling her fingers into the cold mud and the thorns, feeling old moss. And then, away from Gravenhead and digging in the wild, natural undergrowth, I knew she had *felt* it; a smooth, cold surface beneath her fingers:

A brick.

And another. And another! Her fingers digging at the mud, forming a smooth arch, before briars and hawthorn branches took over.

I knew her thoughts were travelling back, to a time when she was wandering alone with my gran on the hill during that blazing summer. When *her* side of the folly was just shallow, brackish water. All that was left of...

'Morwen, does this mean...' she whispered -

'That no-one ever thought that the diggers might be digging... *up?* From Gravenhead itself through the hill to the other side?' I asked her gravely. 'Yes, I think so. I think it means all of that.'

Bethan fell suddenly silent. *The savage wall of water blasting its way out of the hill; shattering the nearest houses into smithereens as the lake above them drained.* How could she not be thinking the same as me: the people alive in the tunnel as the hill was breached; the villages who sacrificed themselves for the great secret; the waiting Cowminster survivors in the manor house.

Behind her cupped hands, she said: 'You have to tell somebody, Morwen!'

I shook my head, 'but then they'd want to know *why,*' I murmured simply.

Bethan told me later that her memories flooded into her head, then; they tore themselves apart on the briars it seemed to her, for she really remembered them only in fragments; her conversation with my gran, high up on the hill, that blazing summer:

'I mean, he didn't really have the first idea where Gravenhead was, or even if it ever existed in the first place.'

'I *did.*'

Richard Thorns

'Yes, but you never thought to say anything?'
'Would you?'

But that was for later! Now, in the shady scratchiness, she simply said to me: 'You're your Grandmother's Granddaughter, Morwen.'

'And when I go to university,' I said to her in the darkness of the undergrowth, 'it might all be different between us from now on. I'd like you to know this... before I go.

'Yours as a souvenir, Bethan,' I said to her, 'greetings from Gravenhead.'

So as I say, that's what happened and that's how it ended that bleak, gusting day in August. Morwen went on to do really well in Years twelve and thirteen and as you'll have seen in the ~~epolge~~ epilogue of our book she DID get into the London School of Journalism and she is doing well. We say hi when she comes back. She kept all her "books" and she made me PROMISE to keep sending her mine as we put this together. If you are reading this, it means it is finished. I've done my best and what you saw there was all I can remember. I'm just glad Morwen has had the most to write.

I think this is because Morwen doing a lot of writing is good for her course and not just because she found Gravenhead (despite what she says about that diver finding it first). She wants to do it as her final diss-whatever but most important of all, I think it means she's moving away. ☺

Write it all down!" is what everyone says to do if you want to escape bad thoughts. Morwen's doing good she has a boyfriend and she's living in a flat with two other girls. I have to retake because I went a bit off the rails and started drinking a bit too much, so I'm selling shoes in Meeks's on Saturdays but it's ok I'll be doing it all myself in a year's time I PROMISE!! :-O

Garreth and me broke up. We never really recovered from what I said to him in Gravenhead; as much as I reassured him all the time about why I said it, how scary it was there and everything, the fact that I said I was seeing someone else probably wasn't a good idea (I think we would have recovered if I hadn't said that). Anyway, this meant he caved into his nerves (which Morwen once commented were like toffee-apple) pretty quickly after that, and his constant questioning of me meant the end.

I wasn't as devastated as I thought I would be; when I'd made that call to him from Gravenhead I was surrounded by such sadness, and all my memories of the part I'd played in Morwen's suffering. I suppose subconsciously I'd felt it was time to let go. Garreth would have found out eventually what I'd done and he would have dumped me anyway, so I guess I got in first. :-D . I wanted Morwen to go out with him but she wouldn't; she said it would be disloyal, which was typical of her.

Anyway, I mentioned I went off the rails and started drinking, but it wasn't any kind of teaching from Mam and it wasn't because of Garreth either.

You see, on the good days when the sun isn't shining I tell myself it was probably nothing, but when we climbed up the basin to leave Gravenhead behind, I took a rest about halfway up. And I looked behind me and the weathercock was facing in a different direction from when we'd started. And at nights when I wake up and I lie awake in bed I find myself wishing I'd checked on the trees at the same ~~hieght~~ height as the weathercock that day, to see if they were moving, or blowing in any wind, as well.

I think if I'd done that at the time I'd sleep better now. So that's why.

I think that's it really.

Richard Thorns

Gravenhead

Richard Thorns

Proof

Made in the USA
Charleston, SC
24 November 2015